"Are you a spy, Drummond?"

She put her hands on his chest to push him away, but then she looked up at his face.

His green eyes were much too attractive and much too intent.

He brushed his knuckles against her cheek. She didn't retreat. Nor did she tell him that he mustn't touch her. She was inviolate, his employer, the Duchess of Marsley. What would anyone say to see him touch her so?

She measured the seconds in held breaths. He didn't rush. He didn't pressure her. Instead, he gave her a chance to protest. Or to caution him. Or to pull away.

She remained silent, even as he reached out and cupped her face with both hands . . .

By Karen Ranney

To Love a Duchess

🍃 AN ALL FOR LOVE NOVEL 🍃

KAREN RANNEY

AVONBOOKS

An Imprint of HarperCollinsPublishers

TO LOVE A DUCHESS. Copyright © 2018 by Karen Ranney LLC. All rights reserved. Printed in the United States of America. No part of this book may be used or reproduced in any manner whatsoever without written permission except in the case of brief quotations embodied in critical articles and reviews. For information, address HarperCollins Publishers, 195 Broadway, New York, NY 10007.

First Avon Books mass market printing: August 2018
First Avon Books hardcover printing: July 2018

Print Edition ISBN: 978-0-06-284104-9
Digital Edition ISBN: 978-0-06-284105-6

Cover design by Patricia Barrow
Cover illustration by Patrick Kang

Avon, Avon & logo, and Avon Books & logo are registered trademarks of HarperCollins Publishers in the United States of America and other countries.

HarperCollins is a registered trademark of HarperCollins Publishers in the United States of America and other countries.

FIRST EDITION

18 19 20 21 22   QGM   10 9 8 7 6 5 4 3 2

To Love a
Duchess

Chapter One

September 1864
Marsley House
London, England

*H*e felt the duke's stare on him the minute he walked into the room.

Adam Drummond closed the double doors behind him quietly so as not to alert the men at the front door. Tonight Thomas was training one of the young lads new to the house. If they were alerted to his presence in the library, they would investigate.

He had a story prepared for that eventuality. He couldn't sleep, which wasn't far from the truth. Nightmares often kept him from resting more than a few hours at a time. A good thing he had years of practice getting by with little sleep.

He'd left his suite attired only in a collarless white shirt and black trousers. Another fact for which he'd have to find an explanation. As the majordomo of Marsley House, he was expected to wear the full uniform of his position at all times, even in the middle of the night. Perhaps not donning the white waistcoat, cravat, and coat was an act of rebellion.

Strange, since he'd never been a rebel before. It was this place, this house, this assignment that was affecting him.

For the first time in seven years he hadn't borrowed a name or a history carefully concocted by the War Office. He'd taken the position as himself, Adam Drummond, Scot and former soldier with Her Majesty's army. The staff knew his real name. Some even knew parts of his true history. The housekeeper called him Adam, knew he was a widower, was even aware of his birthdate.

He felt exposed, an uncomfortable position for a man who'd worked in the shadows for years.

He lit one of the lamps hanging from a chain fixed to the ceiling. The oil was perfumed, the scent reminiscent of jasmine. The world of the Whitcombs was unique, separated from the proletariat by two things: the peerage and wealth.

The pale yellow light revealed only the area near the desk. The rest of the huge room was in shadow. The library was *ostentatious*, a word he'd heard one of the maids try to pronounce.

"And what does it mean, I'm asking you?" She'd been talking to one of the cook's helpers, but he'd interjected.

"It means *fancy*."

She'd made a face before saying, "Well, why couldn't they just say *fancy*, then?"

Because everything about Marsley House was ostentatious.

This library certainly qualified. The room had three floors connected by a circular black iron staircase. The third floor was slightly larger than the second, making it possible for a dozen lamps to hang from chains affixed to each level at different heights. If he'd lit them all it would have been bright as day in here, illuminating thousands of books.

He didn't think the Whitcomb family had read every one of the volumes. Some of them looked as if they were new, the dark green leather and gold spines no doubt as shiny as when they'd arrived from the booksellers. Others were so well worn that he couldn't tell what the titles were until he pulled them from the shelves and opened them. There were a great many books on military history and he suspected that was the late duke's doing.

He turned to look at the portrait over the mantel. George Whitcomb, Tenth Duke of Marsley, was wearing his full military uniform, the scarlet jacket so bright a shade that Adam's eyes almost watered. The duke's medals gleamed as if the sun had come out from behind the artist's window to shine directly on such an exalted personage. He wore a sword tied at his waist and his head was turned slightly to the right, his gaze one that Adam remembered. Contempt shone in his eyes, as if everything the duke witnessed was beneath him, be it people, circumstances, or the scenery of India.

Adam was surprised that the man had allowed himself to be painted with graying hair. Even his muttonchop whiskers were gray and brown. In India, Whitcomb had three native servants whose sole duties were to ensure the duke's sartorial perfection at all times. He was clipped and coiffed and brushed and shined so that he could parade before his men as the ultimate authority of British might.

His eyes burned out from the portrait, so dark brown that they appeared almost black, narrowed and penetrating.

"Damn fine soldiers, every single one of them. All mongrels, of course, but fighting men."

At least the voice—surprisingly higher in pitch than Adam had expected—was silent now. He didn't have to hear himself being called a mongrel again. Whitcomb had been talking about the British regiments assigned to guard the East India Company settlements. He could well imagine the man's comments about native soldiers.

What a damned shame Whitcomb had been killed in a carriage accident. He deserved a firing squad at the very least. He wished the duke to Hell as he had ever since learning of the man's death. The approaching storm with its growling thunder seemed to approve of the sentiment.

As if to further remind him of India, his shoulder began to throb. Every time it rained the scar announced its presence, the bullet wound just one more memory to be expunged. It was this house. It brought to mind everything he'd tried to forget for years.

Adam turned away from the portrait, his attention on the massive, heavily tooled mahogany desk. This, too, was larger than it needed to be, raised on a dais, more a throne than a place a man might work. A perfect reflection of the Duke of Marsley's arrogance.

The maids assigned this room had left the curtains open. If he had been a proper majordomo he would no doubt chastise them for their oversight. But because he'd been a leader of men, not of maids, he decided not to mention it.

Lightning flashed nearby, the strike followed by

another shot of thunder. The glass shivered in the mullioned panes.

Maybe the duke's ghost was annoyed that he was here in the library again.

The careening of the wind around this portion of Marsley House sounded almost like a warning. Adam disregarded it as he glanced up to the third floor. He would have to be looking for a journal. That was tantamount to searching for a piece of coal in a mine or a grain of sand on the beach.

This assignment had been difficult from the beginning. He'd been tasked to find evidence of the duke's treason. While he believed the man to be responsible for the deaths of hundreds of people, finding the proof had been time consuming and unsuccessful to this point.

He wasn't going to give up, however. This was more than an assignment for him. It was personal.

One of the double doors opened, startling him.

"Sir?"

Daniel, the newest footman, stood there. The lad was tall, as were all of the young men hired at Marsley House. His shock of red hair was accompanied by a splattering of freckles across his face, almost as if God had wielded a can of paint and tripped when approaching Daniel. His eyes were a clear blue and direct as only the innocent could look.

Adam always felt old and damaged in Daniel's presence.

"Is there anything I can do for you, sir?" the young footman asked.

"I've come to find something to read." There, as an excuse it should bear scrutiny. He could always claim that he was about to examine the Marsley House ledgers, even though he normally performed that task in his own suite.

"Yes, sir."

"I think we had a prowler the other night," Adam said, improvising. "One of the maids mentioned her concern."

"Sir?"

Daniel was a good lad, the kind who wouldn't question a direct order.

"I'd like you to watch the outer door to the Tudor garden."

"Yes, sir," Daniel said, nodding.

"Tell Thomas that I need you there."

"Yes, sir," the young man said again, still nodding.

Once he, too, had been new to a position. In his case, Her Majesty's army. Yet he'd never been as innocent as Daniel. Still, he remembered feeling uncertain and worried in those first few months, concerned that he wasn't as competent at his tasks as he should be. For that reason he stopped the young man before he left the library.

"I've heard good reports about you, Daniel."

The young man's face reddened. "Thank you, sir."

"I think you'll fit in well at Marsley House."

"Thank you, Mr. Drummond."

A moment later, Daniel was gone, the door closed once again. Adam watched for a minute before turning and staring up at the third floor.

The assignment he'd been given was to find one particular journal. Unfortunately, that was proving to be more difficult than originally thought. The Duke of Marsley had written in a journal since he was a boy. The result was that there were hundreds of books Adam needed to read.

After climbing the circular stairs, he grabbed the next two journals to be examined and brought them back to the first floor. He doubted if the duke would approve of him sitting at his desk, which was why Adam did so, opening the cover of one of the journals and forcing himself to concentrate on the duke's overly ornate handwriting.

He didn't look over at the portrait again, but it still seemed as if the duke watched as he read.

At first Adam thought it was the sound of the storm before realizing that thunder didn't speak in a female voice. He stood and extinguished the lamp, but the darkness wasn't absolute. The lightning sent bright flashes of light into the library.

Moving to the doors, he opened one of them slightly, expecting to find a maid standing there, or perhaps a footman with his lover. He knew about three dalliances taking place among the staff, but he wasn't going to reprimand any of them. As long as they did their jobs—which meant that he didn't garner any attention for the way he did his—he wasn't concerned about their behavior in their off hours.

It wasn't a footman or a maid engaged in a forbidden embrace. Instead, it was Marble Marsley, the widowed duchess. She'd recently returned from her house in the country, and he'd expected to be summoned to her presence as the newest servant on the staff and one of the most important. She hadn't sent for him. She hadn't addressed him.

He had to hand it to the duke; he'd chosen his duchess well. Suzanne Whitcomb, Duchess of Marsley, was at least thirty years younger than the duke and a beautiful woman. Tonight her dark brown hair was arranged in an upswept style, revealing jet-black earrings adorned with diamonds. Her face was perfect, from the shape to the arrangement of her features. Her mouth was generous, her blue-gray eyes the color of a Scottish winter sky. Her high cheekbones suited her aristocratic manner, and her perfect form was evident even in her many-tiered black cape the footman was removing.

Did she mourn the bastard? Is that why she'd remained in her country home for the past several months?

From his vantage point behind the door, he watched as she removed her gloves and handed them to the footman, shook the skirts of her black silk gown, and walked toward him with an almost ethereal grace.

He stared at her, startled. The duchess was crying. Perfect tears fell down her face as silently as if she were a statue. He waited until she passed, heading for the staircase that swooped like a swallow's wing through the center of Marsley House, before opening the door a little more.

Glancing toward the vestibule, he was satisfied that Thomas, stationed at the front door, couldn't see him. He took a few steps toward the staircase, watching.

The duchess placed her hand on the banister and, looking upward, ascended the first flight of steps.

He had a well-developed sense of danger. It had saved his life in India more than once. But he wasn't at war now. There weren't bullets flying and, although the thunder might sound like cannon, the only ones were probably at the Tower of London or perhaps Buckingham Palace.

Then why was he getting a prickly feeling on the back of his neck? Why did he suddenly think that the duchess was up to something? She didn't stop at the second floor landing or walk down the corridor to her suite of rooms. Instead, she took one step after another in a measured way, still looking upward as if she were listening to the summons of an angel.

He glanced over at the doorway, but the footman wasn't looking in his direction. When he glanced back at the staircase, Adam was momentarily confused because he couldn't see her. At the top of the staircase, the structure twisted onto itself and then disappeared into the shadows. There were only two places she could have gone: to the attic, a storage area that encompassed this entire wing of Marsley House. Or to the roof.

He no longer cared if Thomas saw him or not. Adam began to run.

Where the hell was the daft woman?

Adam raced up the first flight of stairs, then the second, wondering if he was wrong about Marble Marsley. He'd overheard members of the staff calling her that and had assumed she'd gotten the label because she was cold and pitiless. A woman who never said a kind word to anyone. Someone who didn't care about another human being.

In that, she and her husband were a perfect pair.

But marble didn't weep.

He followed the scent of her perfume, a flowery, spicy aroma reminding him of India. At the top of the staircase, he turned to the left, heading for an inconspicuous door, one normally kept closed. It was open now, the wind blowing the rain down the ten steps to lash him in the face.

He'd been here only once, on a tour he'd done to familiarize himself with the place. Marsley House was a sprawling estate on the edge of London, the largest house in the area and one famous enough to get its share of carriages driving by filled with gawping Londoners out for a jaunt among their betters.

Not that the Marsley family was better than anyone else, no matter what they thought. They had their secrets and their sins, just like any other family.

He kept the door to the roof open behind him, grateful for the lightning illuminating his way. If only the rain would stop, but it was too late to wish for that. He was already drenched.

In a bit of whimsy, the builder of Marsley House had created a small balcony between two sharply pitched gables. Chairs had been placed there, no doubt for watching the sunset over the roofs of London.

No one in their right mind would be there in the middle of a storm. As if agreeing with him, thunder roared above them.

The duchess was gripping the balcony railing with both hands as she raised one leg, balancing herself like a graceful bird about to swoop down from the top of a tree.

People didn't swoop. They fell.

What the hell?

He began to run, catching himself when he would have fallen on the slippery roof.

"You daft woman," he shouted as he reached her.

She turned her face to him, her features limned by lightning.

He didn't see what he saw. At least that's what he told himself. No one could look at the Duchess of Marsley and not be witness to her agony.

He grabbed one of her arms, pulling her to him and nearly toppling in the process. For a moment he thought her rain-soaked dress was heavy enough to take them both over the railing.

Then the daft duchess began to hit him.

He let fly a few oaths in Gaelic while trying to defend himself from the duchess's nails as she went for his eyes. Her mouth was open and for a curious moment, it almost looked like she was a goddess of the storm, speaking in thunder.

He stumbled backward, pulling her on top of him when she would have wrenched free. He had both hands on each of her arms now, holding her.

She was screaming at him, but he couldn't tell what she was saying. He thought she was still crying, but it might be the rain.

He pushed away from the railing with both feet. He'd feel a damn sight better if they were farther away from the edge. As determined as she was, he didn't doubt that she would take a running leap the minute she got free.

The storm was directly overhead now, as if God himself dwelt in the clouds and was refereeing this fight to the death. Not his, but hers.

He was a few feet away from the railing now, still being pummeled by the rain. Twice she got a hand free and struck him. Once he thought she was going to make it to her feet. He grabbed the sodden bodice of her dress and jerked her back down. She could die on another night, but he was damned if he was going to let her do it now.

He made it to his knees and she tried, once more, to pull away. She got one arm free and then the second. Just like he imagined, she made for the railing again.

He grabbed her skirt as he stood. When she turned and went for his eyes again, he jerked the fabric with both hands, desperate to get her away from the edge.

The duchess stumbled and dropped like a rock.

He stood there being pelted by rain that felt like miniature pebbles, but the duchess didn't move. Her cheek lay against the roof; her eyes were closed, and rain washed her face clean of tears.

He bent and scooped her up into his arms and headed for the door, wondering how in hell he was going to explain that he'd felled the Duchess of Marsley.

Chapter Two

$\mathcal{A}$dam's luck ran out on the family floor. He nodded to the footman stationed outside the duchess's suite, wondering what kind of training the man had received from the previous majordomo. The young man's eyes didn't reveal any emotion at the sight of Adam carrying an unconscious duchess, both of them dripping on the crimson runner. All he did was open one of the doors and step aside to reveal the sitting room.

The lamps had been left lit inside the room. Adam expected the duchess's maid to greet him. No one did.

The scent of the duchess's perfume was even stronger in the sitting room. He stood there uncertain, glancing over his shoulder only when the door closed softly behind him.

He had never been in the duchess's chambers before. The sitting room alone looked as if it took up half this wing. The walls were covered in a pale ivory silk patterned with embroidered branches complete with birds of different colors.

Two sofas sat perpendicular to the white marble fireplace on the far wall. They, too, were covered in ivory silk. The crimson-and-ivory rug was woven in a pattern similar to the silk on the walls. The furniture was mahogany and crafted with feminine touches, like curved legs ending in delicate paws.

The tenement in Glasgow where he'd been born and raised could be put inside this room and still have space left over. The cost of the ivory silk curtains alone could probably have fed his family for a year.

The duchess lay like a black cloud in his arms, her head lolling against his chest. Her cheek still bore a red mark where she'd struck the roof.

Should he attempt to apologize? Or explain? Or simply hope that she'd forget the entire incident?

Why had she tried to throw herself off the roof? Had she loved the bastard that much? The Duke of Marsley didn't deserve her devotion, especially two years after his death.

He wanted to give instructions to the footman to keep her inside her suite, but doubted that would work. The duchess was their employer, the goddess in this little kingdom of Marsley House. None of the servants would go against her for fear they would be dismissed.

Maybe the duchess's maid was close enough to the duchess to be able to alter her behavior. She might have some influence. If she didn't, maybe she'd know someone who would.

But the maid wasn't here, even though she should have been waiting for the duchess to return.

He strode across the room, uncaring that his shoes squished on the expensive carpet or that the duchess's skirt dripped a path to her bedroom.

This chamber was as richly furnished as the sitting room. The bed was easily four times the size of his in the servants' quarters and, no doubt, four times as comfortable.

Here the ivory color was featured again, in the bed coverings and the curtains on the floor-to-ceiling windows. Even the vanity was swathed in ivory silk.

He glanced at the silver brushes and assortment of jars. His late wife, Rebecca, or his sister would have loved this room. He could almost imagine each woman sitting there, delight sparkling in their eyes as they used the downy powder puff or that pink stuff. What did women call it? Pomade? He really didn't know.

He pushed the ghosts of his past away and walked to the bed, depositing the duchess on the spread before stepping back.

He'd thought she was marble, but it was all too clear she wasn't. Not with that agony in her eyes.

She'd wanted to die.

He stretched out one hand and pulled the bell rope beside the bed. A night maid, in addition to a night footman, was on duty in the kitchen, ready to serve the duchess if she required anything. This time she didn't need tea or digestive biscuits. Only Ella, the lady's maid who should have been here.

She wasn't his responsibility, thankfully, but was disciplined by the duchess or Mrs. Thigpen, the housekeeper, if the duchess preferred.

After opening the chest at the end of the bed, he found a blanket, which he draped over the duchess. She needed to be undressed, and quickly, before she caught a chill. But he wasn't about to compound his sins of the evening by attempting that.

Her lashes were incredibly long, brushing her cheeks. Her face was as pale as any of those poor souls they'd found at Manipora. Death, or almost death in the case of the duchess, had bestowed a marble purity to their faces. The duchess's lips were nearly blue, and he found himself wanting to warm them, to bring back some color. If for no other reason than to prove that she wasn't dead after all.

At least she hadn't died tonight, but what would happen tomorrow? Would she succeed in her aim?

When the night maid arrived, he had her send for Ella. The girl was a gossip, but one quick glance at him froze any future words she might have spoken. If anyone talked about him standing in the duchess's bedroom, or her looking nearly like a corpse, he knew where to go. The young maid knew it, too, if the wide-eyed stare she gave him was any indication.

She nearly flew from the room to fetch Ella, leaving him alone with the duchess once more.

He didn't move from his stance beside the bed. *Stand easy* was a pose he'd learned as barely more than a boy in the army. He assumed it now, his hands interlocked behind his back, his legs spread a foot or so apart. His gaze didn't move from the woman on the bed. If he'd looked away, he would have missed the fluttering of her lashes.

"It's awake you are," he said.

He cleared his throat, annoyed at himself. When he was tired, or under the effect of strong emotion, he sometimes fell into the Glaswegian accent of his youth, the same cadence of speech he'd been at pains to alter once he'd left Scotland. It returned now, as did his accent, belying the twenty years or so since he last set foot on Scottish soil.

She appeared to still be unconscious, but he wasn't fooled. The duchess was playacting.

Should he apologize or simply pretend that the incident on the roof hadn't happened?

If he didn't appease her, he'd probably be dismissed on the spot, and he'd have to go back and admit that he'd failed spectacularly at his mission.

That was not going to happen.

She turned her head slowly, her eyes opening reluctantly.

He felt a jolt when she pinned him with her stare. "Who are you?"

He'd been introduced to her when she arrived back in London a few days earlier. She hadn't looked up from her task of removing her gloves, one finger at a time. He hadn't even warranted a quick glance. He'd opened the door for her on two other occasions and she'd sailed past like a schooner in full wind.

This was the first time she actually looked at him. He didn't move from his stance, but he allowed himself a small, cool smile.

"I am your new majordomo, Your Grace," he said. "Your solicitor hired me two months ago."

She closed her eyes again and turned her head once more.

"Go away," she said softly, her voice sounding as if it held unshed tears.

"I've sent for your maid," he said. "She should be here any moment."

"I don't want her here, either," she said.

He knew hell all about a woman's relationship with her maid, but he suspected it must be a close one. After all, the latter helped the former dress, cared for her clothing, fixed her hair, and was no doubt the recipient of confidences. Evidently, the Duchess of Marsley and her lady's maid didn't share that bond.

He wasn't going to send Ella away. In fact, he would feel much better if Her Grace had a companion at all times, especially if she got a yen to throw herself off the roof.

She didn't say anything further. Nor did he. Instead, they were separated only by a few feet, two silent people in different poses and in vastly different roles in society. They might as well have been on different sides of the world.

He brought his feet together, released his arms, and took a deep breath. Walking to the opposite wall, he used a finger to lift one of the curtain panels, then stared out at the night. The rain was still falling steadily. The lightning was giving a show in the distant sky, but the thunder had been muted. Here, in this room, in this house, the silence was almost absolute but for the plaintive cry of a cat.

The duchess didn't have any pets, so he reasoned it was probably a stray cat that had taken up residence somewhere close by and wasn't happy about the rain. When he finished with the duchess, he would go find the poor animal and give it some shelter. No creature deserved to be cold, wet, and probably hungry.

The door opened, then closed. Footsteps heralded Ella's arrival. A moment later she stood in the doorway to the sitting room, her attention first on the duchess and then on him.

Ella was of an uncertain age, past the first blush of youth and slightly older than the duchess. She always appeared to be judging something, most often standing rigid with her hands clutched tight to each other at her midriff. She rarely smiled and although he'd heard other members of the staff laugh on numerous occasions, he'd never heard Ella. He didn't think she was capable of it.

The word *dour* had been invented to describe people like Ella.

He didn't like the maid, an instant judgment he'd made the third day after the duchess had arrived from the country. He and Ella had passed each other on the servants' stairs and she'd given him a contemptuous look.

He'd wanted to stop her right then and ask her why she thought she was so much better than the other staff. Was it because she served a duchess? Did she somehow believe that she possessed some power because she'd laundered a member of the peerage's unmentionables? Or did her hair?

As a real majordomo, he needed to be familiar with the various hierarchies in the world of servants. He wasn't since he'd never employed a servant. Nor had he grown up around them, so he'd needed to do some research.

A lady's maid was a position that required some skill and experience. One needed to know— according to a book he'd found in the library—how to care for her employer's clothing. She was to direct the staff that would care for her employer's belongings, such as the maids who would clean the duchess's suite. She ordered items of clothing, gifts, and other necessities as dictated by her employer.

In Ella's case, another one of her duties was to be as insufferable as possible.

The maid's expression was continually haughty. She didn't dine with the rest of the staff, but planned her meals so that when everyone was finished she could eat in relative privacy in the small dining room set aside for the servants. No doubt she would've preferred to have a sitting room attached to her bedroom, but those two suites on the third floor had been set aside for the housekeeper and the majordomo.

"Her Grace needs your assistance," he said to Ella.

The fact that he didn't explain any further earned him a glance from the duchess.

When he returned her look she closed her eyes, but not before giving him a quick impression of gratitude, which didn't make any sense.

Ella removed the blanket from the duchess. She shook her head when realizing the state of the younger woman's attire. He didn't know if the black silk dress was ruined and he didn't care, but the duchess needed to change as quickly as possible and get warm.

So did he, for that matter.

"I don't understand," Ella said. "What happened?"

He had a feeling that nothing would satisfy Ella but the absolute truth. However, she wasn't going to get it from him. Let the duchess tell her maid whatever she wanted.

He moved toward the doorway, wanting his bed and his solitude.

"Airson caoidh fear gun onair a tha gòrach," he said to the duchess before making his way out of her suite.

He was rewarded with a frown from both women.

Chapter Three

"What happened, Your Grace? Why are you wet?"

She really wished Ella wasn't here. She could have done for herself quite well if the room wasn't suddenly spinning. She needed to compose herself and take a few minutes to blink back the dizziness, but Ella had an arm around her back and was insisting that she sit up.

"What happened?"

Suzanne swallowed against the sudden sourness on her tongue. She still tasted the wine she'd drunk at her father's dinner. Too much wine. How many glasses had she consumed? Too many if she couldn't remember.

"Your Grace, why are your clothes sodden?"

Here she needed to be careful. Drummond had surprised her by not revealing the entire story. But if she wasn't cautious now, Ella would summon her father to Marsley House and Suzanne would be forced to endure his scrutiny and lectures.

She opened her eyes. Ella looked even more angry tonight than she normally did.

"The storm was spectacular. I went on the roof to see it."

"The roof?" Ella said.

"I wanted to see the display of lightning."

There, that was plausible enough. In addition, it sounded slightly idiotic, which wouldn't disappoint either Ella or her father.

"But on the roof, Your Grace?" the maid asked, her voice conveying some degree of skepticism.

"The rain had momentarily stopped," she said.

"Your dress is wet, Your Grace."

"It started to rain again," she answered as Ella began unfastening her clothes. She was wet and the cold was finally beginning to penetrate the gray fog that always surrounded her.

"Where is your other hair clip?" Ella asked.

"My hair clip?"

"Yes, Your Grace," Ella said, her voice just this side of rude. "Your hair clip. One of two that you inherited from your mother. The ones that look like leaves, Your Grace, and are filled with diamonds."

Suzanne kept her eyes closed. She really didn't want to see the maid right now. She didn't want to see anything at all. How odd that she could still see the newly hired majordomo standing there in his militaristic way, his eyes heated with fury. How very strange to be hated by one's servants.

"Where is the hair clip?" Ella asked.

Suzanne raised her right hand. Georgie's mourning ring was still on her third finger. That, and her mourning brooch, were the only pieces of jewelry she cared about right now.

No doubt Ella would inform her father of her laxity. The maid was fawning but only toward her father. Not a foolish thing to be, all in all. Had he encouraged her to spy on Suzanne? Sometimes she felt herself being observed by Ella, as if the maid were making mental notes of what to write at a later date. Did she journal as assiduously as her late husband, George?

How odd that she didn't know. Nor did she care. If she could have, she would have dispensed with Ella entirely, but her father would no doubt hire someone else in her stead.

Ella was extremely proficient at her position. She hadn't lost a collar, cuff, or corset cover since Ella had come to Marsley House six months ago. All of her lace was laundered to perfection. Her unmentionables were darned when necessary and replaced otherwise. A summons from Ella would bring all manner of tradesmen, seamstresses, and jewelers, each one of them eager to be recognized as providing trade to the Duchess of Marsley.

If she cared about any of those things, she'd be quite content with Ella's execution of her duties. Since she didn't, Suzanne felt apathetic and wished she could feel the same about Ella.

She didn't like the maid, and that feeling seemed to be growing every day. How very odd. She hadn't objected to Ella at the beginning, but then she hadn't felt much of anything. Now the only emotion she felt was antipathy.

She looked at Ella, trying to figure out what it was about the other woman that was sparking so much sudden feeling.

Ella's hair was much lighter than Suzanne's own dark brown. Instead, it was almost the color of honey and seemed to have a will of its own, one of constant disobedience, frizzing when it rained. The maid's eyes were brown, almost the color of whiskey. Her lips were thin, the better to disappear in her face when she was in a critical mood, and her nose was slightly askew, as if it had been broken once. Or perhaps the Almighty, having seen Ella's character as an adult, had tweaked it in remonstration.

She'd never asked Ella about her parentage, her childhood, her wishes or wants, or anything remotely personal. She hadn't asked if the other woman liked chocolate or had a dog as a child, or what kind of weather she preferred. She knew as little about the other woman as she could and only wished that she could say the same about Ella's knowledge of her.

She kept her thoughts to herself. At least Ella could not invade them. She never willingly confided in Ella. Instead, she watched every comment she uttered in the maid's presence, which meant that she hadn't spoken freely for months.

Her majordomo hadn't been as constrained, had he? What had Drummond said to her? Had it been Gaelic? How strange that her solicitor would hire a Scotsman, especially since her father didn't like Scotland or its people. She'd often heard him complain about them for some reason or another. Either they were too penurious or they had a tendency to speak their thoughts too honestly.

One did not challenge Edward Hackney without paying a dear price.

"Your Grace?"

She met Ella's eyes.

"The hairpin?"

She didn't know where the hairpin was. She didn't care. But if she said such a thing, Ella would tell her father and she'd receive an involved speech about treasuring the possessions of her dear departed mother. As if she needed a lecture.

How many times in the past two years had she wished her mother had survived the cancer that had taken her life? How many times had she spoken to her in the quiet of the night, as if praying more to her mother than to God Himself?

"Why was Drummond in your bedroom?"

She didn't remember that part. When she remained silent, Ella continued.

"You returned from the dinner early, Your Grace."

Was the woman going to challenge everything she did? Yes, if Ella proved faithful to her past.

Suzanne was so tired, almost too tired to care that she was wet and had probably soaked the mattress. Her head hung down, her hair plastered against her cheeks. She didn't bother removing it.

She stood, finally, a little wobbly and using the mattress behind her as a bulwark. Each separate garment was stripped from her, Ella's ministrations not requiring any thought. All she needed to do was stand as straight as she was able, given that the room was spinning again, and obey her maid's commands. *Lift that foot, then that one. Raise your arm. Lower it, Your Grace.*

Ella led her into the bathing chamber, handed her a cloth to wash her face as she washed and dried the rest of Suzanne's body. In earlier days, before Ella, she would have dismissed her maid and bathed in the polished marble tub across the room.

If she hadn't been so tired. If she had cared a bit more. If it hadn't been beyond her.

She raised her arms again when Ella dressed her in a voluminous silk nightgown. Once attired for the night, with all her other needs taken care of, she was led to the vanity, where Ella removed the rest of her hairpins and began to dry her hair with a thick towel.

"I've looked through your garments, Your Grace, and I can't find it."

She stared at Ella's reflection in the mirror, uncertain what the other woman was talking about.

"Your hairpin. Your mother's hairpin."

Did she truly need to care about her mother's hairpin? Would her mother mind if it was lost? Did angels care about such things?

She was so very tired, but she tried to remember what had happened tonight. Her father had been displeased. She'd taken too many glasses of wine from the footmen circulating in the public rooms. She'd dared to look unimpressed at some official's title. Or perhaps she'd done something else for which she'd been summarily banished.

Earlier, however, she'd pretended attentiveness as she was introduced to her father's newest protégé. She'd answered the questions put to her with a half smile on her face. She'd endured the endless conversations swirling around her.

Now she just wanted to be left alone.

No one seemed to understand that. Not Ella. Certainly not her father. Not even her Scottish major-domo.

She opened her eyes and stared at her image in the mirror. There was a red mark on her cheek. When had that happened? She suddenly remembered. She'd fallen and he'd picked her up as if she'd weighed no more than a feather.

Abruptly, Ella thrust a glass in front of her.

Without looking she knew what the glass contained. A green liquid that smelled of grass and promised oblivion.

"I don't need it," she said. The wine had dulled her wits, numbing her to everything.

"I'm instructed to give it to you, Your Grace."

Her father's orders. *Keep Suzanne in a half-dazed state both day and night. She's more amenable that way. She smiles more. She will agree to almost anything.*

She took the glass, but didn't drink it.

Ella didn't move. She would remain where she was until Suzanne downed the contents. Part of her didn't want to drink it. Another part, more the coward, craved the stupor that would come over her when she did.

To forget, that was the aim. To pretend that nothing had ever happened. To live in a perpetual dream. If only she could. If only she didn't have to wake every day.

"You can leave, Ella. I'll drink it later."

How strange that it hurt to talk. She pressed her fingers to her cheek.

"If you don't mind, Your Grace, I'll stay until you finish the draught."

Leave me. Words she didn't say. What difference did it make, in the end? She would take the potion and sleep. Tomorrow would be the same as today. *Dress, Suzanne. Be pretty, if vacuous. Smile when commanded. Turn this way, then that. Nod or shake your head, depending on the situation or the dictate.* She was only a body, not unlike those marionettes she'd once seen at Covent Garden. No one cared what she felt

or thought. Why shouldn't she live in the gray beyond?

She downed the contents of the glass and handed
it back to Ella, who smiled. Was that triumph she saw
in the other woman's eyes? She didn't care about that,
either.

Chapter Four

Adam took one of the Marsley carriages to Schomberg House in central London, but he made a quick side trip first.

Mrs. Ross, a widow and his landlady, had begun taking in boarders of a certain type to stave off loneliness, a fact she shared with him when he'd first arrived in London.

"I'm partial to military men, myself," she'd said. "They can handle themselves, and they're handy to have around. They know what's what."

He'd only nodded at the time, but she'd called on him over the years. He'd fixed a broken table leg, escorted a boarder who hadn't paid her for three weeks back over the threshold, examined an oil lamp and declared it inoperable, moved countless pieces of furniture, and had been as helpful as he could be when he was there.

Whenever he announced that he'd be away for a few weeks, she only nodded and asked him if he knew when he'd return. On some occasions, he'd been able to give her an answer. Most of the time he could only give her a general idea, but he always paid his rent ahead of time so she'd keep his rooms and dust and tidy up as needed.

She'd taken one look at the scrawny black kitten he'd found trapped outside the duchess's sitting room and welcomed him into her home.

The poor thing had been shivering and terrified when he'd finally found it. Somehow it had crawled under an outcropping, a bit of decorative brickwork where there was some shelter from the storm. He'd wrapped it in a towel, warmed it, and managed to feed it some of his breakfast before bringing it to Mrs. Ross.

"Oh my, yes, what a little darling. Of course he can be our mouser."

She'd welcomed him back to England with the same generosity of spirit. He'd been ill on the ship, suffering the effects of a lingering fever, and Mrs. Ross had nursed him back to health. He didn't have any doubt that she'd treat the kitten with the same kindness.

Some people in the world were generous and caring. Mrs. Ross was one of those.

What type of person was the duchess?

He hadn't been able to stop thinking of her, and that both annoyed and concerned him. If she attempted to end her life again, would someone be there to prevent it?

The carriage rolled to a stop in front of Schomberg House. The place was rumored to have once been a gambling den and a brothel. Now the redbrick-and-stone four-story building housed the organization for which he worked. They were housed here almost as an afterthought, but close enough to the War Office in Cumberland House, like misbehaving children under an adult's stern guidance.

The quarters were nothing like the site of the new Foreign Office building on King Charles Street that, along with the India Office, was going to be an example of Palladian architecture gone amok. Evidently, anyone visiting the buildings was supposed to come away impressed at the empire's use of columns, decorative molding, and polished marble.

The building he entered was devoid of columns or marble floors. Instead, there were hallways with doors, none of them marked save for a number. He took the first turn to the left and walked down a hallway tinted yellow by the sunlight spilling in through a far window.

He might have been walking through a deserted building for all the sounds that reached him. The silence was profound, broken only by the muffled noise of a door closing on the second floor and the footfalls on the nearby stairs.

The place smelled of dust and something else: strong black tea. Behind these doors were no doubt small braziers with kettles bubbling away. He was, after all, in the middle of a government building.

Seven years ago, when he'd left the army, Sir Richard Wells had made him a proposition. "Come and work for me. It's a new branch of the War Office. Something that might interest you."

Despite his questions, he'd only been given a cursory explanation of exactly what kind of branch it was, to whom they reported, and why. After a few dozen assignments, he had a better idea.

What he was doing wasn't officially sanctioned, but it benefitted the empire. He'd become a member of a group Sir Richard called the Silent Service, men who might never be recognized for their actions, but who were—one assignment at a time—making the empire safer.

Adam stopped before a room bearing a thirty on the plaque and placed his hand on the wooden knob. When he opened the door, his first sight was of Oliver Cater sitting at his desk in the outer office. He'd been a corporal in their regiment, a young man with a subdued personality and a terror of loud noises. Roger had been his protector of sorts, making sure that Oliver wasn't taunted for his lack of courage. The younger man had reciprocated by being intensely loyal.

Adam hadn't been surprised that Oliver had followed Roger to the War Office.

He glanced up as Adam entered, his bushy eyebrows drawing together. When he got older, Oliver's eyebrows would probably turn gray, get longer, and act like a forest in front of his small brown eyes. Adam couldn't help but wonder what age would do to the moles that dotted Oliver's face.

He pulled out the handkerchief from his pocket, unwrapped it, and placed the candy on Oliver's desk.

"Grace's licorice?" Oliver asked.

Adam nodded. Grace, the cook at Marsley House, had a sweet tooth and kept several treats around for herself and the other servants as well. Adam always took a few from the jar when he was reporting to Roger and gave them to Oliver.

He glanced toward the closed door. "Is he in?"

After selecting one of the candies and popping it into his mouth, Oliver nodded. "He's waiting for you."

Adam entered the office, closed the door behind him, and turned.

Roger was his age, a little shorter and heavier, but possessed of an affable smile that he often used. He was smiling now, an expression that was lost on Adam. He always looked at a man's eyes and he never missed the calculating glint in Roger's, as if he were measuring the worth of someone even as he was convincing them to throw in with one of his schemes.

The outside corners of Roger's eyes turned down, giving him the appearance of a bloodhound. A very trustworthy, kind, and loyal bloodhound.

Appearances could often be deceiving, however.

If anyone could find an easy way to do something, it was Roger. In India he'd gotten a reputation for being able to procure those items a soldier wanted and was willing to pay for. The East India Company had been an unwieldy bureaucracy. The talk had always been that if you needed something found, Roger Mount was your man. Roger had gotten a reputation for finding things that couldn't be found, for obtaining the unobtainable, and for making things happen.

Until he'd been sent to Lucknow, a neighboring garrison, Roger had been making a tidy sum for himself.

When they'd met again a few years ago, Adam hadn't been surprised that Roger had achieved some of his goals. He was no longer just a former soldier, but had risen to the rank of Assistant Undersecretary for Foreign Affairs, a position that allowed him to act as a liaison to the Foreign Office. He didn't doubt that Roger's promotion was due in part to the other man's ability to recognize a fortuitous circumstance when it appeared. The advantageous marriage he'd made had also helped. Roger was, simply put, ambitious.

"I'm not right for this assignment," Adam said, taking the chair in front of Roger's desk. "I haven't found the damn journal and I'm probably on my way out."

Roger Mount sat back in his desk chair, steepled his fingers, and regarded Adam as if he were much older and wiser. The pose was a wasted gesture. He and Roger had fought together in India. He knew the other man's peccadilloes and failings. Nor was he impressed by this large office or the desk that looked as if it had cost a family's yearly wages.

"What makes you think you're wrong for the position?"

He debated telling Roger about his actions of the night before, then decided against it. For some odd reason, he didn't want to divulge the duchess's suicidal intentions to anyone. He couldn't rid himself of the image of her face lit by lightning and the agony he'd seen in her eyes.

"I just know I am," Adam said.

A muscle in Roger's cheek clenched and released several times before the other man spoke again.

"You're the best I've got for the position," Roger finally said. The words were uttered calmly and spaced apart to give them more weight.

"Why, because I'm a Scot?"

Dispensable, in other words. Easily explained away. *Oh, yes, Drummond. Good man, but he was a Scot, you know.*

They stared at each other. They'd had this discussion many times in the past and here it was again.

"No, not because you're a Scot, damn it. You're good at fitting in. People like you."

"I'm a lousy majordomo."

"On the contrary. I've heard very good reports about you."

Adam didn't say anything for a moment. When he did speak, his voice was tight. "Do you have someone else at Marsley House? Someone spying on me?"

Roger leaned forward, all earnestness and honesty. Adam wasn't fooled by that pose, either.

"You didn't want to be a servant, Adam. Do you blame me? I had to protect the mission. It's important."

"Who is it?"

Roger shook his head.

He wasn't unduly surprised that Roger had sent someone in to check on him. Roger was capable of smiling to his face and saying something snide about him the minute Adam was out of his office.

He'd never had any delusions that he and Roger were friends, not like Roger pretended. They hadn't been friends in India and they weren't friends now, especially since fate decreed that he had to report to the other man, albeit temporarily. He'd much rather have had his original boss, Sir Richard Wells, but Sir Richard had agreed with Roger that Adam would be best on this assignment. It had been Roger's idea from the beginning to send someone into Marsley House.

"I'm not sure I can find the damn thing."

"You'll find it. If you don't give up," Roger said. There was a look in his eyes that dared Adam to argue.

"The man wrote in a journal every day of his life. I've found journals that began from his boyhood."

"But nothing from India?"

"I've found some from India, too, but they haven't revealed anything."

He'd never failed before and he didn't like the idea

of failing now. But there were times—and he was very much afraid that this was one of those—when circumstances were arrayed against him.

"I need you there," Roger said.

He'd heard that same sort of speech two months ago when he'd first been sent to Marsley House.

Adam rolled his shoulders and angled himself in the uncomfortable chair.

"You have to go back and find the damn journal. We can't afford a scandal like that being made public. The Foreign Office is making amends in India, Adam. We're trying to atone for the mistakes we made there. Can you imagine what would happen if it got out that the Duke of Marsley betrayed his own men? The world would see that whole business of Manipora in a different light."

"God help us," Adam said dryly.

He doubted that anyone would ever discover the duke's confession. Most of the journals he'd read looked as if they hadn't been moved since first being placed on the third floor of the library. However, it wasn't his place to argue with a superior and for this assignment, that's what Roger was.

"Who the hell confesses to treason in a journal?" Adam asked.

"Perhaps someone who wants to justify the action," Roger said. "Or feels a sense of guilt?"

He wasn't familiar with questioning his superiors, but in this instance he couldn't bite back his curiosity.

"How do you know he wrote about Manipora? Or about what he did?"

"The information was passed to us from a person very close to the duke," Roger said.

"Who?"

He was coming close to insubordination, but he didn't pull back the question. Instead, he waited, anticipating that Roger would tell him it wasn't any of his business.

"A member of his staff, someone who was very concerned about what he'd learned."

In other words, he wasn't going to get an identity of the informant.

"I know you disliked the duke," Roger said.

"The man was an idiot," Adam said, stretching out one foot and tapping it on the bottom of the desk in front of him.

The duke was not, contrary to his own estimation, a military genius. He'd been arrogant but also impulsive, a deadly combination. He hadn't thought it necessary to solicit the advice or opinions of others, several of whom knew significantly more than he. Consequently, he'd often gone off without the whole story, leading his men into skirmishes that had proved deadly.

Adam had lost his share of friends, not to the glory of the British Empire as much as the stupidity of one of its peers.

"You've never let your personal opinions blind you on an assignment, Adam. Don't do it on this one."

Roger let that comment linger in the air for a moment or two before sitting back, smiling, and offering tea.

Adam didn't want tea; he wanted answers, but he knew Roger wasn't going to be forthcoming. He might get one piece of the puzzle. Another operative would get a second piece. The only person who could put the entire puzzle together was the man heading the assignment. As an operative, Adam wasn't supposed to know every reason and rationale. He was only supposed to be a good civil servant and obey his directives.

Most of the time he didn't have a problem with that. This assignment was different. Of course his personal opinions were going to surface.

Roger rang a bell on the corner of his desk, and a few minutes later Oliver came through the door with a tray containing a teapot, two cups and saucers, a small pitcher filled with milk, and a bowl of sugar.

"I hear the duchess has returned to London," Roger said after preparing his cup and taking a sip. "What is she like?"

Adam did the same, more to give himself time to think than because he wanted tea, especially something that was yellow, smelled of flowers, and reminded him of India. He threw in a teaspoon or two of sugar to make it palatable and managed a sip. He preferred coffee, but that was tantamount to treason here in this War Office warren.

What was the duchess like?

Sad, for one. Intriguing, for another. He wanted to ask her questions he had no business asking. Why had she married the duke? Why did she mourn the man with such ferocity two years after his death?

He couldn't banish the memory of that look in her eyes.

"Maybe the duchess knows where the journal is," Roger said. "Perhaps you could wheedle the information out of her."

He doubted that was ever going to happen, especially after the events of the previous night.

"Someone else would be better in this position," Adam said.

"You're doing fine," Roger said. "You're one of the Service's most trusted operatives. No one else could do better than you, Adam."

If that was true, why had Roger sent another agent in to Marsley House?

He stood, knowing that they were about to go into a circular argument. Nothing he said was going to make any difference to Roger. Either Adam would have to walk away from his position at the War Office or he'd have to go back to Marsley House.

"Make a friend of her," Roger suggested. "Be a confidant. You might even hint that you knew her husband in India. That could form a bond between the two of you."

He doubted the duchess had much to do with her husband's prior military career. The fact, and it disturbed him to admit it even to himself, was that he didn't want to return to Marsley House, not even to submit his resignation and pack his belongings. He didn't want to see the duchess again. He didn't want to explain how resentful he felt about her grief. He didn't want to feel a surge of compassion for her. Nor did he want to have this odd compulsion to explain that he was trying to find proof that the Duke of Marsley had been a son of a bitch and responsible for the deaths of hundreds of people.

The duchess wouldn't mourn the bastard if she knew the truth.

Chapter Five

"$\mathcal{I}$ have been unable to find the hairpin, Your Grace."

It wasn't fair that she had to wake to Ella's complaints. If she put the pillow over her face would that silence the woman? Suzanne doubted it.

"I'm certain it will turn up," she said, blinking open her eyes.

Staring up at the sunburst pattern of silk over the bed didn't banish the sound of Ella's voice. Had it always been this grating?

"It is not among your things, Your Grace. And I've had the coachman check the carriage. Could you have left it at the dinner party?"

The dinner party had been a political event, a way of advancing another young man's career. She'd gone because it had been a command from her father, only to discover that there were a great many people in attendance, more than could be adequately seated at her father's expansive dining table. Instead of offering his guests service à la Russe, the dinner courses were arranged on the sideboards in the dining room, with the guests free to mill about or return to the food of their choice.

Had anyone else dared to entertain in such a fashion, the result would probably have been chaotic, but of course it wasn't. Her father left nothing to chance. A bevy of footmen wandered among the guests, ready to take plates or glasses or to offer more wine.

"Your Grace?"

Suzanne opened her eyes and turned her head to find Ella standing beside the bed as she did most mornings. At least the woman retired to her own chamber at night, giving Suzanne some much needed solitude.

If she had her way, she wouldn't have a lady's maid at all. But George had insisted. She'd quite liked Lily, the maid who'd abruptly quit six months ago. Ella had come to Marsley House then, recommended by her solicitor. Her father had also approved of the woman, and it had just been easier to keep Ella on after that.

Ignoring what was around her, be it people or things, made life so much simpler. What did anything matter, after all? It was easier to close her eyes and pretend she was somewhere else, a special place in her mind where she was alone and not bothered by anyone's questions or concerns.

He was suddenly there, in her mind like a storm god. A Scot wreathed in a blinding flash of lightning. Who did he think he was, speaking to her with such contempt in his voice? She'd had to endure a great deal in the last six years, but he had gone over the line. She was not going to be spoken to in such a way or be physically assaulted.

Perhaps her irritation at the majordomo was the reason she waved Ella away now.

"I don't need your help this morning," she said.

Ella ignored her. "Would you like to wear the silk with the ruching or the gathered skirt?"

Did it matter what she wore? That was not a comment she made to Ella. If she had said something so improvident to her maid, the woman would've responded with a lecture on mourning. She had passed two years, so technically she could don lavender if she wished or another subdued shade. But the color of her garments didn't matter. She would carry around a hole in her heart for the rest of her life.

"You have a visitor, Your Grace."

She looked at Ella in surprise. "A visitor? What time is it?"

"Nine thirty, Your Grace."

No one called at that hour in the morning. To do so was the height of rudeness, especially when she wasn't expecting them.

"Who is it?"

"A Mrs. Noreen Armbruster."

"Tell her I'm not receiving visitors. Tell her I'm away. Tell her anything."

"I would have done so ordinarily, Your Grace, but she said that you told her to call this morning, that the two of you talked last evening and specifically made an appointment. Nor does she look the type to leave without getting her way."

Ella sniffed, which was her way of expressing disgust. Evidently Mrs. Armbruster had annoyed the maid. For that alone, Suzanne should make the effort to visit with the woman.

She didn't remember a Mrs. Armbruster, but she didn't say so to Ella. Nor did she confide that the night before had been a blur.

No wonder her father had insisted that she depart

for home. She had probably embarrassed him in some way, but then she often did simply by being herself.

Once she would've cared. Once, years ago, she would've felt bad that they clashed so often. She would have felt that she'd let her mother down in some way.

"He doesn't mean to be a hard man, Suzanne," her mother had often told her. "It's just that he wants to accomplish a great deal in his life and the rest of us are slower and get in his way."

Edward Hackney had already accomplished a great deal. Was it enough for him? She didn't know and she'd never ask. They didn't have that kind of relationship. Not one of true thoughts and honest answers. Instead, he told her what he wanted her to do and she, for the most part, acceded without much clamor or fuss.

"Be kind to your father, my dearest Suzanne," her mother had said. "Try to understand him. If something happens to me it will just be the two of you." Had her mother known that her words would be prophetic? She'd died less than a month later.

At least her father hadn't married again. Was that because he'd truly loved her mother and mourned her still? Or because of expediency? He couldn't take the time or the energy to court another woman?

Another instance of never knowing.

She chose the silk with the ruching on the top of the bodice. She added a small black mourning cameo of a mother and child at the base of her throat.

"I'll get your tonic," Ella said.

"Not this morning."

She stared at herself in the mirror. She was too pale. Once she might have cared more about her appearance. Now all that mattered was that she was clean and presentable.

"Your tonic, Your Grace," Ella said.

Suzanne stood, moved away from the vanity, and headed for the sitting room door. She wasn't going to take that vile stuff this morning. Perhaps after her meeting with the majordomo. Until then, she needed to keep her wits about her and it was difficult to do that after ingesting the green potion.

Ella trailed after her instead of remaining behind and straightening up her chambers. Ella insisted on doing the cleaning herself, rather than allowing one of the upstairs maids into the suite. Suzanne knew exactly why she did that. It was yet another way she could maintain control.

The same reason the maid was now following her down the grand staircase.

At the bottom, Suzanne turned and faced Ella, uncaring that there were at least three footmen who could overhear their conversation. She had ceased having any privacy the day she moved into Marsley House. Over the years, she'd gradually become accustomed to the fact that she would always have people listening or watching her. In a sense, the green potion had helped with that, too.

This morning, however, she was herself, albeit with a headache. "That will be all," she said.

Her look defied the other woman to argue with her. It was probably the fact that there were witnesses that made Ella simply nod in response.

"That will be all," she repeated.

Ella nodded once more, but this time she turned and began ascending the staircase.

Mrs. Armbruster had been put into the Persian

room. George's grandfather had named this parlor after all the artifacts he'd collected from Persia and the Far East.

Suzanne hesitated in the doorway, realizing that it had been months since she'd been in this room. Thankfully, Mrs. Thigpen was an excellent housekeeper and didn't require daily monitoring. She felt a surge of gratitude toward the woman as well as the staff. There was no dust anywhere. The floors were swept and polished. The brass gleamed. The windows sparkled.

If only she were as well kept as her house.

Someone had had the good sense to offer Mrs. Armbruster refreshments, and the woman was sitting in the pasha's chair next to the window. George's grandfather claimed the chair was a throne used by a ruler of one of the disparate tribes in Persia. Its upholstery was crimson, and its arms and legs ended in lion's paws. A gilded wooden crown in a pattern that no doubt meant something to someone of Persian descent stretched four feet above the back of the chair. The morning sun danced on the gold, then came to rest on Mrs. Armbruster's bright red hair.

It was the hair Suzanne remembered more than Mrs. Armbruster's doughy, kind face. The woman had sparkling blue eyes that seemed amused as she placed her teacup on the table beside her.

They had indeed spoken last night, but Suzanne could not remember one single thing either of them had said.

"Mrs. Armbruster," she said. "I'm so sorry to make you wait."

"Your Grace, it's no bother at all. I have spent the time admiring this surprising room."

Suzanne glanced around at the shelves and the hundreds of knickknacks.

A crimson sofa sat in front of the fireplace and a primarily crimson carpet was underfoot. Even the wall covering was crimson, patterned in France and no doubt extraordinarily expensive.

She always thought of blood when she entered this room and from the history of Persia, she thought it was an apt comparison.

"It was an interest of my husband's grandfather," she said.

The man had a great many interests. One of them wasn't fodder for polite conversation.

Infidelity had been a hobby among the Whitcomb men.

"I'm very much afraid I don't have an apron, Your Grace."

Suzanne looked at the other woman. "I don't understand, Mrs. Armbruster."

"That lovely dress might be ruined."

She still didn't understand.

Mrs. Armbruster stood.

The woman was formidable, a presence in the room. It had nothing to do with her height, which was considerable, or her girth, or even the jutting of her bosom that made her look like the figurehead of a clipper ship. No, Mrs. Armbruster had something else, a quality that reminded Suzanne, oddly enough, of her father.

He, too, could quell anyone's comments or rebellion with a glance.

"Shall we go?" Mrs. Armbruster asked, heading for the parlor door.

"I beg your pardon? Where?"

The older woman glanced over her shoulder at Suzanne. "To the hospital, of course. We discussed it last night. We most desperately need your patronage, Your Grace."

She was marshaling her arguments as to why she couldn't possibly leave Marsley House when Mrs. Armbruster came to stand in front of her.

"You promised, Your Grace."

She'd never willingly broken a promise, even during these ghastly past years. Her mother had been her example in that.

"A woman's word is as good as a man's, Suzanne. Men aren't the only ones to live by a code of honor."

She wanted to ask her mother, then, if her father had a code of honor. But her mother had been ill and she hadn't. There were some questions that could never be asked and some answers that would never be given.

Mrs. Armbruster placed her hand on Suzanne's arm. That's how they left the Persian Parlor and headed for the front of Marsley House: Mrs. Armbruster sailing through the corridors and Suzanne feeling like she was being towed after the woman.

At the door, the footman furnished Mrs. Armbruster with her shawl while another servant fetched Suzanne's cloak.

"Where is that fascinating majordomo of yours, Your Grace? He's a military man, isn't he? You can always tell. They have a certain air about them. Not to mention that yours is a phenomenally handsome creature."

She focused on what Mrs. Armbruster was saying. "You've met my majordomo?"

"Indeed I have. You may not realize this, my dear,

but I came to see you a month ago, not realizing that you were at your country home. It was only the very best of circumstances that my husband and I were invited to your father's dinner party. Such a fascinating man, your father."

She didn't know which comment to respond to first. Thankfully, Mrs. Armbruster didn't seem to expect a response.

"It's a beautifully sunny day, my dear. You shan't need that," the older woman said, eyeing Suzanne's black wool cloak. "However, it might serve as an apron of sorts, especially when we get to the nursery."

Her hands froze in the act of putting on her gloves. "Nursery?" Her feet felt embedded in the marble of the foyer. They wouldn't move. For the love of all that was holy, she couldn't visit a nursery.

Mrs. Armbruster glanced at her.

"Trust me, Your Grace. Please."

"I can't," she said.

"You must."

Suzanne shook her head. She didn't care how insistent the other woman was, she couldn't.

Chapter Six

*A*dam arrived back at Marsley House in time to see a carriage pull away from the front entrance. He gave the signal to the driver to halt for a moment as it passed. Her Grace, the Duchess of Marsley, turned a white face toward him. He had the curious sensation that she needed assistance and that he was the only person who could help her. Their eyes met. Hers widened just for a moment before she composed herself once more, facing forward.

She'd been on his mind ever since last night, but the fact that no gossip had surfaced about the duchess being ill reassured him somewhat.

After the carriage passed he gave the signal for his driver to take him around the back of the house to the stables. The encounter, brief as it was, disturbed him. This assignment had been difficult from the beginning, but she was at the root of his sudden wish to be gone from Marsley House.

Until last night, he hadn't been excessively impatient with the slow pace of his investigation, knowing that it could take some time to find proof of the duke's treason. Now he wanted it done, completed, and over.

He hadn't wanted to come back to the house, but he'd done so because *duty* was a word that meant something to him. He'd been a dutiful soldier in India despite the stupidity of the orders he'd been given. Now he was a dutiful servant of the War Office and the Silent Service. Duty, however, sometimes required a sacrificial commitment. He'd learned that at Manipora.

He'd been a boy when he entered the army and it had molded and shaped him. Growing up in the tenements of Glasgow, he'd been concerned with elemental things like eating and keeping warm. It was only later, after comparing himself to his fellow soldiers, that he'd realized how much he was missing.

He could read, thanks to his mother, who'd died early of a lingering cough, but not before she had instilled some knowledge in her son and daughter. It was Mary, his sister, who had insisted on him learning his numbers and practicing his reading. After enlisting in the army, he'd begun to procure books, spending his hard-earned wages on a volume that he carried around in his knapsack. He would sometimes trade with another soldier. One of the wives at the British Legation in India had given him two books. He still had them at his lodgings and they were among his most treasured possessions.

A book, to him, was like a portable school. A book, unlike a headmaster, didn't care in what area of Glasgow he'd been raised, or whether he'd had the time or the energy to haul a bucketful of water up three flights of stairs so that he could wash. A book didn't offer judgment about his accent or his profanity. But the words, assimilated at his own pace, taught him.

So did his fellow soldiers. He emulated those men who'd purchased their commissions for a lark. He learned to eat with manners, figured out which words were insulting and not to be used often. Over time he softened his Glaswegian accent so that people didn't have any trouble understanding him.

"You're like a hawk," one of the women at the garrison once said to him. "You watch everything, Drummond, but you rarely speak. Why is that?"

He hadn't been able to explain it to her. Thankfully, she'd turned away so he was spared the necessity of trying to be polite.

His early years had been like barren soil. Only two flowers had brightened the landscape: his mother and his sister. They'd both been gone too soon, leaving him nothing but a brown-and-gray existence. Ever since being sent to India, however, he'd gradually begun to realize that life—for most people—was a flower garden.

They took for granted that they would be healthy and, for the most part, happy. They smiled and laughed, rejoiced in their children, good food, and companionship.

He had wanted that and he'd cultivated it for himself. At the same time, he decided that he would never willingly go back to that barren world of barely existing, of drawing breath but resenting even that because nothingness was so much more preferable to his current life.

He read philosophy and poetry and, like the Duke of Marsley, military theory. A few times, he even read novels, although in some cases he found the prose overblown and the dialogue ridiculously dramatic.

Nor was he like any of the heroes portrayed in

some of those books. He might have been considered brooding, but that was only because he believed in thinking more than speaking.

But he certainly wasn't a duke or a count or a mysterious owner of a deserted castle. He was only himself, and while he might be proud of some of his accomplishments, he doubted that they would be of interest to any woman like the heroines in some of those novels.

He made his way upstairs. From the information he'd acquired from Mrs. Thigpen, he knew that Marsley House was one of the largest private homes in London. He couldn't help but wonder if the builder, the third duke, had wanted to rival a palace. He'd come close to doing exactly that with the building's seventy-eight rooms. No wonder the staff was almost as large as a company.

In addition to all the bedchambers there were rooms to polish shoes and rooms to trim lamps and rooms to clean cutlery, press the newspapers, store the common dishes, and dry the dish towels. There was even a room that was set up with a broad oak table, stools, and a wooden clock over the door. On a shelf was a book on the peerage and one on etiquette. He'd taken that to be where the newest members of staff were educated on their duties. He'd had more than one peek at both of those books, but had found even more information in the library.

When Adam had first arrived, there were additional footmen assigned night duty—one for each of the wings and one outside the duke and duchess's quarters.

He'd gradually limited the number of personnel assigned to night duty. One of the reasons was simple logistics. He couldn't explore the library—and any of the other rooms—if he had to avoid eleven footmen. The second reason was that they didn't need all those footmen whose sole duty was to stand there and try not to fall asleep.

Because of his position Adam had a corner suite on the third floor with a bedroom, a sitting room that had been converted into an office, and a bathing chamber. He returned to his rooms now and spent several moments changing. He'd become accustomed to a uniform in the army, but a majordomo was supposed to dress in formal attire day and night. He wore black trousers, well-shined black shoes, a black tailcoat over a white shirt that had been starched to the point it could almost stand alone, a white waistcoat, and a white tie.

Once dressed, he walked into the office. The room was plain, devoid of any furnishings but his desk and one straight-backed chair. Someone had tried to add a touch of color to the room in the draperies, a crimson-and-beige stripe that looked as if it had been taken from one of the downstairs parlors.

He had not, despite the length of this assignment, attempted to personalize the space. Depending on who he was supposed to be, he often furnished personal items: a picture of a wife, or a sweetheart, a book or two, a watch inscribed with the name he was using at the time. They all went toward corroborating his false persona.

At Marsley House, his bedroom and office had been left bare. Perhaps because he had a more personal connection to this assignment.

For a few hours he occupied himself with the tasks of his role. The sheer volume of documents he needed to read, approve, sign, or forward to the family solicitor seemed to increase every day.

He arranged for the alterations to the uniforms of two fast-growing footmen. After writing down a recipe for silver polish, he tucked it into his pocket to give to the head footman who was responsible for making it, showing how it was to be applied, and supervising the staff in its application. Adam would inspect the silver later and arrange for it to be returned to its place in the pantry. It was his responsibility to count the damn stuff every night and make sure that one of the staff hadn't made off with a fork or spoon. At least he wasn't required to sleep next to the pantry, although Mrs. Thigpen had informed him that such had been the arrangement for years. That's why there was a room across the hall now used for extra china and stemware.

Before coming to Marsley House, he'd always thought that a housekeeper was responsible for everything that happened in an establishment. His assumption was incorrect, at least here. Adam was tasked with Marsley House running smoothly, which meant that if the roof needed retiling he had to ensure it was done. The same went for filling the pavement in front of the house. Last week he had the bother of getting one of the wrought iron gates at the front of the drive repaired.

He'd replaced an elderly majordomo, one Mrs. Thigpen called Old Franklin.

"The poor man became so forgetful and hard of hearing that he needed help with his tasks," Mrs. Thigpen had told him. "Sankara helped him a great deal. Sankara Bora. He was the duke's secretary and handled a great many details about the house. And Fairhaven, the family's house in the country."

Adam had found that Mrs. Thigpen was a font of knowledge. He went back to the well now, finding the housekeeper in her office beside the kitchen. The room smelled of cinnamon, but all of Marsley House was perfumed in some way. One maid was assigned to exchange the potpourri in all the rooms on a weekly basis. The scent was different depending on the chamber.

Mrs. Thigpen—or Olivia, as she insisted he call her—was eating what looked to be a raisin biscuit and passed the plate to him.

He smiled his thanks, sat on the chair next to her desk, and took one of the biscuits. Like anything Grace cooked, it was delicious.

Olivia had a long thin face with a broad nose, an appearance that made him unfortunately think of a horse. She had a similarly horsey laugh and large teeth. In addition, she had a curious gait. Not a limp exactly, but she tended to list a little to the right side when she walked.

He'd wanted to ask if she'd had a childhood accident that affected her, but it was too personal a question. However, he tried to ease her burden whenever he could, giving orders to all the footmen to assist her if they saw Olivia carrying anything.

"Have you any idea where the duchess has gone?" he asked after spending a few minutes in pleasantries. He helped himself to two additional biscuits, which only prompted Olivia's smile.

"Has she gone somewhere? Not very usual of her, Adam. I don't know. Shall I ring for her maid? Ella will probably know. She doesn't share much about the duchess, however."

"Never mind," he said. "It isn't important. I merely saw her on my way in."

"She may have gone visiting," Olivia offered. "The new duke is a second cousin of the late duke. They socialized some. Perhaps she's gone to see him."

Was she even considered a duchess if there was a new duke? He didn't know. Nor was he comfortable in sharing his ignorance with Olivia.

A good deal of the time he had to hide his lack of knowledge from the rest of the staff. To do that, he had to appear standoffish, demonstrating a haughty kind of arrogance that always irritated him when he had to face it in another individual. He'd managed to frighten a good percentage of the maids, most of whom did a curious little curtsy when they saw him. It wasn't until Olivia said something that he understood why.

"You're new," she said. "A great many of the staff are frightened of you, Adam. You could let anyone go at any time."

"I have no intention of letting anyone go, Olivia," he'd said.

"Well, if you don't mind, Adam, I shall convey that to the rest of the staff. I know it would reassure everyone."

Now whenever he encountered one of the frightened maids, he went out of his way to smile. They still acted nervous, but if they'd come from a background similar to his, he could understand their fear. Being a servant helped them escape from grinding poverty. Of course, nowadays, there were other avenues as well. A girl could find work in the shops or the factories. They didn't have to go into service. But it seemed to him that working at Marsley House wasn't a bad plan for making your way in the world.

He advised Olivia that he was ordering another two bolts of cloth for uniforms and was sending the monthly expenditures to Mr. Barney, the family solicitor. She nodded and said she'd tell the seamstress who made most of her living sewing livery for the Marsley House staff. She informed him that one of the maids had tearfully left their employ this morning, citing homesickness. He would be responsible for hiring a replacement.

He thanked Olivia for the biscuits and headed for the library, specifically to the third floor and the shelves containing the duke's journals.

When he'd first begun his assignment, he'd started with the duke's years in India. None of those books had furnished the proof that he needed. Then he took the last book and moved backward through time. A gap existed between that journal and the date of the duke's death, but there had been other times when the duke had simply stopped writing for a while. Adam had finally started over at the beginning, giving himself the chore of reading all of the Duke of Marsley's self-indulgent writings. So far he'd learned a great deal about the duke and most of it was boring.

This week he'd reached the man's early twenties. George Whitcomb had written extensively about his conquest of the ladies. On more than one occasion he'd seemed to delve into self-examination and said something cogent like, "It is my title, I am sure, that brings them like bees buzzing around the garden." Then he'd added a comment that made Adam realize he wasn't aware of himself at all. "But it is my title, after all. It is part of me. My heritage. I was reared to be the Duke of Marsley. And as such, I will accept any bounty that my title delivers to me."

The duke had had the same attitude in India, the same self-glorification. It was as if, when he spoke, he simply amazed himself and had to spend several minutes in silent awe of his own brilliance. Of course, his aides and the other men surrounding him acted as impressed as George no doubt felt.

Beware a man who holds power with no one to check it. One of the many lessons Adam had learned in the army.

He grabbed two of the journals and returned to the desk on the first floor. It would be better if he could examine the books without the possibility of being interrupted by a maid. However, he didn't want to change the schedule and therefore incite curiosity. The less attention he attracted, the better.

At least there was no threat of the duchess coming into the library.

Where had the duchess gone and why had he gotten the feeling that she needed to be rescued?

The sooner he found the proof he needed, the better. He wanted to be gone from Marsley House and its duchess in all possible haste.

Chapter Seven

Suzanne had no idea how she'd been manipulated into entering Mrs. Armbruster's carriage. She hadn't had much of a choice. Her only alternative had been to strike the older woman. Or perhaps scream at the top of her lungs.

She'd been impotent in the face of the older woman's implacable determination.

The vehicle was not as luxurious as her own, but then, her carriage had been a gift from her husband on their second anniversary. As if a vehicle was enough of an inducement to ignore George's straying from the marital bed. She'd pretended not to notice and, later, not to care. The terrible thing about pretense was that sometimes it became real.

Her hand on the bottom of the window was warm even through her gloves. The sun was insistent about brightening the day. She pulled her hand down and placed one atop the other at her waist.

"It's not just money we're after," the older woman said. "These poor babies need more than that. Food first, it's true, but they also need kindness. They need someone to care for them, Your Grace, and you struck me as the type of person who would care."

"You don't know me, Mrs. Armbruster. Nor did you when you first came to see me. What gave you the notion I would be interested in a hospital?"

The other woman shook her head. "No, Your Grace, not just a hospital. It's called Haven Foundling Hospital."

She was going to be sick. She couldn't possibly visit such a place, but she had the inkling that whatever she said would be countered by this most insistent woman. She had to do something, anything, to get Mrs. Armbruster to turn the carriage around and take her home. She just wanted—desperately needed—an end to this. Hopefully before anything more terrible happened.

"Recently we took a few babies from St. Pancras Workhouse," Mrs. Armbruster was saying. "That despicable place stank of sewage, Your Grace. Flies were allowed to breed everywhere and the poor infants had been left to lie for hours in their own waste."

Suzanne closed her eyes and wished that the woman would stop talking. She and God had an arrangement. He would no longer punish her and she wouldn't pray. She was not going to betray their truce now by slipping and praying that He would do something to quiet Mrs. Armbruster. Not that God would listen. He hadn't been listening for two years.

"I realize that Spitalfields is a terrible place, Your Grace. Father Gilbert and the Sisters of Mercy have recently opened a refuge on Providence Row. It's a place where destitute women and children can find a meal and a bed at night. But we know there is always more of a need than there is an answer to that need."

She'd heard of Spitalfields at one of her father's innumerable political dinners. Someone had described it as Hell on earth and had then apologized profusely to the assembled guests.

She mutely nodded, turning to the window again.

In the past few minutes the merry sun had vanished. Houses leaned together, obscuring the view of the sky. The crowded London streets had altered as well. The color of the pavement was darker and had a slick and slimy look to it. An odor came to her then of an open sewer or the Thames in previous summers. She held her handkerchief to her nose and wondered if Mrs. Armbruster came this way every day. Or was this journey only to impress upon Suzanne the dire conditions of the people living in Spitalfields?

Only a few people were visible. The women who stood on the street corners had stark white faces with pale mouths and dark shadowed eyes. How odd to realize that she and a woman of the streets had the same lack of hope, the same disinterested view of the world.

The men were thin, startled easily, and glanced around nervously before their eyes settled on the passing carriage. Their looks were hungry and not simply for food. They wanted what she had without knowing the price she'd paid for it.

"Why?" Suzanne asked, turning to Mrs. Armbruster.

"Why you?" The woman smiled brightly again.

Suzanne shook her head. "No. Why you?"

For the first time, Mrs. Armbruster looked taken aback. Suzanne could see that she was formulating an answer. No doubt something that sounded good but was far from honest.

She pressed her advantage. "Why you, Mrs. Armbruster? What about the situation inspired you, particularly, to do something? To raise money? To attempt to change the conditions of these children?"

The other woman's gaze settled on her hands. Although Mrs. Armbruster wore gloves, Suzanne could tell that her knuckles were swollen and her thumbs disfigured from arthritis.

"I had a maid," she finally said. "A good girl. Tenny was her name. She came from Ireland and was as bright a soul as you could ever meet. She and I looked like mother and daughter with our red hair. But Tenny's eyes were as green as the hills of Ireland."

Suzanne didn't interrupt the woman, even though she was certain the tale didn't end well.

"She left my employ, I'm sorry to say, but at the time I was happy for her. She benefitted herself by taking up service in a wealthy merchant's home." Mrs. Armbruster took a deep breath, let it out, and continued Tenny's story. "It wasn't an advancement at all, poor thing. Instead, she got herself with child and was dismissed."

The older woman stared out at the sight of Spitalfields.

"She didn't come to me, and I wish she had. I would have spared her the agony of her actions. She put her child in the care of a woman who promised to look after it while Tenny worked. The infant died only three weeks later and Tenny was beside herself. She passed not long after and although the physician said she died of natural causes, I think it was a broken heart, myself."

She turned to look at Suzanne. "Had she placed the infant with an orphanage or a workhouse, the effect would have been the same. The child would probably still have died. Most infants do in those circumstances."

A band tightened around Suzanne's chest, keeping her heart from bursting. She could barely breathe, but somehow she asked a question of the older woman. "But they don't with your organization?"

"No," Mrs. Armbruster said flatly. "They don't. We give each baby individual care and pride ourselves on the fact that each thrives under it. Yet we have a list of nearly five hundred women and their children who desperately need help. I don't know how many of them are still alive, Your Grace. I do know that we could have saved most of them."

"Have they no place to go?" she asked.

"One would think their families would take them in, but that isn't the case, regrettably. They've shamed their relatives and they want nothing to do with them."

"Not even for the sake of the child?"

"Unfortunately, the child is seen as expendable." Mrs. Armbruster's voice was dull. Gone was her bright smile, and tears pooled in her eyes. "That's why, Your Grace, I'm appealing to you."

She didn't want to help. She didn't want anything to do with Mrs. Armbruster and her Foundling Hospital. She wanted to be returned to Marsley House now, as swiftly as the horses could carry her. She wanted to retreat to her suite, bolt the door behind her, and take some of Ella's tonic, the better to forget everything.

"We exist not only to save those poor children, Your Grace, but to give their mothers a chance once more to enter society. We teach them to read, do sums, and write. We train them in various positions so that they are able to support their children. When the children get older, we provide a school for them."

"All of which sounds exceedingly virtuous, Mrs. Armbruster. If you'll return me home I'll communicate with my solicitor and ensure you are given a generous sum."

"But that's not enough, Your Grace."

It was assuredly going to have to be. She could not tolerate much more. Her hands were clammy. Her heart was beating entirely too fast. Her stomach was churning. She was going to be deathly sick in front of the woman, in front of all of London, but she didn't care as much about that as the feeling that she was breaking in two.

What had she said to the woman to give the impression that she was interested in this cause? She suspected that she'd said almost anything in order to keep the woman from going on and on about her charity. People normally didn't mention children around her. They knew enough to keep silent on that topic. She doubted that Mrs. Armbruster had been as tactful and now she was trapped in a carriage with the woman.

Any moment now and her heart was going to spill out of her chest. It would go tumbling down over her bodice, her skirt, and throw itself out the door of the carriage, there to be run over by the wide wheels.

What did she need with a heart, anyway? Hers had been dead for years.

She closed her eyes and leaned her head back against the seat.

"Please, Mrs. Armbruster. I'm feeling unwell. I need to return home."

"But Your Grace, we're here. We'll get you a bracing cup of tea and all will be well, you'll see."

Chapter Eight

$\mathcal{M}$rs. Armbruster didn't offer her tea. Instead, she led Suzanne to the main part of the hospital.

Suzanne didn't know what she expected, but it wasn't a neat row of cribs, each sitting next to an iron cot with a thin mattress. Every cot had a small table next to it with a lamp and a Bible and a small trunk at its foot.

Only five of the twenty beds and cribs were currently occupied.

"They've just given birth," Mrs. Armbruster whispered. "The girl at the end, the one with the short black hair, is our newest patient. Amy was found in the ocean. It was thought that she tried to drown herself, but she was rescued by a kindhearted sailor and brought here. I shudder to think what would've happened to her if she'd been taken anywhere else."

"Where are the rest of the girls?" she asked.

"Some might be with the physician. Others might be in the garden. We have a small yard in the back. We want them to take their babies with them, of course. There will be plenty of time for them to be separated. Now it's important that they get to know each other."

She turned and walked with Mrs. Armbruster as they headed down a wide corridor with windows at each end, flooding the space with light. Everything was painted white, but instead of giving it a sterile look, the absence of color merely brightened the space and allowed the sun to tinge everything a pale yellow.

Mrs. Armbruster opened a door at the end of the hall to reveal a room with a wall of windows. The space was bright and sunny, and the yellow, green, blue, and pink cribs added color to the space. Here there were no cots, only cribs, each one of them occupied.

There was a curious sweetness to the air, as if there were flowers somewhere nearby. Was the Foundling Hospital normally this clean or had it been straightened for her arrival?

Suzanne froze in the doorway, watching as three girls went from crib to crib, caring for the infants.

One girl went to the crib closest to Suzanne and lifted an infant from it.

"Henry, what have you done so soon? You just want to make sure I can't sit down for a moment, don't you?"

The baby drooled happily down the shoulder of her dress, reached out, and batted her nose with his clenched fist. The girl laughed as if it was a game they had played many times before.

"Come, my dear," Mrs. Armbruster said.

The woman grabbed Suzanne's arm and nearly hauled her into the room, making a sweeping gesture with her free hand to encompass all the cribs.

"These are our foundlings, Your Grace. These poor babies have either lost their mothers or they were found on our doorstep."

She couldn't imagine anything more terrible, having to give up a child in order to ensure its life. Would she have done that? Yes, in a heartbeat.

The young girl assigned to care for Henry turned and walked toward them.

To her absolute horror, the young girl thrust Henry at her.

"Would you like to hold him?"

Suzanne broke free of Mrs. Armbruster's grip and stepped backward, away from the infant, and kept going until she hit the far wall.

Henry didn't like being held with hands beneath his arms and began to wail. The young girl pulled him back into her embrace, cradling him until he was calm. Mrs. Armbruster nodded at the girl, and she took Henry to the changing table and replaced his diaper.

Suzanne crossed her arms in front of her, expecting a lecture, a verbal treatise on the joy of caring for an innocent child. At the very least, she anticipated a solicitation for funds.

Instead, Mrs. Armbruster approached her slowly, almost as if Suzanne were a rabid dog or a fox that had been cornered and was now snarling and threatening to bite.

The woman reached out and touched her arm again.

"I know, Your Grace. I know."

That's all she said before dropping her hand.

No one ever said a word. No one offered condolences or sympathy. Not one person had, in these last two years, ever come to her and said, *I am sorry, Suzanne.*

Yet Mrs. Armbruster had done more than that.

There were tears in the older woman's eyes. Suzanne closed her own eyes, kept her arms folded, the better to prevent herself from shattering.

The silence lengthened and strengthened, creating a bubble around them. No doubt one of the babies cried. Or was soothed by one of its minders. Perhaps someone even spoke or crooned or laughed. But here, in a room set aside for orphaned infants, neither of them spoke.

Words were beyond Suzanne. Nor would she have been able to listen to anything Mrs. Armbruster had to say.

Finally, when she could bear the silence no longer, the other woman said, "We should return to Marsley House, Your Grace."

Suzanne only nodded, so grateful she nearly wept.

Suzanne walked swiftly back to the entrance, nodding to the driver, who dismounted from his perch and opened the carriage door. Once inside, she settled herself in the corner of the seat.

Mrs. Armbruster remained silent for long moments.

Suzanne studied the passing scenery. Not that there was anything to admire about what she saw. The darkness, the grayness of the very air pushed down on her. She pressed her handkerchief to her nose in an effort to tolerate the stench.

"I'm sorry, Your Grace," Mrs. Armbruster finally said. "I should not have taken you there. But I'd heard that you were a kind woman and thought you might be able to help. Those poor babies need someone to care."

Suzanne didn't respond. At least she hadn't burst out wailing in front of Mrs. Armbruster. For a good many months she had done that, to the shock of the servants. That's why she'd finally gone to their country house, where there were fewer witnesses to her grief.

"You expect too much from me."

"Yes," Mrs. Armbruster said, surprising her. "I have, Your Grace, and that is my failing. I sometimes push too hard, and I ask your forgiveness."

Her hand curled below the window, the knuckles showing white. When the carriage turned left, an errant beam of sunlight danced along her skin. She pulled her hand back and buried it in her cloak. She wasn't dead, but sometimes she felt guilty for being alive. Why should she feel the sun when he didn't?

"What will happen to them? All those infants?"

"There aren't that many," Mrs. Armbruster said, a touch of defensiveness in her voice. Suzanne wanted to tell her she wasn't being critical, merely curious.

"That's why we keep our numbers down, Your Grace. We want to ensure a favorable outcome for each child we take in."

"Is there a reason for the different colored cribs?"

She glanced over at Mrs. Armbruster. The other woman had tilted her head slightly, reminding her of an inquisitive bird.

"The pink, blue, yellow, and green," Suzanne said. "Is there a reason for those colors?"

Mrs. Armbruster shook her head. "No, but how wise of you, my dear. Perhaps we should make it mean something. An infant below six months could go in a blue crib. One below three months might go in the yellow. That sort of thing. We don't do that now, but it's definitely an idea."

"And the girls, assigned to care for the babies," Suzanne said. "You might have them wearing a different colored smock depending on what age they are assigned to."

Mrs. Armbruster smiled slightly as she nodded.

"To answer your earlier question, Your Grace, some of the infants will be sent to foster homes until they're four or five years old. At that time, they'll come back to the hospital to live. In a different section, of course, but there all the same."

"Isn't that cruel? To pull them away from the only family they'd ever known?"

"Most foster families are not equipped to raise a child, but they're willing to help one get past infancy."

"And the girls? The girls who stay with their children? Is there a favorable outcome for them?"

Mrs. Armbruster gave her a look that she couldn't interpret. It was almost as if the older woman didn't wish to speak any further. As if Suzanne had asked her an intimate question, one that was rude by its very nature.

"Your Grace, does it matter? You've already given me the impression that you prefer to have nothing to do with the hospital. I can certainly understand why."

Suzanne wanted to explain, to offer some kind of justification. But what would she say? She didn't expose her grief. She didn't parade it, unveil it, and hold it aloft for other people to see. It was hers and perhaps some would say that she had breathed life into it, that she'd made it substantial and real. Perhaps she had, but who could blame her?

Perhaps little Henry.

"I know what you're feeling, Your Grace. You think that if you put aside your grief, even for a moment, it means you didn't love him. But I can assure you that caring about something else will not mean that you love him any less. Or that you've ceased to mourn him."

She glanced at the other woman to find Mrs. Armbruster regarding her with kind eyes.

She'd gone along with the woman practically kidnapping her, thrusting her into a carriage, and taking her to the Foundling Hospital. She'd endured a tour, and then, when it was too much, demanded to be returned home. She would not tolerate being lectured on grief.

What did the woman expect? That she would want to hold each and every one of those infants? That she would kiss a downy head and smile at an infant's grin? That she would put out a finger to have a chubby fist grip it?

The ache was back, but then it had never truly gone away. It sat there, waiting, for something to unfurl it. A sight, a sound, a thought was all it needed and then the ache became a very real pain.

She was not given to being direct in her speech, but it seemed as if Mrs. Armbruster was demanding it of her. Whatever happened to tact or a little reticence in manner? The woman had said it herself. She pushed too hard. Perhaps she deserved Suzanne pushing back in turn.

"What is it you want from me, Mrs. Armbruster?"

"I didn't have the opportunity to show you our other project, Your Grace. The Institute. We're taking in girls who have gotten themselves in trouble. That is not the proper way to call it, of course. They did not do it to themselves, but the law does not see that as correct. Society punishes only the female in this case."

Mrs. Armbruster turned a little so that she was facing Suzanne.

"Until they give birth, they have a home and a roof over their heads. They are fed and kept warm and out of the elements. I want you to meet some of them. They aren't terrible girls, Your Grace. They might have been foolish. They might have listened to the blandishments of young men. Some of them were even taken advantage of by their employers.

"In addition, I would like to name the Institute after you, Your Grace. That is, if you wanted to become one of our patrons."

She looked at Mrs. Armbruster, stunned. She hadn't agreed to any kind of financial backing. In fact, she didn't have the kind of funds the other woman evidently hoped she'd donate.

The only money George had left her was what remained of the huge amount her father had settled on him at their marriage. A dowry, if one was kind. Payment for taking her as his bride if one was more realistic. While her husband hadn't been profligate, he hadn't been a miser, either. No doubt he'd purchased a few baubles for his mistresses. She knew, from his bragging, that he'd bet on more than one horse.

But to sponsor—and fund—an organization the size of Mrs. Armbruster's? No, she didn't have the ability to do that.

What on earth was she supposed to say?

Thankfully, the carriage was turning into the drive, through the wrought iron gates, up the slight incline to the circular approach to Marsley House.

Mrs. Armbruster was still looking at her.

The carriage rolled to a stop and the footman was opening the carriage door.

Suzanne murmured something about speaking with her solicitor and said her farewells as quickly as politeness dictated before descending from the carriage. She climbed the steps faster than she could ever remember doing and entered the door with a sigh of relief. After she removed her hat and gloves and placed both on the sideboard, the footman helped her off with her cloak.

Where was Drummond?

Another irritant—this one, at least, she could do something about.

Chapter Nine

Drummond was nowhere to be found. The annoying man was not in the pantry supervising the polishing of the silver. Nor was he in his office—and she'd sent a maid to fetch him.

"He's often in the library, Your Grace," one of the footmen said, bowing slightly to her.

Why on earth would he be in the library? He hadn't struck her as being particularly scholarly the night before.

He wasn't there, either.

Rather than send the entirety of the staff looking for him—and causing a great deal of speculation, not to mention gossip—she sublimated her irritation and set herself on another course, that of finding her mother's hair clip.

The roof was bathed by sunlight. There were only a few tiny puddles here and there as proof of the storm the night before. A cool wind brushed the tendrils of hair away from her cheeks. The air smelled fresh with no tinge of decay. The sky was a brilliant blue and from here, atop Marsley House, she could see the skyline of London stretching out before her. No hint of Spitalfields was visible.

Although the house boasted a formal Tudor garden, she missed the valleys and fertile fields of the country. Summer seemed to last so much longer there until, at last, autumn reluctantly arrived, turning the leaves brown and scattering them across the lanes.

Standing here she might have been a princess in a castle, one elevated away from the masses. Instead, she knew she wasn't royalty. Nor was she exempt from the emotions any other person felt.

At the moment it was anger. Anger at Mrs. Armbruster, at her father, at Drummond. Some of that anger—perhaps most of it—was set aside for herself. She should have been stronger. She should have refused to go to the Foundling Hospital. She should have stayed in the country.

Perhaps she should only be angry at circumstances. Fate had decreed her life, altered her destiny, and changed her future.

She walked to the edge of the roof, putting her hands on the banister, and looked down at the gravel approach below her. The height made her dizzy and more than a little nauseous. Cautiously, she stepped back.

A sparkle caught her attention. Something was lodged not far from the railing, an object gleaming in the afternoon sun. She was bending to retrieve it when she was suddenly grabbed about the waist and jerked back a few feet.

"Och, you daft woman," an accented voice said.

"Let me go!"

"Why, so you can try to throw yourself from the roof again? Not on my watch."

She tried to wrench herself away, but Drummond

had a good grip on her. His arms were wrapped around her midriff and were pressing upward on her breasts. She hadn't been touched like that by a man for years. She had certainly never been assaulted by one.

She tried to use her elbows to punch him but he didn't release her. Instead, he pulled her backward until the heels of her shoes were grinding into the surface of the roof.

"Let me go, you idiot. I wasn't going to throw myself off the roof. I was looking for something."

"And is that what you were trying to do last night, you daft woman?"

"Would you stop calling me that," she said. She'd never been talked to in such a manner. Who did he think he was? "Let me go," she said, calming herself so she could speak. Her heart was racing and she could barely breathe. "I didn't. It was a mistake. You misinterpreted everything."

"Did I misinterpret you crawling over the railing last night?"

"Did I really do that?" she asked, startled.

"Aye, you did, and very determined you were."

"I had too much wine," she said, embarrassed to be making such a confession to someone she didn't know. Someone who was in her employ, at least for now.

"I've had my share of nights like that, Duchess. I never once tried to end my life."

She didn't have anything to say in defense of herself. Was there a defense she could offer? Not one word came to mind. Prior to last night she couldn't remember ever being on the roof.

"How did you know where I was?" she asked.

"I was told you were looking for me when I got back from the stables."

"And you naturally came here to see if I was intent on throwing myself to my death again?"

"Something like that," he said, not relaxing his hold.

"You can let me go," she said. "I can assure you that I have no intention of ending my life."

In the past few minutes she'd allowed herself to relax in his grip. She lay her head back against his chest. Anyone looking at them might think they were lovers who'd slipped up to the roof for a few moments alone and now stood there, captivated by the sight of London lit by the sun.

No one would think that the two of them were antagonists.

"I don't know what came over me," she said, compelled to say something. "I don't remember wanting to end my life. I'm glad you stopped me."

"He isn't worth it, you know. Not all your grieving."

Anger suddenly bubbled up from where it had been hiding. She pulled free of him and turned.

"How could you say such a hideous thing?"

"Because it's the truth."

She hadn't meant to cry. She really hadn't. Especially not in front of him. But she couldn't hold back the reservoir of tears, all that weeping she wouldn't permit herself to do at the hospital. She took a step back, but he wouldn't allow her that. Instead, he reached out and grabbed her wrist and pulled her to him. Only then did she realize that she'd been backing up to the edge.

For some reason, that made her cry harder. Then he was holding her again. His arms were around her back, his hands flat against her cloak. She couldn't reach up and brush her face, so she had no other choice but to lay her cheek against his jacket and let it soak up her tears.

He said something in Gaelic to her, some barely whispered words in a voice that sounded reluctant and ill at ease.

When she tried to move away, he shushed her and pulled her close once again.

"I'm sorry," he said. "I had no right to speak of your husband that way. Of course you mourn him. That's what wives do, don't they?"

She held herself still, closing her eyes against her tears. He thought she was crying for George. He thought her grief was for a man she'd never truly understood, for a stranger with whom she lived for six years.

She moved her arm up and placed her hand against Drummond's chest. His heart thundered against her palm.

"*Gabh mo leisgeul,*" he said. "I didn't mean to ridicule your pain."

"What are you saying?"

"I'm sorry. It's Gaelic for *I'm sorry*, and I am."

He confused her. What kind of man was this Scottish majordomo? On one hand, he was vicious in his speech, yet he'd tried to save her not once but twice.

She pushed free finally, taking a step back and keeping her gaze on the surface of the roof. She couldn't look at him. She couldn't acknowledge this moment of intimacy. He was the first man who'd touched her or attempted to comfort her for years.

Also, he was the only man who'd ever apologized for his actions.

"I was going to release you from my service the minute I saw you today," she said, her voice low. "I was going to demand that you leave Marsley House within the hour, without recommendation or reference. I was going to tell you how much I detested your speaking to me in that way and that I considered you a despicable creature."

She dared herself to look up at him.

Mrs. Armbruster was right.

Why hadn't she noticed how handsome he was until this exact second? His eyes were a soft green. His hair was thick and black, and he had a dimple on the left side of his mouth. His was a strong, square face, one that would probably be transformed by a smile. Now it was stern and somber and a little daunting.

"But I can't do any of those things now, Drummond. Not after coming to the conclusion that you saved me from myself. That was last night, however. Today I only came here to find something."

He didn't look as if he believed her and she regretted that.

"I do not mourn my husband," she said, giving him the truth as a gift, a payment for his protection of her. "God forgive me, but all I felt was relief at his death."

She turned and headed for the door to the third floor. How odd that she could feel his eyes on her all the way down the stairs.

ADAM WALKED TO the edge of the roof, stood where the duchess had been, and looked around. It took him a moment, but he saw what she'd been reaching for, a leaf-shaped diamond brooch. He bent and picked it up. The brooch rested in his palm, the diamonds glittering and sparkling like fire was in their depths.

What kind of woman treated this bauble with such disdain? The kind who had been, no doubt, raised with no fear. Not like his mother, who worried about each meal or if the landlord was coming before she'd earned the rest of the rent. He'd been twelve when she died of a cough that had consumed her.

If she'd still been alive or if Mary had lived, he would've stayed behind in Glasgow. He would've made his way, somehow, maybe at the foundry or one of the cotton mills. He'd have been determined to support them. But that was water into the Clyde, wasn't it? They hadn't lived and there'd been no reason for him to stay there.

He pushed the thoughts of his past down deep. What good was it to dwell on something he couldn't change?

He closed his fist around the brooch so tightly that he could feel the diamonds pressing into his skin. Marble Marsley—hardly that, though, was she?

Whom did she mourn? He hadn't asked Mrs. Thigpen enough questions about the Duchess of Marsley, and he was determined to correct that oversight as quickly as possible.

First, however, he had an obligation to return to his pose as majordomo and then to his assignment. Along the way, if he could forget the surprising duchess, all the better.

Chapter Ten

$\mathcal{S}$he really should have dismissed Drummond on the spot. Instead, she'd allowed him to comfort her. She wasn't acting anything like a duchess, was she? First going to the Foundling Hospital and then being embraced by a servant.

Perhaps she'd simply needed to be held. For those few minutes when he'd put his arms around her she'd allowed herself to weaken. In that short space of time she didn't have to be the Duchess of Marsley. She didn't have to be possessed of poise and reserve. She didn't have to be strong.

Drummond hadn't told her that she should get over her loss. He didn't say that she needed to put her past behind her. Not once had he uttered those despicable words: *Sometimes things happen. We need to get beyond them.*

What was the recipe for getting beyond this? What, exactly, did she do? Did she burn a certain herb? Did she utter an incantation? Did she memorize a certain verse or a whole book from the Bible? Did she prostrate herself on the chapel floor? Did she summon a wise woman or a physician? Did she consult the most learned men in London?

She would've done all of those things eagerly, but nothing would have altered the reality of her life. Nothing would have ended the cavernous emptiness she felt.

Instead of entering her suite she hesitated at the door, unwilling to go inside and face Ella. The fact that she was hiding from her maid was yet another embarrassment. When would she cease being a person subject to the whims of others?

She walked to the end of the corridor where George's rooms were located. Slowly, giving herself time to reconsider, she opened his sitting room door and slid inside.

The smell of beeswax permeated the room, an indication that the maid had been diligent. Although he'd been gone two years, his suite was dusted every day. Every morning the curtains were opened as if someone might wish to witness the view of the approach to Marsley House. Once a week the windows were polished, as were the mirrors. The cushions on the yellow-and-brown-striped sofa and chairs were fluffed. The pale yellow carpet with its brown frame was brushed once a month and twice a year taken outside to be beaten.

Yet no one would ever return to take up residence in this suite again.

She went to the small desk between the two floor-to-ceiling windows and extracted the key from the center drawer. It never used to be here, but she kept it in this place for safekeeping. Her life was not her own and any semblance of privacy was laughable with Ella going through her pockets, reticule, and anything else she wished on the premise that she was caring for Suzanne's belongings.

The one thing Ella hadn't yet done was prowl through the duke's suite.

Suzanne pocketed the key, turned, and surveyed the room. She would have to commend Mrs. Thigpen for assigning a conscientious maid to the suite. Whoever had been in charge had done an admirable job. Even George couldn't have faulted the girl. Even though he would have tried, unless she was pretty enough to seduce.

She opened the door to the duke's suite slowly, looking down the hallway to ensure that Ella wasn't coming or going. When she saw no one in the corridor, she slipped out of the room and closed the door quietly behind her.

Although the servants' stairs would have been closer to the room she sought, she took the main staircase to the third floor. The chances of encountering one of the maids were greater in the afternoon. They worked from seven until eleven and then again from one until dark, going through Marsley House from the first floor to the third, with the public rooms rotated on Mrs. Thigpen's schedule.

No one, however, ever entered the room that was her destination. She'd given orders that it was to be considered sacrosanct. No one was to dust or rearrange anything. Everything was to be left exactly as it had been that day. That terrible day. The day that essentially ended her life.

She didn't allow herself to come here often, because the temptation would be to remain in here, cloistered, with memories of happiness like bubbles surrounding her. She might have turned insane in this room from longing or grief.

She stood outside the door with her hand gripping

the key as she willed her heart to slow its frantic beating and her lungs to fill with air. After the events of this morning, she needed to remind herself of things gone and over, but never forgotten.

Sadness felt sentient, reaching out with a clawlike grip and holding on to her soul.

Slowly she inserted the key in the lock and turned it, hearing the click as loud as a gunshot. Here, in this quiet corridor, every sound was magnified.

She turned the latch and stepped inside, then closed the door swiftly behind her. As it was most times, the room was shadowed and still. Because she knew the space so well, she didn't need light to see her way to the windows. She opened one set of curtains and then another, turning and surveying the room in the bright sunlight.

She could feel the warmth of the sun on her shoulders. How strange that she felt so cold inside, as if she could never truly be warm again.

The wind sighed against the windows, promising the chill of winter soon to come. Winter was the dead season when everything, perhaps even life itself, went dormant.

There, in the corner, was the crib he was so proud to have outgrown. Next to it was the small bed with its pillow and bright blue coverlet. At three years old he had been his own person with his father's arrogance and her humor.

The silence in the nursery still shocked her. It grated on her, reminding her at the same time it enshrouded her. There were no soft giggles. No remonstrances from the nurse. No excited, "Up, up," demands from Georgie. Nothing but an eternal quiet that must mimic the grave.

Here, in this room, she remembered happiness and joy. Here, as in no other space on the earth, she remembered a small voice asking innumerable questions and demanding that the world slow and stop for him.

She walked toward the crib, reached out, and put her hand on the ornate carving of the spindles. The crib was an heirloom, like most of the furniture at Marsley House. George had used it, but there would never be another child to use the crib. Memories would have to be enough. Georgie bouncing up and down, impatient to be about the investigation of his day. Her raising him up in her arms as he grinned at her.

He had been just like Henry in his optimism and joy.

Henry had few chances in life, while Georgie had had the world spread out before him. Whatever he'd wanted to do, however he'd wanted to accomplish it, both his mother and father would have moved mountains to ensure he could have done it.

In their love for their child she and George were united. It was in everything else they were separate.

She sat on the end of Georgie's bed, staring at the far wall where all his toys were arranged. His toy soldiers would never again fight imaginary battles. His stuffed rabbit would never be clutched to his chest as he fought sleep. A wooden horse on wheels sat next to a wagon filled with blocks, all waiting patiently for their owner to return and play with them.

For the first time in two years, her tears were manageable. She wasn't assaulted by the strength of her grief. Because she had already wept in her majordomo's arms? Or had she begun to realize, finally, inexorably, that she might wish it and will it and pray for it but she was never going to see her darling child again. He would forever be three years old and she would forever be his grieving mother.

Henry didn't have a mother. She pushed that thought away but it surfaced again. None of those babies at the Foundling Hospital had a mother to care for them. They'd been made artificial orphans because of shame. Those poor children would always be known as foundlings. They'd go through life with that stigma, being branded as a child even their own mother hadn't wanted.

Life was sometimes cruel; she knew that only too well. Was that why she'd tried to scale the railing and fall from the roof? She couldn't honestly remember wanting to end her life. She couldn't imagine doing that despite everything.

Had the wine dulled her wits? Or had it merely allowed her true wishes to come out?

She clasped her arms around her waist, feeling cold. She hadn't known the pastor who'd officiated at her husband and son's service. He'd been an acquaintance of George's and had pontificated at length on her husband's glorious military history. He'd offered a dozen platitudes in the guise of comfort, none of which had penetrated her gray haze. Something about God never making mistakes and reuniting under faith and other sayings that made absolutely no sense.

Nothing made sense in her life right now. Suddenly she was feeling a myriad of emotions—anger, curiosity, rebellion—added to the grief she almost always felt. Yet this sadness was different and it took her a moment to isolate why. She felt as if she were mourning not only her son, but the fate of Henry and those other babies.

Mrs. Armbruster had a great deal to answer for.

Chapter Eleven

The duchess hid for a week. At least, that's what it felt like to Adam. She didn't go anywhere. Nor did she entertain visitors. No one came to call.

After his last encounter with the duchess he'd gone to Mrs. Thigpen, knowing that the woman would know the answer to his question.

She insisted on him joining her for lunch, and since the meal was a beef-and-pork pie, he wasn't adverse. When he finished and he put his fork down, he complimented Mrs. Thigpen on the talents of the cook. For a few minutes he listened as she detailed all the dishes in which Grace excelled. When the housekeeper was done he leaned forward and dropped his voice. Although there was no one else in the staff dining room, he didn't want his question overheard by anyone passing in the corridor.

"Olivia, I have a favor to ask. I realize that what I'm asking is somewhat intrusive, and I apologize for that. My curiosity, however, demands an answer."

"Of course, Adam. What do you want to know?"

"Who does the duchess mourn?"

She sat back in the chair and regarded him solemnly. Had he overstepped? For several moments he thought she wouldn't answer him, but then she sighed.

"Georgie," she said. "Her son."

When he didn't say anything, she continued. "We didn't think the poor dear would survive it," Mrs. Thigpen said, dabbing at the corners of her eyes with a lace-trimmed handkerchief. "It was such a terrible dark time. She doted on Georgie. I think he was the light in her life."

She didn't add, and he was probably wrong in assuming, but he wondered if her son was the only bright spot in the duchess's life. He could only assume what marriage to the duke had been like.

He'd gotten to the duke's thirties and had to read page after page of the man's bragging about his conquests. The duke had been proud of his sword—as he'd called it—and the wide swath he'd cut through the female population. From what Adam had read, he hadn't limited his swordplay to London, but had taken advantage of more than one young girl who'd come to work at Marsley House.

He hadn't respected the man in India, a feeling that had led to loathing soon enough. His memory summoned up images of the duke ordering the rebels to be blown from cannons, reason enough to despise the man. The more journals he read, the more his opinion was reinforced. The Duke of Marsley was morally bankrupt and ethically challenged.

"The darling died in the accident, of course," Olivia said. "Drowned, poor mite. I can still hear the duchess's scream when she was told."

She shook her head, her attention on the table-top, but Adam could see that she was reliving that moment.

"Why does no one ever mention his name? Or say anything about him?"

Mrs. Thigpen glanced at him. "It wasn't for lack of love for Georgie. We all loved him as well. But it was out of respect for the duchess. Poor thing, to lose her husband and her son in the same accident. We all decided—the previous majordomo, the stable master, the land steward, and me—not to mention the child. And we gave the order that the staff was not to speak of either of them, for her sake."

He only nodded in response. He didn't have a thing to say.

As the days passed he started to look for her. She hadn't come to any of the public rooms. He'd even unbent enough to ask Ella where the duchess was.

"Why would you want to know?" she asked, giving him a narrow-eyed look.

"I need to speak with her about a matter."

"I'll tell her you need to see her," she said, but he didn't believe her.

If it suited her purposes, Ella would say something. If not, she'd remain silent. It wasn't loyalty to the duchess as much as it was power. People like Ella hoarded information because it might prove valuable to them in the future.

Nor was the Silent Service forthcoming with information. He was never told more than he absolutely needed to know. The temptation was to do the same in return, to keep back a few details to protect oneself. He'd run into those kinds of people, too.

"Where is she?" he asked, a mistake the minute the words came out of his mouth.

"Is that any of your concern?"

The tone of Ella's voice was one of disdain, as icy as the duchess.

Except that the duchess hadn't seemed cold a week ago.

He watched as the maid sauntered off without another word. Too bad he didn't have the power to dismiss Ella.

Over the past two months he'd established a pattern of behavior for himself as majordomo. The week was filled with approving expenditures or meeting with the upper staff or interviewing the maids and footmen. He believed in information filtering up the chain of command. He was also able to head off any misunderstandings about new rules and regulations that he'd initiated.

Every morning he inspected the staff along with Mrs. Thigpen. That was another change—he wanted to ensure that the staff knew that the housekeeper was well respected and someone they could go to if they had a problem.

Unless there was a visitor expected—which rarely happened at Marsley House—he did not man the door. Instead, a senior footman was assigned that position along with a junior footman in training. Adam was a stickler for training, and no doubt it was because of his time in the army. He never wanted to be surprised. Instead, he believed in preparing for every contingency.

He'd been woefully unprepared for the duchess. Nor had he counted on her father.

Chapter Twelve

"What do you mean she doesn't want to see me?"

The man's voice carried to the third floor of the library, where Adam was starting to read the duke's confessions about his forties. He'd had to wait until late afternoon, when the three maids assigned to the room had finished dusting it. At the slow pace he was going, a few more midnight visits were in order. Few people bothered him in the middle of the night.

He bit back an oath, stood, and straightened his jacket before descending the staircase and heading toward the front door.

The junior footman in training looked terrified, a strange sight since he towered over the man being refused admittance. The senior footman, on the other hand, was trying to appear conciliatory. Adam counted three bows from Thomas by the time he made it to the front door.

"What's going on, Thomas?" Adam asked.

"I'll tell you what's going on," the visitor said. "This damn fool is keeping me from my daughter."

Evidently, the short man with the voice of a giant was Edward Hackney. Adam had heard of the man in India. Hackney had been one of the directors of the British East India Company, making a fortune over the years.

He wondered if it was just a coincidence that both the late duke and Hackney had deep ties to India. So did he, since he'd been in the country at the same time.

Hackney's head seemed oddly out of proportion to the rest of his body, as if God had created a man of small stature and then had only large heads left over. Nothing matched. His nose was long, his mouth almost too broad for his face. His neck was a little squat, giving the impression that his shoulders were too close to his ears.

What he lacked in physical presence, however, Hackney made up for in sheer determination.

"You will take me to my daughter this instant."

Adam glanced at Thomas. "Have you let the duchess know that she has a visitor?"

"Not just a visitor, damn it," Hackney said. "I'm her father."

"Her Grace is not receiving, sir," Thomas said, his expression deadpan while Daniel still looked terrified. It couldn't have been easy to refuse Hackney.

At Thomas's words, Hackney grew even more belligerent.

"Like hell. Where is she?"

Daniel looked at Adam. "She's in the conservatory, sir."

When Hackney would have pushed past both the footmen and strode into the house, Adam held up his hand.

"If you'll wait a moment, sir, I will inquire of Her Grace if she wishes to see you."

He'd been in command of hundreds of men. He

knew just what kind of tone to employ to a recalcitrant soldier or an idiot general. In this case he chose something halfway between either extreme, but that left Hackney no doubt that he wasn't going to enter Marsley House.

"Who the hell do you think you are?"

"A member of your daughter's staff, sir," he said. "I will ask the duchess what she wishes to do."

As he turned and left, Adam thought the older man might be on the verge of apoplexy.

At least the duchess had come out of her room.

According to Mrs. Thigpen, the conservatory was one of the duchess's favorite rooms, and he could well imagine why. It was one of the brightest rooms at Marsley House in a building that had hundreds of windows to let in the light. Here the windows jutted out and met at the ceiling to form a roof of sorts. He'd been in this room during a storm once. Nature had surrounded him, the sound of the rain against the windows like a giant drum.

He stood in the doorway, admiring the various kinds of plants for a few seconds. He knew nothing about growing things. In Glasgow, they'd never been close to a garden. In India, he had been too busy to learn about the native flora and fauna.

There was a small enclosed area to the left with a table and two chairs against the window. The Duchess of Marsley was seated there, her hands clasped together on the tabletop, her face turned not toward the conservatory, but toward the back of the house and the kitchen garden.

At his appearance, she turned her head and regarded him with a steady look. He fingered her brooch in his pocket and thought about returning it now.

Instead he said, "Your father is here to see you."

"I know." Her voice was calm, almost too calm. "I can hear him."

He took a few steps toward her. "He seems intent upon seeing you, Your Grace."

"Does he?"

She didn't say anything else. Nor did she look away. She blinked slowly, as if she were half-awake.

"Some people always get what they want. Have you ever noticed that, Drummond?"

"I have," he said, wondering if he should summon some tea for her. Something strong to wake her. Or had she been drinking?

"My father always gets his way. He demands it."

"He doesn't have to in this case, Your Grace."

"Oh, Drummond, you must take my word for it. He will never accept no. Not from me. Not from anyone. He can be quite ferocious."

She smiled lightly, but it wasn't an expression of amusement.

"Would you like me to send him away, Your Grace?"

"I should like that very much, Drummond, but I'm afraid it will not work."

She looked almost fragile sitting there in the sunlight in her black dress. Her blue-gray eyes seemed to see down into his soul. No doubt it was only his guilty conscience that made him think that. Why the hell should he be feeling guilty? It was her husband who was the traitor.

"What did you say to me?"

He frowned, not understanding.

"The other night, on the roof. And then in my bedroom. You said something to me. In Gaelic, I think. What was it?"

He toyed with the idea of lying to her. It hadn't been the most polite of expressions.

"What the hell are you doing hiding out in this place, Suzanne? You're the Duchess of Marsley. Act like it. You don't need to go to ground like a damn fox."

They both turned to see Hackney pushing his way into the conservatory, the two footmen following. Short of physically accosting the man, there was nothing they could have done. A determined bully could outmaneuver a servant trained in tact and politeness any day.

Adam was slightly different.

He caught the duchess's flinch and saw her face pale slightly.

Turning, he stood between her and Hackney. He braced himself with his feet apart, his arms crossed in front of him.

"The duchess is not at home," he said, parroting an expression he'd been taught. The art of lying was specific among the upper class. You didn't actually come out and say that you didn't want to see someone. Instead, you implied that you weren't there, even though everyone knew you were.

"Get out of my way, you damn fool," Hackney said.

He outweighed the man by at least fifty pounds and a good six inches. Plus, he wasn't a normal majordomo. He'd been a soldier in Her Majesty's army, with experience in the Sepoy Rebellion, and countless skirmishes before and after. He'd been wounded twice and promoted for his stubbornness.

He didn't back down easily.

"The duchess is not at home," he repeated, more

than willing to act as a human bulwark against Hackney and his daughter.

He felt her hand on his shoulder and smelled her perfume as she came to stand beside him. The scent was different from what she'd worn that night on the roof. Light yet lingering and suiting her better.

She trailed her hand over his sleeve to rest at his elbow.

"That's all right, Drummond," she said. Her voice was calm, as if he were a wild animal and she his trainer. "I'll see my father."

Without a word she left them, leading the way, evidently, because Hackney followed her. Adam wanted to as well, but remained in the conservatory with the two footmen.

"She could have made our job a damn sight easier, sir, if she'd agreed to see the man in the first place."

Adam looked at Daniel. "That is the last time I'll hear criticism of the duchess, do you understand? If you value your place here."

To his credit, Daniel looked a little abashed. He nodded. "I understand, sir. It won't happen again."

Adam dismissed them and as they went back to their post, he turned and looked at the view the duchess had found so interesting.

What was wrong with her? And why did he care?

Chapter Thirteen

"*Y*ou look worse than you did the other night," her father said. "You're not going to be of any use to me, Suzanne, if you don't at least look the part. People are impressed to meet a duchess, but not if she looks like a chambermaid."

She had heard it all before. Countless times, as a matter of fact. On so many occasions that whenever her father started on this tirade, she stopped listening.

Instead, she chose to think about Drummond. Drummond had protected her. He'd stood there, defying her father in a way no one else ever had. How odd that she could see him in a kilt, perhaps with a broadsword strapped across his chest.

She led her father into one of his favorite rooms, the Green Parlor, so called because of the predominant color. A mural of a forest had been painted on three walls, with the fourth wall being given over to three ceiling-to-floor windows. Despite the sensation of openness, she always felt closed in when she came here.

He hadn't come to Marsley House to comment upon her appearance. Nor to criticize her in other ways, although that would surely come. No, her father wanted something.

Planning was what separated the successful man from the failure. Her father had imparted that bit of wisdom to her when she was a child. After she'd married, he'd used that axiom with George on numerous occasions. Although he hadn't considered George a planner. More a quintessential example of failure, which of course he was.

George hadn't added to the family coffers. Every attempt at investing had ended in ruin. Even his military career was speckled with rumors. Other men had been singled out for their courage or their brilliant tactical minds. Sometimes, George had been invited to those functions, only to return and pepper the air with oaths and questions she couldn't possibly answer.

Didn't the fools know what I did in India? I defeated the damn rebels, didn't I? Did I ever get any credit for it?

Occasionally, they would get visitors, men who'd once reported to George. He would be in his element, the magnanimous duke in command of the troops. For days a glow would seem to surround him.

Her father sometimes had that same effect on George, his flattery not the least bit subtle. Yet George had been an easy pawn to manipulate, someone who could be called upon to attend any dinner or ball, thereby granting to her wealthy father the social standing he craved.

Since George's death and after a suitable period of mourning—according to her father's decree more than society's—she'd been expected to attend all of her father's gatherings as a hostess of sorts. In actuality, she was not permitted to do more than smile and

make a few inane comments. She wandered from
room to room in the palatial home her father had
built, ensuring that people saw her and knew that
she was the Duchess of Marsley. In other words, she
was her father's placard, an advertisement as glaring
as those men who marched up and down the street
selling something.

"Are you ailing?" her father asked now. "If so, I
have an excellent physician you should see."

"I'm fine, Father. Truly."

He didn't say anything out of any concern for her,
not really. She'd always realized what kind of man
he was. He wasn't cruel as much as unaware. He was
so driven that he didn't understand that other people
might not possess the same ambition or need.

She'd never liked riding, but as a child she'd been
forced to learn because her father believed all proper
gentlewomen were also good with horses. Once her
mount had gotten spooked and raced down the lane
at a terrifying speed. Everything was a blur until the
mare finally stopped. Suzanne imagined that's how
her father went through life, at such a fast pace that
he saw other people only as indistinguishable patterns.

She didn't know anything about his past. He'd
never discussed his childhood and refused to answer questions. She always thought it was because
his upbringing embarrassed him, but that wasn't a
comment she'd ever make. If her father had his way,
everyone would believe that he'd just appeared on
the earth one day, fully formed and grown.

To the best of her knowledge she didn't have any
paternal grandparents. She didn't know if he had any
other relatives. Whenever she asked, which hadn't

been for years, he changed the subject. For that reason, she'd always suspected that he came from poor, if not desperate, conditions. He'd made himself wealthy, a fact that should have been an object of pride instead of shame.

After selling his shares of the East India Company, yet another topic she wasn't supposed to discuss, he'd delved into politics, of all things. Her father had no political ambition for himself. In this he wasn't lacking in self-knowledge. She'd once overheard him discussing the matter with one of his secretaries and his frankness had so surprised her that she hadn't been able to forget his words.

"I'm too blunt," he'd said. "I have a way of speaking that puts people off. And I don't look the part. I'm too short and I'm not a pretty boy. It's best if I become the power behind a candidate instead of being the candidate. That way we can win."

Her father's motives had always been shrouded in mystery, but she couldn't help but wonder, after hearing his words, if the reason he was doing this—and had become so wealthy—was to prove to the world that he was just as good as anyone else.

That was another subject she could never discuss with him. He didn't require her understanding, only her presence at the gatherings he arranged. Each one was designed to introduce one of his protégés, men he was sponsoring for public office.

He liked taking an ambitious young man, grooming him, ensuring that he became known, and doing everything within his power to help that individual win his first election.

So far he'd done that three times and, as his successes mounted, so did his resolve. Now he was concentrating his efforts on potential members of Parliament.

His power base might be growing, but Suzanne wished he would keep out of her life.

"I'm having a luncheon," he said now. "Several highly placed personages will be there."

She only nodded. He didn't ask if she would attend. He merely informed her what time and what event and she was expected to dress accordingly and be there.

"I'm getting tired of seeing you in black, Suzanne. I think you should give some thought to another color."

This was a conversation they had every time they met. Normally she remained silent, allowing him to rant without her participation. Today, however, she felt compelled to answer.

"It wouldn't be proper, Father," she said, moving to the end of the couch. As he did every time he came into this room, he chose the opposite chair. "People would talk."

"I don't think so. I've consulted experts on the subject, Suzanne. They concur with me. Two years is long enough for you to wear black."

She shouldn't have said anything, but silence was getting more difficult. She was not going to wear lavender simply because he didn't want to remember. He'd done the same with her mother. Two weeks after her death he'd begun to distribute her belongings to her friends and the servants. He was so determined to erase every trace of her that it was as if she'd never existed.

"I don't need trinkets," he'd said when she confronted him about his actions. "I'll never forget your mother. She'll always remain in my heart."

She wasn't entirely certain her father had a heart, but maybe he'd been telling the truth. In the last ten years he hadn't found another woman to take her mother's place. To the best of her knowledge—and thanks to information parlayed by chatty servants—he didn't entertain on his own. Every dinner party, every social event, was a result of a calculation. Who should attend? Who should be singled out for attention? Who was more valuable?

"I expect you to be there," he said. "You need to get past your sorrow, not wallow in it."

She stared at him. "Wallow in it?"

He nodded. "You need to devote yourself to a few good causes. If you like, I'll have Martin send you a list of acceptable activities."

She stood and looked down at her father. Anger surged through her, banishing the last of the gray haze from Ella's tonic.

"How could you say such a thing?"

"Sit down, Suzanne. We have a great deal more to discuss."

"No, we don't," she said. "I'm not one of your political cronies. I'm not a pawn on your chessboard."

She was not going to stay here and listen to him berate her. Instead, she walked out of the room. Let him condemn her for being rude; she didn't care.

Chapter Fourteen

Adam made his way back to the library, trying to dismiss the image of the duchess leaving the conservatory with her father. There was something about the set of her shoulders that disturbed him. Almost as if she were curving into herself.

Edward Hackney was one of those men who saw nothing wrong with browbeating someone in his employ or the women in his life.

Adam knew quite well that the man was rich, but he didn't give a flying farthing. Men with that kind of wealth were as arrogant as the peerage, thinking that they were better than other people.

They weren't, but the problem was that no one had the nerve to tell them. Most of the time they were allowed to get away with their arrogance. They'd been born and one day would die like everyone else. Between those two dates it seemed to be important for them to let everyone know exactly who they were and what they possessed.

A title might be bestowed upon a man at his birth, but Adam doubted that Saint Peter would be reading out the name of the Duke of Marsley. Instead, it would be George Whitcomb who stood there, waiting to be judged.

As for himself, Adam was all too aware of his own sins as well as his failings.

It would be better to quickly finish up this assignment and get back to his lodgings. He wanted to stop worrying about whether he fit the majordomo template or how to handle personnel problems.

Granted, he would miss Mrs. Thigpen, who turned out to have a surprising sense of humor and a practical grasp of life itself. He would miss several of the footmen who looked to him as an older brother.

He wanted an assignment that was more professional and less personal. Perhaps without a woman who sparked his protective instincts. Or made him think, even once, how beautiful she was.

Being at Marsley House was not good for him, and it didn't matter how many times Roger implied that this assignment could easily advance his career. Roger had been guilty of promising too much and delivering too little before. He'd be a fool to take him at his word.

Adam made his way back to the third floor, staring at the shelves filled with the duke's journals. He had a suspicion that they had not originally been stored up here. He couldn't imagine, given the duke's character, that he would want his personal journals so far from hand.

The duke had been remarkably thin-skinned. When he perceived an insult, he recorded the slight along with the name of the infringing individual, the situation, and the date—the better to remember. It was a good thing that he hadn't been able to read the minds of the men under his command. There weren't enough journals in the world to record all those comments.

Adam reached for the fourteenth volume on the third shelf from the bottom, knowing that he probably wasn't going to get anything of substance from this book, either. Chronologically, Whitcomb had just arrived in India. Four years would elapse before the Sepoy Rebellion. Until then, the duke would have enough time to make a complete ass of himself and reveal the depth of his incompetence.

The man's appointment had been a royal favor and one that had surprised a great many people. It was entirely possible that Whitcomb, as the Duke of Marsley and the heir to a distinguished family, had some sort of relationship with the Queen. If he did, Adam doubted if the information would ever be passed along to him, a Scot from Glasgow, and the poor part of Glasgow, at that.

He heard the library door open and swore beneath his breath. He should have taken one of the journals back to his office to read the duke's increasingly indecipherable handwriting at his leisure.

Silently, he made his way to where the circular staircase ended, peering down into the cavernous first floor. To his surprise, the duchess stood there, her fists clamped on the black skirt of her dress, her lips thinned.

A second later Hackney entered the room, nearly slamming the door behind him.

"Have you lost your mind, Suzanne? Or all semblance of manners?"

"You would push yourself into my home, Father, and then lecture me on manners?" she asked, turning to face him.

"What's gotten into you?"

"I didn't feel like having a visitor," the duchess said. "Yet you didn't feel it necessary to respect my wishes."

"Are you drinking, Suzanne?" Hackney put both fists on his hips and glared at his daughter.

"You needn't be insulting, Father."

"And you needn't walk away when I'm trying to talk to you."

"You're not talking to me. You were beginning to lecture me again. I don't need to be lectured."

"Evidently you do, or you would've behaved much better than you have today."

Hackney's florid face was made even redder by his irritation. There was no doubt that he was furious with his daughter.

Adam couldn't see the duchess's face from here because her back was to him. However, she didn't sound as dazed as she had earlier. Whatever she'd taken or drunk had evidently worn off.

"You've changed, daughter, and it isn't becoming."

"I've changed?"

"Your grief has turned you into a harridan."

The duchess took a few quick steps back, almost as if Hackney had announced that he carried the plague.

"Behave like the widow of a duke, daughter. Georgie's dead and the sooner you come to that realization and accept the permanence of it, Suzanne, the better you will be."

She took another step back, her fingers now pressed to her mouth.

Hackney, to his credit, looked as if he realized how damaging his words had been. He reached out one hand then dropped it when she took another step back.

"I think you should leave," she said, her voice tight. "I really don't want to see you right now."

"I think that's a good idea," Hackney said. "I'll send you notice of the luncheon. I expect you to be there."

Hackney didn't say anything else as he turned and left the room.

She was weeping again, the sound like a spear to Adam's chest. He wanted to pummel Hackney.

What kind of father talked to his daughter that way?

Adam waited a few minutes until he was certain that the man wasn't returning. He left the journal flat on the bookshelf and was descending the staircase to talk to the duchess when she left the library.

Was she going back to the roof?

He understood her grief now, in a way he hadn't before.

Adam caught sight of the edge of her black skirt as she made it to the second floor landing. She wasn't going to the roof, but to her own suite.

He went up the stairs anyway, just in time to see her enter the duke's sitting room. He was descending the stairs when she came out again. He pretended to be testing to see if there was dust on the wainscoting just in case she interrogated him as to his actions. But the duchess didn't come to the first floor. Instead, she headed for the third.

He followed her, hoping to God she wasn't going to the roof after all. Once again, however, she confused him, turning left toward a part of the wing that wasn't used for servants' quarters. Nor was it near the entrance to the roof.

A door closing behind her was the only clue to where she'd gone.

Adam remained at the end of the hall, watching. A few minutes passed and she didn't emerge.

He walked to the door and stood in front of it. Twice he raised his hand, debating about whether to knock. Twice he lowered it. Should he interrupt her? Should he offer his condolences?

What the hell should he do about the Duchess of Marsley? He couldn't, in all good conscience, call her Marble Marsley anymore.

Perception was based on perspective, another lesson he'd learned in the army, but not from his superiors. He'd watched as one indignity after another was dealt out to the native population by the British East India Company. He hadn't been able to understand how an organization as expansive and all-consuming had been so blind to its own actions. They had no inkling that a great many of their policies were insulting to the populace, like the idiotic decision to use beef tallow to grease the cartridges for the new Enfield rifles. By doing so, they managed to offend the Hindu population, for whom the eating of cows was forbidden.

He'd been as blind about the Duchess of Marsley, judging her by his own personal prejudices and biases.

At least he'd tried to comfort her. He could still feel her standing close to him, her arms around his waist, her cheek against his chest. He felt her tears against his knuckles, and more than once he looked at his hand as if to see evidence of them still there.

He, too, knew what grief was. It was a cruel emotion, one that sapped your energy and gave nothing in return. Anger sometimes brought wisdom. Fear encouraged caution. Love? Love was perfect in its own sense. But grief? All it brought was anguish and despair and the pitiless certainty that you would always feel it in some degree.

Rebecca's death still weighed heavily on him, as well as the loss of his mother and sister. He'd had friends he'd watched die for no more reason than they were serving in the army. He knew grief only too well.

If the duchess was cold, if she held herself stiff and aloof from others, it could be that she was like Mrs. Anderson in India. The poor woman had watched two of her children die of fever. He'd been assigned to take her to the ship bound for England. She'd barely spoken, but when she had, he could hear the despair in her voice. He'd wanted to say something then, too, but what words could possibly ease someone trying to cope with that kind of loss?

He didn't have anything to say now, either, so he turned and walked away.

Chapter Fifteen

$\mathcal{T}$wo days later Adam entered the housekeeper's office, only to be informed that the duchess wished to see him. Mrs. Thigpen looked worried, which was not a good sign. The housekeeper normally remained calm and unmoved even in the worst of crises.

"Do you know why?" he asked her. "Have I done something wrong?"

That was always a possibility. He had navigated many roles in the previous seven years, but this stint as a majordomo had been the most difficult one of all.

"I don't know," Mrs. Thigpen said, sighing. "She does seem in a mood, which is strange. The duchess is normally very sweet and unassuming."

He hadn't seen that side of the duchess yet, but he wisely kept silent.

"I do wish her father would not come and visit," Mrs. Thigpen said, surprising him. "She's always so agitated after he leaves."

"The duchess doesn't seem to be very much like him."

"She doesn't, does she? From the very first moment she moved into Marsley House, I liked her. She never put on airs and she always treated every member of the staff with kindness. She went out of her way to say please and thank you, which is more than I can say about Mr. Hackney. Or the duke, for that matter."

"He was in India, wasn't he?" Adam asked, trying to sound as nonchalant as he could. He'd never considered that Mrs. Thigpen might be a source of information about India, but the woman had been employed at Marsley House for two decades. The duke might have said something to her about Manipora.

"That he was, and very enthusiastic about the prospect. At least, that's what his valet told me. Of course, Paul didn't last long in his employ. Once he got to India, His Grace replaced him."

The duke had been surrounded by a coterie of people who either protected him from others or the rest of the world from George.

She glanced at the clock. "Best be off, then, before she rings again."

He entered the library, closed the door behind him, and walked to the desk where the duchess was sitting. She kept him standing there while she pretended to be interested in the account books in front of her. He saw those once a month when they were sent from the solicitor. He was expected to make comments and notations, and enter in any unexpected expenses that hadn't been otherwise listed. The books were then sent back to the solicitor for evaluation. He hadn't realized a step in the process was that the duchess reviewed them as well.

She finally looked up, her face wiped of any expression, and said to him, "Your penmanship leaves a great deal to be desired, Drummond."

He bit back a smile. If that's all she could find fault with, then he was in no danger of being dismissed.

"I apologize, Your Grace," he said, bowing slightly. "I will attempt to do better."

She glanced away and then back at him. "See that you do."

He nodded, moved to stand at parade rest position, his legs slightly apart, his hands clasped behind him. He could stand for hours if need be. At least the sun wasn't beating down on his head and shoulders. Plus, he'd had a good breakfast, so he was prepared to remain here for as long as she kept him.

Somehow, he'd annoyed her. No doubt protecting her from her father had been one of his sins. Another might be that he'd held her in his arms. Was she going to call him out on that, too? If so, he was tempted to tell her that, if he'd known about Georgie, he would have done even more. He would have embraced her fully, let her cry as long as she wanted, knowing exactly how she felt.

"You've spent entirely too much on the conservatory," she said.

"Two of the window panes were broken, Your Grace. With the winter coming on, I didn't want the damage to go unrepaired. Otherwise, the plants would've suffered, resulting in an even greater expenditure."

She looked annoyed at his answer.

She was evidently fishing for something to complain about or some reason to have him stand in front of the desk like a supplicant. Very well, he would play this game. While she was looking for some reason to upbraid him, he would admire the picture she made, framed by the windows behind her, with the sun dancing on her dark brown hair.

Her nose was perfect for her face, neither too large nor too narrow and aristocratic. A woman's mouth was a fascinating thing. Hers was perfect. The upper and bottom lip were exactly the same size. Both full, but not overly so. Nor was it too small for her face. It was another perfect feature, as were her eyes. He couldn't remember ever seeing that shade of blue before. It was almost as if God couldn't decide whether to give her gray eyes or blue and combined the two.

Her long and slender fingers trailed down the notations he'd made, one by one, as if seeking an error.

He much preferred her as she was now, annoyed and determined, than how she'd been that day in the conservatory.

She looked up then and said, "You've never been a majordomo before, have you, Drummond?"

He forced a smile to his face. "Why would you ask that, Your Grace?"

"For the simple reason that I desired an answer, Drummond."

Her eyes were narrowed and that beautiful mouth of hers thinned. He might not be able to charm her with his answer, but he had every intention of doing the very best he could.

"Your Grace, I was a sergeant in the army for many years. I was responsible for a hundred men, their welfare, their deportment, and whatever was needed to ensure their well-being. I was promoted to lieutenant, which meant that my responsibilities increased. Instead of simply a hundred men it was ten times that. When I gave your solicitor my qualifications, he thought that I would serve the position and Your Grace well. Have I not done so?"

They exchanged a glance. He almost dared her to tell him where he had not done his best in this position. If he'd erred, and they both knew it, it was in being too familiar with her.

He would not apologize for that.

After a moment, she stared down at the account book. "You may go, Drummond."

That was all. Not an explanation of why he'd been called into the library. Not an apology for wasting his time or insulting him. Nothing. Just a dismissal by a duchess.

He stood there wrestling with himself. He needed to finish his assignment. He didn't need to cause any more conflict between the two of them. That was not his mission. The man he was, however, separate and apart from being a member of the Silent Service, wanted to ask what she'd objected to the most, that he'd treated her like a woman or that he had no intention of changing his behavior?

Instead, he did a smart about-face and left the room, feeling that a great many things had been left unsaid.

SUZANNE WATCHED THE library door close behind Drummond before sitting back. She gripped the arms of the chair tightly with both hands, her fingers resting on the indentations of the lion's paws.

Why had she summoned him? She hadn't seen him for two days. Two days in which she'd heard his voice from time to time. He had a low laugh, one that captured her attention. His instructions to the staff were done in a no-nonsense kind of voice as if he would brook no disobedience.

He'd stared down her father. For that alone, he should be rewarded.

The man was entirely too attractive, however. Dressed in his majordomo uniform he almost looked like a prince leaving for a night of revelry. He moved as if he were comfortable with himself. She doubted if his hands ever trembled. Or if he ever looked uncertain.

He was entirely too intriguing.

Was that why she'd summoned him?

He hadn't looked afraid. Instead, there had been a look in his green eyes that was almost insulting. No, not insulting. Challenging, perhaps. Almost as if he'd been daring her. To do what? Dismiss him? He was an excellent majordomo. Even the account books indicated that. He actually requested bids from several tradesmen instead of paying anything they demanded like Old Franklin had. In addition, he'd questioned several expenditures they'd normally always paid with the result that they were saving money at the greengrocers and the butcher.

Besides, he was excellent at protecting her.

Was that why she'd summoned him?

Had she felt the need to be protected? Perhaps she had, but how absolutely idiotic of her to think of her majordomo. He was a member of her staff. He was in her employ. She paid his wages.

She really shouldn't have any curiosity about the man. Still, it had been nice to see him. He was looking well, fit and hardy. It was important to ensure the well-being of her staff. That's the only reason she'd summoned him, of course.

She shook her head at that thought. She wasn't given to lying to herself and she didn't intend to start now.

For some reason, he made her feel safe. He inspired something within her, some kind of admiration she hadn't often felt. He hadn't sought her out in the past two days, reason enough to send for him.

She missed him. There, the truth, as idiotic as it was.

Chapter Sixteen

$\mathcal{A}$dam was almost to the grand staircase on his way to the library when he saw the light beneath the mysterious door. He didn't think. He didn't consider the matter before putting his hand on the latch and pushing the door open.

He didn't know what he expected, but it wasn't what he saw. The Duchess of Marsley was sitting on the side of a small bed. In her lap was a well-worn floppy yellow rabbit with one eye slightly askew. When the door opened, she looked up.

What surprised him was her silence. She didn't demand that he leave or close the door behind him. She didn't say a word.

He should have respected her privacy. At the least he should have realized that he'd erred in opening the door. Overriding that was a curious and instinctive response to the picture of her sitting there, her eyes filled with tears. He didn't want to leave her alone.

After entering the room he closed the door behind him.

The walls of the nursery were painted a soft blue. Some shelves on two walls were filled with toys and some with books. He'd never imagined that one child could have so many possessions, but Georgie had been the heir to a dukedom. A child feted from the moment he'd drawn breath.

He had the feeling that rank hadn't mattered to the Duchess of Marsley. She would have cherished her child regardless. His own mother had been like that, making no secret of her love for him and Mary. She told him often, cupping her hand against his cheek, smiling into his eyes.

"I love you, *mo mhac*. Never forget that, my lad."

Only later, when he'd been far away from Glasgow, had he realized how rare that devotion had been.

Georgie had been loved the same way, he suspected, not in poverty but plenty.

He came and, no doubt in defiance of every kind of etiquette, sat next to her on the bed. She looked startled for a moment, but she didn't move away.

The room smelled of cloves and oil from the lamp mixed with the duchess's perfume. For a few moments they didn't speak, sitting in companionable silence with Marsley House quieting around them.

He turned his head to look at her. The duchess had a beautiful face, but the angle of her chin seemed too sharp. Was she eating enough?

"Are you hungry, Suzanne? Can I bring you anything? Some pastries, biscuits? Cook made a roast and I know she'd be pleased if you had some."

"It's nearly midnight, Drummond, and you're offering to feed me?" she asked, brushing away one lone tear from her cheek.

"Have you eaten lately?"

"Now you're my nanny?"

He didn't answer, merely watched her.

"I had quite a lovely dinner, as a matter of fact," she said.

He was somewhat satisfied, but he would alert Mrs. Thigpen as well. Perhaps the duchess had some favorite dishes that Grace could make to tempt her appetite.

"How old was he?" he finally asked.

She blinked at him. That was all. For a moment he didn't think she was going to answer, but then she did, the words filled with tears.

"Georgie was three," she said.

"Gabh mo leisgeul."

"You've said that before. *I'm sorry.* Is that what it means?"

He nodded.

Her gaze went back to the stuffed animal on her lap. "Thank you."

"What happened?" he asked.

"I had a cold," she said, brushing the fur on the floppy-eared rabbit. "Isn't that odd? I haven't had a cold since."

She didn't speak for a moment and he didn't urge her to continue, content to sit and wait.

"George was impatient with sickness. George was impatient about most things. He was all for visiting his second cousin," she added after several minutes. "He's the current Duke of Marsley. Poor man never expected to be duke and was shocked by it, I think. He married an heiress, which is a good thing because there's no money to go with the title."

She looked at the ceiling and the walls of the nursery as if to encompass the whole of Marsley House. "This is an expensive place to maintain. You might call it the price of George's bachelorhood. My father bought him for me. He'd always wanted to be connected to the peerage and now he has a duchess for a daughter."

She smiled slightly, but the expression had no humor in it.

"That day, George wanted to take Georgie and his nurse with him. I asked him to wait, but he wouldn't. I told him that it was too cold, that the weather would warm in a few days, but he didn't listen. No one could get George to do something he didn't want to do. So I waved them goodbye from the front steps. I expected them back by nightfall and when they didn't return, I knew. I knew something terrible had happened, although I didn't learn exactly what until the next day."

She lifted her eyes to him. In them was the same expression he had seen that first night, endless grief.

"The bridge collapsed. Who expects a bridge to collapse? But it did and the carriage plunged into the water. The coachman was saved and the nurse, but not Georgie or his father."

She arranged the rabbit on her lap and took a deep breath before continuing. "I've often thought of them together in those last moments. George would hold Georgie in the freezing water and reassure him. He wouldn't let Georgie be afraid, of that I'm certain."

He didn't know what to say to comfort her. He suspected that mere words wouldn't help.

"I didn't really wish to throw myself off the roof that night," she said. "At least, I don't think I did." She glanced over at him. "I had too much wine and that's never happened before."

"I've known a great many men who swear that

they wouldn't have done something if they hadn't been intoxicated."

Her smile was barely a curve of her lips. "There is that, I suppose. I think it would be wise for me to avoid spirits of any kind from now on."

"That might be a good decision."

The room was shadowed, lit only by a small lamp beside the bed. Ever since he'd entered, they'd spoken as contemporaries. He hadn't called her *Your Grace* and she hadn't banished him from the room.

He was loath to leave, even though it would've been the right thing to do so.

"I should have known you were in the military," she said.

The statement surprised him. "Why?"

"You have a military bearing. An acquaintance of mine mentioned it."

"Do I? No doubt it's from hours of standing at attention."

"Why did you leave? My husband used to say that only failures leave the army. Good men stay and retire."

He didn't give a damn about what her husband used to say, but he tried to answer her without revealing his contempt for the duke.

"I found myself at odds with the aims of the army," he said.

Her smile made an appearance again. "Then the army's loss is our gain."

He had expected her to question him further, but she only cradled the bunny against her chest, pressing her chin against the stuffed animal's head.

"This was Georgie's favorite toy," she said. "He didn't take it with him that last day. His father didn't approve of toys." She looked at the rabbit and then at Adam as if introducing them. "His name is Babbit because he couldn't say rabbit."

He looked around him, at the evidence of a child who had been loved and cherished.

"Do you come here often?"

Had he dared too much with his question? He thought so when she didn't answer him.

"Less now than I once did," she finally said. "I used to find some comfort here. I pretended that Georgie was with his nurse and that he'd return in a little while." She didn't say anything for a moment, and when she spoke again, there were tears once more in her voice. "Now it's almost too painful. I can't pretend anymore and this is just a reminder of everything that was, but will never be again. I've finally realized that nothing will be the same. He isn't coming back. He won't ever be older than three."

She didn't say anything further.

He remembered the cruel comment her father had made.

"You will always be his mother," he said. "He'll always be alive in your heart."

She took a deep breath and looked at him again. "How wise you are, Drummond. Do you often counsel the grieving? Or do you mourn a loss of your own?"

"A great many people."

She surprised him by reaching over and placing her hand on his wrist. Her hand was warm, the connection something he hadn't expected.

"Who?"

He hadn't thought of the duchess as being determined, but the steady look in her eyes indicated that he had underestimated the strength of her will. She wanted an answer. Very well, he would give it to her.

"My mother, first," he said. "And then my sister. Friends, men I knew in the army." He hesitated for a moment. "My wife, Rebecca."

Her hand closed around his wrist as if she measured his pulse or wanted to keep him seated there.

"Tell me about her."

He smiled, but it was an effort. He rarely talked about Rebecca. Doing so filled him with regret. He couldn't alter the events of the past, but it didn't stop him from wanting to do so.

"Please," she said.

Because there were still tears in her eyes, he began to speak.

"When I think of Rebecca I think of sunshine," he said. "She had light blond hair and a bright smile and a laugh that could make you laugh along with her. She was the sister of one of my lieutenants and had come out to India with a few of her friends."

He stared down at where Suzanne's hand rested on his wrist, remembering.

"We've come to find husbands," Rebecca had said when he'd been introduced to her. *"At the end of six months, if we haven't succeeded, we're going back to England."*

She was like that, without guile or shame or even embarrassment. Yet she was so charming and pretty that most people forgave her any gaffe she might have uttered.

He and Rebecca had married five days before she was due to return to England.

"What is your name?" the duchess asked now.

He glanced at her.

"Your given name," she said.

"Adam."

"Thank you, Adam."

She stood and went to the door, opening it. He stood as well, knowing that he was being politely invited to leave. She surprised him, however, by going to the bedside table and extinguishing the light, then joining him in the corridor. She closed and locked the door before pocketing the key.

He wanted to say something to her. A caution along the lines of, *Don't come here that often. Don't punish yourself.* Instead, he looked down at her, standing in the shadows.

He took a step toward her, unable to bear the anguish in her eyes.

"Suzanne."

She only nodded. When he went to her and pulled her into his arms, a space that she seemed to fill so perfectly, she sighed deeply again and sagged against him.

They stood like that for several moments.

"Some people cling to grief," he said. "As a way to keep their loved one close." He wanted to tell her that it didn't work. It didn't make the passage through anguish any easier. Nor did it bring a loved one back.

She stepped away, keeping her head down. Had he angered her? Perhaps that would be better than her sorrow.

"Good night, Suzanne."

Only after he left her, heading back toward his room, did he remember that he hadn't given her the brooch in his pocket. He didn't call out to her, merely watched as she descended the staircase to the second floor. He would see her tomorrow and give it to her then.

The anticipation of that moment was a warning. He'd go back down to the library in a few minutes and start searching again. Once he'd found that damn journal he'd leave Marsley House and its surprising duchess behind.

That day couldn't come fast enough.

Chapter Seventeen

"Where have you been, Your Grace?"

At her entrance into the sitting room, Ella stood. She'd been occupying Suzanne's favorite wing chair in front of the fire. A cup of tea sat on the table beside her. Where was the footstool and a pillow, perhaps, for her back? Suzanne was only surprised that her maid hadn't ordered a tray of cake and biscuits.

But Ella had always made herself at home in the duchess's suite, hadn't she?

As she walked into the bedroom, Suzanne held up her hand. "I really don't need your help tonight, Ella," she said.

She wanted to be alone, to think about the surprising events that had just transpired. Tonight, she'd acquired a friend. A strange and unexpected friend in her majordomo. His words had been so welcome and his understanding so complete that she couldn't help but be grateful.

She turned to see Ella standing in the doorway. Evidently, she was not going to get rid of the maid until she performed her duties.

"I still haven't found your hair clip, Your Grace. I've gone through both armoires and the carriage and I haven't been able to find it. It's very valuable, Your Grace. Your father will not be happy that it's missing."

"Then we don't need to tell him, do we, Ella? Unless, of course, you insist on reporting to him every week. Or is it more often than that? I noticed a flurry of correspondence leaving the country for London. Do you write him every day?"

Ella didn't wilt under her questions. Instead, the maid got a mulish look on her face: flat eyes, clenched lips, and a silence that dared Suzanne to question her further.

"Tell him what you want," she said. "I don't care. Tell him I threw it in the Thames. Or out the carriage window."

"I should have accompanied you, Your Grace. I think I should do so in the future."

"That won't be necessary," she said, walking into the bedroom.

She began to unbutton the bodice of her dress. Ella came to stand in front of her, but Suzanne turned.

"You're dismissed," she said. "I don't need help undressing."

"Of course you do," Ella said, coming to stand in front of her once more. She pushed Suzanne's hands out of the way and finished unfastening the row of buttons.

When had she lost all authority? Or had she ever possessed it?

She stepped back, away from Ella.

"Will you please leave me?"

"Your Grace, don't be unreasonable. Let's get you ready for bed, shall we?"

The maid picked up the nightgown draped across

the end of the bed. "We don't need to have an argument about this, do we?"

"No, we don't," Suzanne said.

Grabbing the nightgown, she walked into the bathing chamber and closed the door. Tomorrow she would ask Drummond—Adam—to have someone install a lock on this door. Ella had never disturbed her privacy here, but she didn't have any faith that the maid would continue to leave her alone.

She undressed, unfastening the busk of her corset, her shift, and the rest of her undergarments before washing and brushing her teeth. After removing her hairpins, she threaded her fingers through her hair before braiding it loosely. George had always liked her hair long, and maybe it was for that reason that she now kept it trimmed to just below her shoulders. He wouldn't have approved, but George was no longer here to issue his pronouncements.

She couldn't help but wonder what he would have thought about Ella.

Her previous maid had been from India, coming to England with George and several other people who were added to the staff at Marsley House.

Her father hadn't approved.

"They're damn sly, Suzanne," her father had said. "Always plotting and planning."

Although she didn't agree with her father's words, she understood why he said them. He'd been horrified at the rebellion in India. Because of that, he'd pulled out of the East India Company, severing both financial and personal ties with men with whom he'd done business for decades.

It was in India that he'd met George, a penurious duke who had been giving some vague thoughts to marrying and producing a legitimate heir. At last count George had seven children scattered around London and India. He hadn't cared enough to learn their names, but at least he'd known whether they were sons or daughters.

She had never imagined anyone like George. He was proud of his libertine nature. He made no apologies for the fact that he liked women and had no intentions whatsoever of remaining true to his marital vows. The very thought of having to lash himself to one woman for the rest of his days was an idiotic notion. Once, he'd even gone so far as to attempt to explain his philosophy to her.

"You might think of me as a stallion, my dear. Would a stallion be restricted to one paddock and a single mare? Of course not. He would be given freedom to roam and attract any likely mate."

She could recall the exact moment of his stallion soliloquy. She'd been sitting in the Blue Parlor on the second floor. It had been a spring evening and the windows had been open to let in the air, cooled from an earlier rainstorm. A moth had found its way in to circle the lamp on the table to her left. She'd been reading, a fascinating lurid novel that would have been forbidden to her a few years earlier.

George had come into the room to say good-night. The carriage was waiting. No doubt his fellow revelers were also becoming impatient, waiting for him to arrive. When he'd finished speaking, he had looked at her expectantly, almost as if he wished her approval, which was ludicrous. George required no one's approval, not even God's.

She hadn't been surprised at his words. What had startled her was the fact that he thought it important

enough—that he thought *her* important enough—to
hear his personal philosophy. Of course, it might
have been because she was the mother of his heir.
Georgie was only a few months old at the time.

She'd returned to her book without speaking and
he'd left a moment later. That night was a turning
point, something she'd realized looking back. Once
Georgie had been born, his father absolved himself
of any further marital responsibility. The stallion
speech was just a formal announcement of that fact.

For the great honor of becoming a duchess she
was supposed to ignore George's peccadilloes and
be a supportive and silent wife. Since their marriage had never been based on mutual affection she'd
pushed any thoughts of developing respect for her
husband out of her mind and kept quiet about his
various women.

She and George had lived separate lives. The only
times they were together were when her father invited them to one of his innumerable gatherings.

When she left the bathroom, she encountered Ella
standing there, holding the tonic out for her to drink.

The detestable tonic, something her father and Ella
decided was important for her to drink. She loathed
the taste and the effects.

"No," she said. "I won't take it."

"You must, Your Grace." There was that implacable tone in Ella's voice.

"Why, Ella? Because you say so?"

"It's good for you, Your Grace."

"No."

That's all she said. Just no. She didn't argue or take
the glass. Instead, she skirted Ella and climbed the
steps to her bed, bending over to extinguish the lamp.

"You can stand there until dawn, Ella. I'm not taking your bloody tonic."

Ella gasped. Was she shocked because of Suzanne's profanity? Or simply because she'd refused and this time she hadn't backed down?

When she heard the sound of the door closing behind the maid, she took a deep breath and banished any thoughts of Ella. Instead, she was thinking of Drummond and his revelations. Or how she'd felt when he'd so gently taken her into his arms.

Chapter Eighteen

$\mathcal{A}$dam slept late, something he'd rarely done. In his childhood if he was abed instead of out at first light, it meant that he lost a job with one of the hawkers. He was relegated to selling broadsides for a penny, working eight hours for a pittance. He had to make money every day or they didn't eat. In the army, he would have been cashiered out if he'd acted like a slug.

His night had been filled with wild dreams, things that didn't make any sense in the way of dreams. The duke had featured prominently as well as the duchess. Adam had heard her crying and had been trying to reach her, swimming through icy water to get to her side.

When he finally woke, his first thought was of her. He allowed himself to recall the sight of her profile, the sweet dawning of her smile, and the ballet of her hands.

He needed to be gone from here before too much more time passed.

After dressing in his majordomo uniform and brushing his hair, he descended the staircase to the first floor.

"It's a glorious day, Adam," Mrs. Thigpen said, greeting him when he entered the staff dining room.

To his relief, the housekeeper didn't say anything about his late start to the morning. That was the difference between being a servant and being a majordomo, evidently. Instead, she smiled brightly at him when he asked if he could share her table.

"Please," she said, waving him to a chair opposite her. "There are clouds on the eastern horizon, however. My late husband used to say that if you see clouds before nine o'clock, it means that there will be a storm before seven. He was a great watcher of clouds."

"We called those *banff bailies* in Scotland," he said, sitting. "Big white clouds that promise rain."

"You've been away from your home for a great many years, haven't you, Adam?"

He nodded. "Twenty or so," he said.

"Have you not thought of going back?"

"I've no one there, Olivia, and that's the reason to return, isn't it?"

She left him before he finished his breakfast, allowing him to contemplate his duties for the day. Today was earmarked for interviewing footmen and maids. He staggered the meetings so that he saw each member of the staff at least once a month. That way, he could hear any complaints or suggestions himself rather than allowing them to fester unheard. He also was able to keep personnel disagreements at a minimum. If someone made a remark about another staff member, he disconcerted both of them by having them meet in his office and air out any grievances. In that way, he sent out an unmistakable message: he didn't approve of petty annoyances or disagreements. If someone had an issue with someone else, it was in their best interest to solve the problem before it was escalated to him.

Last week he had the disagreeable task of having to let one of the scullery maids go. She was with child and had kept it a secret until Mrs. Thigpen discovered it one morning. At least, in the maid's case, she had a family to turn to, just as his sister, Mary, had. Hopefully, she would survive childbirth.

"You can always come back here after you have your child, Constance," he told the girl.

She hadn't met his eyes, choosing to stare down at her reddened fingers instead. But she'd nodded her understanding. He'd wanted to know who the father was, but he hadn't asked. Some things he didn't have to know in his post as majordomo. At least she hadn't been impregnated by the duke.

From the records left by Old Franklin, the Duke of Marsley had managed to make himself known to a great many female staff members. Three maids had quit unexpectedly in a one-month period. Two had been dismissed for being with child. Adam had read that an extraordinary measure had been taken to protect the women employed at Marsley House— locks had been installed on all the doors on the third floor.

He was almost to the staircase when he heard Ella. She had a particularly annoying voice, one that grated on him. Something he realized as he listened: the angrier Ella was, the more annoying her voice became.

"It's not proper that you go without me, Your Grace," she was saying.

"Are you implying that I am not a proper companion? How utterly cheeky of you, young woman."

He knew that voice. He stepped into the foyer. The woman who turned and glanced at him before her expression melted into a smile had come to Marsley House once before. He couldn't remember her name, but she'd been pleasant and polite.

Evidently, Ella had the capacity for bringing out the worst in everyone.

The duchess was standing close to the door, her hand on the latch as if she wanted to escape the scene. She glanced at him and to his surprise, her face flushed. Was she remembering their embrace from the night before? He hadn't been able to forget it, either.

Her eyes were clear, her look direct. She was dressed as she'd been since he knew her: in black silk. The meaning for it struck him more today, for some reason. He wanted to go to her, tilt her chin up with his hand, and look into her face. He wanted to ask if she was all right. Had she slept well? Had she eaten? What were her plans for today?

None of those questions would have been proper. Nor was this feeling, this novel and unexpected sensation in his stomach, as if it were suddenly buoyant.

It took a few seconds for him to identify what he was feeling. When he did, he almost stepped back, retreating from the foyer, the sight of her, and his own dismaying happiness.

She'd made his day brighter just by seeing her. She'd caused his pulse to race and his spirit to soar.

Good God, had he gone daft?

"I must insist, Your Grace."

His attention was recaptured by Ella's whine. He stepped forward, putting himself between the stranger and the maid.

"May I be of service?"

"Mr. Drummond," the woman said, "how very nice to see you again."

He bowed slightly, wishing he could remember her name. What had her calling card said? Bruiser? Bullister? He didn't remember names as well as he did facts like geographical details, dates, and troop strength.

"You evidently have enough time on your hands, Ella," the duchess said. "Perhaps Drummond can give you something to do."

That was hardly fair, giving him the task of dealing with the prickly maid.

"Of course, Your Grace," he said, bowing slightly.

He glanced at Suzanne and then away. It wouldn't do to look at her. She was particularly attractive today and he didn't want the temptation.

"Mrs. Armbruster, shall we go?" the duchess said.

Armbruster, that was it. That was the name of the woman.

He nodded to Daniel, who was being put in a difficult position by the duchess's stance. She was gripping the door latch herself, which was a task normally performed by the footman. The young man stood there looking helpless.

Adam walked to the duchess's side and put his hand over hers. You would have thought it was scalding by how quickly she jerked her hand back. Her color grew even deeper as she stood aside, allowing him to open the door for her.

She was wearing a different perfume today, a scent that was spicy yet not overpowering. He'd never been affected by a woman's perfume, but he was by hers. Did she wear it behind her ear? On her neck?

Even as he lectured himself, even as part of him felt as if he stood outside his body and stared in disbelief at his own actions, he wanted to bend closer and breathe deeply. Or take her into his arms and hold her tenderly for a few hours.

He was losing his mind, his determination, and his sense of duty. All because a beautiful woman smelled good.

"I'm certain I can find something for Ella to do," he said, stepping back.

She only nodded, not looking at him.

"Thank you, Drummond," she said as she descended the steps, leaving him staring after her.

Mrs. Armbruster leaned close on her way out the door. "You have the most charming smile, Mr. Drummond," she said. "It's really quite lovely."

He didn't know what the hell to say to that, so he gave her one of his lovely smiles.

When the door closed he was left with the footman and the view of Ella stomping down the corridor on the way to the back of the house. Good, the last thing he wanted—or needed—was to have to deal with a petulant maid.

"Where are they going?" he asked, but Daniel only shook his head.

"I don't know, sir. They didn't say."

Another mystery to solve, but not as important as his tasks for the day. He nodded and headed to his office, all the while attempting to push the thought of the Duchess of Marsley from his mind.

Chapter Nineteen

"*I* was very surprised, Your Grace, that you agreed to this outing, and very pleased as well," Mrs. Armbruster said.

"I'm looking forward to seeing your Institute," Suzanne said.

When she'd received the woman's note this morning, it seemed like an excellent way to get out of Marsley House. She needed to be away, just in case her father called on her again. Plus, she was growing exceedingly tired of Ella and wanted to escape the woman's frowns and snide remarks.

Why had she tolerated the woman all this time? The fact that Ella had been in her employ six months seemed impossible now. But then, she'd been taking Ella's tonic and it had numbed everything.

Evidently, it had also stolen her reason.

Without the tonic, it had taken her longer to fall asleep last night. Her thoughts had been scattered, but they'd kept returning to Drummond. He was an exceedingly handsome man. In addition, he'd been kind and understanding.

People didn't seem to comprehend that it was easier to be alone than to try to pretend that everything was normal, that the world went on, and life still happened.

Drummond—Adam—had seemed to know that. No doubt because he'd his own share of grief with the death of his wife.

Had she said anything comforting to him? She couldn't remember, which made her think that she'd been immersed in her own sorrow. He hadn't been as selfish. He'd wanted to know about Georgie. He'd sat there and listened as she talked.

How natural it had felt to allow him to comfort her.

In those moments in the nursery she'd come to a startling realization. She wasn't numb to all feeling. She noted the strength of a man's embrace, the way he smelled—of bay rum and starch and a faint hint of the potpourri Mrs. Thigpen added to all the drawers. Had the housekeeper made a special recipe for Adam?

She liked the way he spoke, a Scottish accent that was flattened down just a little, as if he'd spent more time away from Scotland than in it.

She also noted the expression in his green eyes. Instead of the almost apathetic look in some higher-ranked servants—as if they'd seen it all and couldn't be bothered to deal further with the vagaries of human nature—Adam's gaze was always interested and curious. And kind. He'd said two words to her—*I'm sorry*—and it had touched her deeply.

"The girls at the Institute are from all kinds of backgrounds," Mrs. Armbruster was saying. "They have each been visited by circumstances that the rest of society deems unfit to contemplate."

"Ignoring something doesn't make it go away," Suzanne said.

Mrs. Armbruster gave her a bright, toothy smile. "How right you are, my dear." She placed her gloved hand on Suzanne's arm and leaned close. "You don't mind if I call you that, do you? You remind me so much of my own dear Diane. It's been four years since she and her husband emigrated to Queensland and I do miss her so."

"Of course not," Suzanne said.

Few people had treated her as if she were human in the past six years. Six years a duchess. Except for having had Georgie, she would much rather have gone back to being Suzanne Hackney. Her father would never have been satisfied with that, however. She was a commodity and he'd made a good bargain, at least according to him.

The Institute was also located in Spitalfields, a place that did not brighten with familiarity. Nor was the smell of it any more acceptable the second time she was here. How did Mrs. Armbruster tolerate it? For that matter, how did the inhabitants of the Foundling Hospital and the Institute?

The carriage halted in front of a two-story redbrick building. The entrance was a single door in the wall.

"We do not advertise what we do here, Your Grace," Mrs. Armbruster said. "There are some groups, unfortunately some that are religious in nature, who take umbrage at the fact that we are encouraging sin, in their words."

"Are you?" Suzanne asked, accepting the coachman's hand as she exited the carriage.

"I suppose that there are some people who think that, but what we do is rescue young women who have gotten themselves into trouble with the help of young men."

Suzanne didn't have a rejoinder to that, so she merely followed the older woman into the building.

Everything about the Institute was bland and neutral. The walls were beige. The wooden floors were covered with a beige runner. The rooms they passed were also beige, as if the entire building had been designed to be as nondescript as possible.

Mrs. Armbruster strode on ahead as if determined to reach a certain point. Suzanne had no choice but to follow her, removing her gloves as she did so and wishing she could dispense of her hat as easily.

The corridor smelled of onions and something sweet, apples. Onions and apples—what a curious combination. The kitchen to their left was filled with women milling about or seated at the long wooden table in the center of the room. Mrs. Armbruster only waved in passing.

The next doorway led to a music room, which surprised Suzanne because she hadn't thought of music as something that might be taught in such conditions. When she said as much to Mrs. Armbruster, the woman smiled.

"Many of these girls are frightened, Your Grace. Music, we've found, is a great equalizer. If you can get a few girls to sing a song they all know together, it eases them, and makes them less afraid."

Mrs. Armbruster finally stopped, turned to the right, and entered a beige room, this one a parlor. Impressively large, the room had two fireplaces on opposite walls. A selection of couches, chairs, tables, and lamps were scattered about the room. Nothing seemed to match and Suzanne couldn't help but wonder if every item in the parlor was a castoff from someone's home.

A great many of the couches and chairs were occupied, all by girls who seemed much too young to be in their condition. All of them were with child. Some looked to be due to give birth at any moment, while others probably had a few months left.

"Do they have no families?" Suzanne asked in a low voice.

Mrs. Armbruster turned to her, her doughy face softened into lines of compassion. For her naïveté? Or for the girls who surrounded them?

"The very sad fact, Your Grace, is that most of them do have families. But their families have thrown them out or locked the doors and banished them for their great sin. You will note, however, that the young men who helped them get into this condition are never punished in any way. Not by reputation. Not by the law. Not even financially."

She'd been sick for the first three months with Georgie, but after that, the entire time until his birth had been one of joy and anticipation. What must it be like to be with child and have no home, no family, no shelter, or anyone to care?

"Is there nothing that can be done?" she asked.

She had so much and they had so little. No, they had nothing except themselves and Mrs. Armbruster, a woman whose zeal was the match of any politician.

"Some brave men in Parliament are attempting to pass laws to effect change, but those are slow measures. In the meantime, we have young women who would suffer without assistance. Everyone is foolish from time to time, my dear. Each one of us has done something we regret. A bad decision, a choice made in the heat of the moment should not result in tragedy." Mrs. Armbruster cleared her throat. "In addition, Your Grace, there are some girls who had no choice in the matter. No choice at all."

Her voice took on a practical tone. "We need to help them provide for themselves. We have classes," she added. "We train them in various skills that an employer might wish to have. A great many of our girls have gone into service. Some work as milliners, some as seamstresses, and a few at nearby factories."

"Surely not when they're with child?"

The older woman nodded. "If they are healthy, yes, Your Grace. We've found that some occupation is harmful for neither the mother nor the child. A girl will remain here until her baby is born. Then she'll stay until she can find employment. We'll give her whatever education she wishes. Several of our girls have gone on to be quite successful, I'm proud to say."

The woman beamed at her. "We have plans to charge the girls a small amount each month to live here after their child is born. Only if they've acquired a position, that is." Mrs. Armbruster leaned close. "It's my fervent wish never to deny a girl a place here, Your Grace. They've already lost so much. I would hate for them to lose this haven as well. But there are those who will disobey our tenets. And some, I regret to say, who have abandoned their babies and left."

Suzanne couldn't imagine such a thing, but she had never been in a similar situation as these girls.

Before she could ask any further questions, Mrs. Armbruster walked to the middle of the room and called for attention.

"Girls, I have a very important visitor to introduce to you."

Suzanne felt her stomach drop and wished that

Mrs. Armbruster had warned her prior to the announcement.

"I'd like to present Her Grace, the Duchess of Marsley. Please welcome her to the Institute."

She was startled to be suddenly surrounded by the occupants of the parlor, most of them wishing to talk to her. Some girls just reached out a hand to touch her shoulder or her arm, almost as if she were an icon of some sort.

Mrs. Armbruster didn't do a thing other than smile toothily at her and leave her there, surrounded and awash in a sea of conversation.

"What's it like being a duchess?"

"Did you marry a prince?"

"Not a prince, a duke. She'd have to marry a duke."

"Are you rich?"

"Of course she's rich. She wouldn't be a duchess without being rich."

"Where's your crown? Why didn't you wear it today?"

"They don't wear crowns. Do they?"

One by one she tried to answer as many questions tossed to her as she could. She had one of her own after glancing at Mrs. Armbruster, who was still grinning at her.

What else was the woman planning?

Chapter Twenty

$\mathcal{A}$dam's first interview of the day was with Daniel. He spoke to the junior footman about his family. Daniel wasn't married. Nor did he have a sweetheart. He did, however, have a mother and five sisters, which probably went far in explaining why Daniel was grateful to have a room in the servant's wing.

"Have I done something wrong, sir?" Daniel finally asked.

Adam wasn't the least surprised to see high color on the young man's cheekbones. Daniel was one of those people who would always reveal what they were feeling on their face.

Adam crossed his arms. "What do you think you've done wrong?" he asked. He always got more information from men under his command when he asked questions than when he made pronouncements.

"I can't think of anything, sir," Daniel said. "I did all my duties today, just like before. Before I went on the door, that is."

"Who did you relieve?" Adam asked.

"Patrick, sir. He takes the early watch."

Adam sat back in his chair and studied the young

man. Even though Daniel was one of two men hired in the previous quarter, Adam doubted he was the spy.

He decided to show the young man some mercy. "I don't know anything that you've done incorrectly, Daniel. In fact, I've heard many good comments about you.

"If you don't mind sending Nathan in," he said, standing and extending his hand.

Daniel looked a little surprised as they shook hands. Adam didn't know if it was something that a majordomo normally did. If it wasn't, perhaps it should have been.

This role was playacting. Granted, there were times in his life—and other roles—when he'd felt the same. Being Rebecca's husband had felt odd to him, a confession he hadn't made to himself until a few years after Manipora. Being considered a hero when he'd only been lucky was another role that hadn't fit. He didn't know what other people thought a hero was, but he had his own definition. A hero was a man who didn't want to die so much that he was willing to do stupid things. For that, the British Army had rewarded him with a lieutenancy and a medal.

Daniel went out the door and Nathan came into the office.

"Close the door," he said, sitting. He indicated with one hand where Nathan should sit, in the straight chair in front of his desk.

Nathan was assigned to the south wing, an area that Adam didn't visit all that much, which meant he didn't know the young man well despite Nathan being a fellow Scot.

The footman was tall and as scrawny as a tree in winter. His neck was long, his chin pronounced, and his ears stuck out on either side of his head like handles.

"How do you like working at Marsley House?" Adam asked the young man as he sat on the chair in front of the desk.

Nathan nodded several times. Adam waited, but that was evidently the only answer he was going to get.

"How do you find London?"

Let Nathan try to answer that question with a nod or shake of his head.

"Crowded."

"And the food at Marsley House?"

"Good."

If Nathan was his spy, then he doubted Roger was getting more than a monosyllabic report.

Adam wasn't an expert at ferreting out confidence men and tricksters, but he did tend to listen to that small voice within, the same one that was now telling him that Nathan wasn't his man. He dismissed the footman after a few more questions and equally short answers.

It was entirely possible that Roger had installed someone at Marsley House before giving Adam his assignment. If that were the case, he would have to go further back and start interviewing staff hired months before he arrived.

That thought had the effect of souring his mood even more. Just add that mystery to another—where had the Duchess of Marsley gone?

Adam continued his planned interviews, which resulted in two surprises. One, that he suspected that one of the upper maids was with child. She'd been tearful throughout the entire meeting and unable to verbalize to him what the problem was.

The second surprise was that there was a Don Juan on the staff. This revelation had been made by yet another maid, one evidently feeling spurned by the man in question. He turned out to be Walter Lyle, who went by the name of Wals to his friends, of which he apparently had many at Marsley House.

The young man was personable, with a ready wit and a quick smile. His flashing brown eyes were probably attractive to women. There was something about Wals that disturbed Adam, however, and it wasn't related to possibly being Roger's spy. There was a calculating look in the footman's eyes, as if he were measuring the vulnerabilities of those he met. In addition, Wals had a propensity for cologne and now smelled like a curious combination of lemon, orange, and lavender.

He didn't know if the footman was responsible for the upper maid's predicament, but he intended to find out. He would have, too, if he hadn't been interrupted by Thomas, who knocked on the office door, then peered inside.

"Sir, Her Grace is asking to see you."

The duchess had returned.

The anticipation he felt was ill-timed, incorrect, and out of place. He was her majordomo. She was his employer. He couldn't forget the role he was playing.

He dismissed Wals with an admonition that they would meet again soon.

"Go back to your room and do a quick wash," he told the footman. "This time don't douse yourself with scent."

Wals looked at him in surprise—evidently, most people didn't comment on his lemon/orange/lavender odor.

Adam followed Thomas downstairs to find the duchess standing in the foyer accompanied by two young women he'd never seen. Mrs. Thigpen was also there, and the older woman was twisting her hands nervously, something she rarely did.

"Your Grace," he said, bowing slightly.

"Drummond," she responded, tilting up her chin at him. "These are your new staff members. I understand from Mrs. Thigpen that you are solely responsible for hiring new staff."

He exchanged a quick glance with the housekeeper. "Yes, Your Grace."

"Ruby and Hortense are to be given light duty only," she said, gesturing to the two young women. "Both of them are with child."

Once again, he and Mrs. Thigpen exchanged a look. Didn't the duchess understand that such a condition was grounds for dismissal?

The look in the duchess's eyes wasn't one of grief. More like resolution, or a steely kind of determination he'd seen before.

Of all the subjects in all the world, he'd never thought to discuss a woman being with child with the Duchess of Marsley.

"There's an upper maid that I suspect is in that condition, Your Grace. She was going to lose her position. Should I reconsider and keep her on?"

She merely blinked at him for a moment, her color steadily rising. In anyone else he might have thought them about to suffer from apoplexy, but he suspected the duchess's courage was hard-won and that she was as embarrassed as he to be discussing this topic in the foyer.

"Would you like to adjourn to the library, Your Grace?"

She nodded, preceding him down the hall and through the double doors.

"I really must insist that you make room for them, Drummond," she said, the minute she entered the room. She whirled and faced him. "It's my home, after all."

"Yes, Your Grace."

"And to dismiss a girl simply because she's in trouble . . . That's not very compassionate."

"No, Your Grace."

"You weren't really going to do that, were you?"

He nodded.

"Why?"

"Each of the girls knows the conditions of her employment."

"That hardly seems fair, Drummond. Do you do the same for the men in that situation?"

"No, but I think we should."

She looked surprised at that.

"They are hardly virgin births, Your Grace," he said, hoping she'd forgive him his plain speaking. "It does take a male and a female."

Her complexion grew pinker.

"I do think she should be allowed to stay on as long as she can," the duchess said. "Does she have any family who will take her in?"

"I don't know," he said.

She looked surprised again. "Well, you should, Drummond."

He nodded once more. "You're right, Your Grace."

Her eyes narrowed. "You're being very agreeable about this, Drummond. Are you just saying what you think I want to hear to humor me?"

He smiled, the expression genuine. "I am not."

"Then you won't dismiss the upstairs maid," she said.

"Not if you don't wish it, Your Grace."

"And the new girls, they'll be welcome?"

"As much as it is in my power to ensure, Your Grace."

"What exactly does that mean, Drummond?"

She had called him Adam last night.

"Human beings sometimes don't act in ways that we would wish them to," he said. "They may be accepted by the rest of the staff. Or not."

"I will not have them called names," she said.

"Of that I can guarantee you," he answered.

His own sister had been called a whore for loving a peer who'd taken advantage of her. He'd do everything in his power to ensure that no one said anything about the two new maids, but he couldn't manage anyone's thoughts.

People were occasionally stodgy in their thinking. They might espouse a more advanced attitude, but they often fell back on tried and true ways. A girl in trouble was not an object of pity as much as derision, especially from other women. He couldn't help but wonder if, behind their criticism, was the thought, *There but for the grace of God go I.*

"Do you disapprove, Drummond?"

"It's not my place to approve or disapprove, Your Grace. As you stated, it's your home."

She regarded him steadily for more than a minute. He returned her look, thinking that she was surprising him again. She wasn't as fragile as he'd thought. Instead, he had the startling notion that the Duchess of Marsley could give as much as she got.

She was, after all, Edward Hackney's daughter. He shouldn't forget that.

"I had to do something," she said finally. "Mrs. Armbruster is one of those people who overwhelms you with good deeds. She's started a Foundling Hospital and an Institute for Women. I couldn't become her patron, so I had to make some gesture. It seemed a good idea to employ two of the girls who were new to the Institute."

He could understand a compassionate gesture gone awry. How many times in his past had he tried to do a good thing only for the outcome to be less than what he'd desired?

"Your Grace," he said, wanting to make her feel better, "it was a very kind thing that you did. I will let the upper maid know that you would like her to stay on for a few more weeks or months. I will find out if she has a family to go to and if she doesn't, we'll make some arrangement for her. As for the other girls, I'm certain that they will work out fine."

"Do you really think so, Drummond?"

He wasn't, no, but he didn't want to disappoint her, so he only smiled in response.

"It's best if I'm not at home when Mrs. Armbruster calls again," she said, her tone one of wry resignation. "Heaven knows how many other maids I'll come home with if I visit with her again."

He wanted to do exactly what he'd done last night, pull her into his arms and hold her there for a moment. Enough time, perhaps, for them to become acquainted with the shape and the warmth of each other. He wanted to breathe in the scent of her hair and feel her breasts pressing against his chest.

He should remember his mission, his assignment, and nothing more.

Stepping to the side, he opened the library door, and bowed slightly to her before leaving. Would she realize how much he wanted to stay?

Chapter Twenty-One

The morning was beautiful, a perfect autumn morning without a hint of clouds in the sky. Suzanne stood at the open window of her sitting room, staring out at the day. The breeze was brisk, carrying a hint of the chill that the night would bring.

The formal Italian garden to the front of the house didn't look any different in autumn than it did in spring. No blowsy, untidy flowers were allowed to bloom here. Nothing but clipped hedges and crushed granite paths.

Everything about Marsley House was manicured for presentation. She'd often felt that way about herself, delivered unto George coiffed and attired, trained and schooled—a *fait accompli*—the perfect duchess.

The trees below her were bathed in the sun, one side of their leaves tinted gold. An errant leaf had escaped the attention of the gardeners and it tumbled across the lawn in a joyous demonstration of freedom.

She wanted to be like that leaf. To throw off her role and race over the grass. The habits of a lifetime were difficult to break, however. Yet wouldn't it be lovely to be someone other than who she was, if only for a few hours?

Who would that be? An image came to her then, a day from her childhood. She and her governess, Miss Moore, had gone on a picnic. Miss Moore believed in a variety of learning locations, and her mother hadn't disapproved. On that day, they'd spread out a blanket beneath a tree. The land had sloped down to a gurgling brook. The passage of time had no doubt painted the scene with perfection. A breeze had blown the glorious perfume of lilacs to her. She could remember laughing, but not the reason.

She'd been ten years old, racing out of childhood with abandon. She wanted to know everything. Why did the bees skip certain flowers? What made the clouds go skidding across the sky? Why had the Egyptians made the pyramids the way they had? Miss Moore answered every eager question, even the ones about India, where her father spent so much of his time.

How strange that she would never feel quite that free again. On his return from India, her father had dismissed Miss Moore, replacing her with a narrow-eyed harridan who reminded her of Ella.

Gone was the appreciation for her childish curiosity. Instead, she'd been stuffed full of information, dates, names, and locations. If she dared to ask a question she only received a frown in return.

Was that child still inside her? Did she have the ability to turn an eager face to the world? She had wanted that for Georgie. She had wanted to show him that there were wonders and marvels to see and share.

Part of her died the day he did. She'd felt as if everything inside had shriveled and burned, leaving nothing but ashes in its wake. Yet now she had the oddest thought. Could something of that young girl still exist?

She was not acting like herself, or at least the person she'd been for so very long. Ever since that night on the roof, she'd changed. She'd refused, again last night, to take the tonic. Granted, it was harder to fall asleep, but she'd occupied herself with thoughts of Adam.

There was something about the way he'd said his wife's name. *Rebecca.* It was spoken in such a gentle tone, almost as if he cradled the word in his hand to mark on its uniqueness.

He hadn't said how his wife had died and she found herself awash in curiosity. Everything about the man sparked her interest. Why had he gone from being in the army to being a majordomo? He hadn't liked that comment she made, repeating something that George had often said—that a man only left the army if he was a failure. Adam's eyes had taken on a flat look and his mouth had thinned.

A proper majordomo, perhaps one without military experience, would have moderated his expression and hidden what he was feeling. Adam hadn't done that.

A month ago she would never have spent significant time wondering about a male in her employ. Yet a month ago she would never have gone to the Foundling Hospital or the Institute. Nor would she have returned to Marsley House with two new servants in tow.

Yes, she was most definitely changing.

She should go and check to see how the new girls

were settling in. While she was at it, she would find Adam and finally get an answer from him about something else. What exactly had he said that night he'd brought her back to her room?

She avoided the bedroom because Ella was going through her wardrobe and sighing in disapproval. Evidently Suzanne had spilled something on a bodice or stained a cuff or dirtied her hem.

She stopped and surveyed herself in the mirror on the wall. She patted her hair into place, practiced a benevolent smile, and straightened the cameo at her neck. Without a word to Ella, she left her suite in search of Adam. How very odd to feel such anticipation.

Her majordomo was flat on his back in the middle of the library.

"Drummond?" she said at the door. "Are you all right?" She flew to his side and stared down at him. "What's wrong?"

"Nothing, Your Grace."

"You haven't fallen?"

"No, I haven't. Nor fainted."

"Then what are you doing on the floor?" she asked.

"Looking at the roof, Your Grace."

She glanced up. "It's not a roof," she said. "It's a cupola."

"Very well," he said agreeably. "The cupola. I'm trying to make out the patterns of the stained glass and I've found that it's much easier to be in this position than bending my neck that far back."

She looked up at the ceiling and realized that she had rarely noticed the stained glass windows.

"What does it signify?" he asked. "I thought, at first, that the windows were religious in nature, that they depicted a scene from the Bible. After studying them for a while, I don't think so."

"All I know is that George had them redone after he returned from India."

He glanced at her. "Did he?"

She nodded.

"How odd if they're Hindu."

"I don't think it would be any more odd than the Persian Parlor or the Chinese Room or the Egyptian Room."

"You have a point," he said. He stretched his hand toward her. "Would you care to join me, Your Grace?"

"I'm the Duchess of Marsley. I don't get on the floor."

Sitting up, he smiled at her. "You look horrified at the idea."

"I am," she said, fingering the cameo at her throat. "I couldn't imagine what the staff might say if one of them saw me."

"Perhaps they'd call you daft," he said. "Or eccentric. 'Did you hear what the Duchess of Marsley did? She was seen on the floor of the library staring up at the cupola. Have you ever heard of anything more ludicrous?'"

"Are you a spy, Adam?"

She'd never seen anyone's face change so quickly. In one instant, there was humor in his eyes and his mouth was curved in a teasing smile. In the next second, his face lost all expression.

He didn't answer her. He got to his feet, brushed off his trousers and the sleeves of his jacket, paying close attention to his cuffs.

"There isn't that much dust on the floor, Adam," she finally said.

She folded her arms in front of her, trying to push down the odd combination of feelings rising up from her stomach. She'd rarely felt anger and fear at the same time, but she did now.

"Are you a spy?" she asked again.

"A spy?"

He was stalling for time, but she'd much prefer if he would just be honest with her.

She nodded. "For my father. Is that why you're in my household? To report back to him? To tell him when I've done anything untoward? Is that why he didn't immediately order me to dismiss you?"

The idea was new, but it made a great deal of sense.

She didn't say anything further, only turned and went to stand behind the desk, studying the view from the sparkling windows. This room reminded her too much of George, especially with the portrait of him in his military uniform hanging over the fireplace. He'd been especially proud of that painting. When it had been completed, he'd invited hundreds of people to the house to marvel at how distinguished and handsome he'd looked.

It felt like he was watching her now in that way of his, as if he were half amused by her youthful naïveté and half bored senseless. She'd been too young for him, too unschooled in certain ways.

"I never met your father until the other day," he said. "I'm not spying for him. Nor am I reporting back to him about anything."

"If you're not," she said, still not turning, "then you would be unusual. Ella is one of his spies."

"Is she? I knew there was a reason I didn't like the woman."

She glanced at him over her shoulder and then back at the view.

"Why do you keep her on?" he asked.

It had been easier to simply endure Ella than to change the situation. What else was she simply enduring? She didn't know, but perhaps it was time she found out.

She turned, finally, to find that he was standing much too close. She should have stepped back, but the window was there. She put her hands on his chest to push him away, but then she looked up at his face.

His green eyes were much too attractive and much too intent.

He brushed his knuckles against her cheek. She didn't retreat. Nor did she tell him that he mustn't touch her. She was inviolate, his employer, the Duchess of Marsley. What would anyone say to see him touch her so? What comment would they make if they noticed that his gaze was particularly tender?

She didn't care.

She shouldn't smile at her majordomo. Or feel as if a rusty door had been opened in her chest. She shouldn't spread her fingers wide against the fabric of his jacket, feeling the pounding of his heart as rapid as her own.

When he lowered his head slowly, she measured the seconds in held breaths. He didn't rush. He didn't pressure her. Instead, he gave her a chance to protest. Or to caution him. Or to pull away. Or, finally, to act shocked and disapproving.

She should have said something like, *You're dismissed, Adam. Leave this moment and I will have your belongings sent to you.*

She remained silent, even as he reached out and cupped her face with both hands now, studying her with intent eyes. Did he wish to remember what she looked like forever? She felt bemused and bathed in confusion.

When his lips touched hers, it was an explosion of feeling. Disbelief banished in the presence of bright sprinkles of delight.

One of the maids had been brushing a threadbare rug from the servants' quarters one day. Suzanne had seen her at her task in the back garden, noting that the sun's rays shone through the worn fibers. She felt like that now, as if her soul, pitted and frayed in places, was being illuminated somehow.

His hands cupped her shoulders and then reached around to her back, slowly bringing her forward, closer to him. Her hands joined behind his neck.

Her mouth opened and he inhaled her breath and gave her back some of his. He tasted of coffee and iced cinnamon buns. His lips were warm, tender, and capable of inducing all sorts of strange and fascinating sensations.

Shivers traveled down her body, seemed to wrap around her stomach, and made their way up to her breasts. Her feet tingled. It was difficult to breathe, to concentrate, and to make sense of what she was doing.

Had he stolen her reason completely with a kiss?

She didn't want to move. She didn't want to become a duchess again. Instead, she wanted to be who she had once been, the young girl about whom she'd wondered earlier.

That Suzanne would have wholeheartedly joined in this kiss. She would've stood on tiptoe as she was doing right now, to deepen it. She would have delighted at the fact that her heart was racing and her body felt as if it were warming from the inside out.

Somehow that girl had taken over, pushing the duchess aside.

Chapter Twenty-Two

*R*eason surfaced gradually, penetrating the haze of pleasure surrounding Adam. What the hell was he doing?

He was jeopardizing everything, his position of majordomo, his assignment, not to mention his honor.

Shame should have suffused him as he stepped back. He should have immediately apologized, explained that it had been a while since he'd kissed a woman. Since he'd even wanted to kiss anyone.

Instead, he shook his head, the gesture substituting for all the words he couldn't say.

She was a duchess and he was as far from the peerage as anyone could be.

She was going to say the words to dismiss him. He waited for them as the seconds ticked past. Instead, she stood there, her fingers pressed to her lips, looking at him as if she had never before seen a man.

"Why did you kiss me?" she asked.

"Do I need a reason?"

"Why, Adam?"

Very well, if she insisted on the truth, he would give it to her.

"Because you're a beautiful woman," he said. "And

you're very kissable." As if that weren't bad enough, he decided to give her another layer of honesty. "I've thought about doing it for days now."

If she was going to dismiss him, let it be for cause. "Have you?"

Her cheeks were turning pink again, a barometer of her emotions. He couldn't tell, however, if she was feeling embarrassment or anger.

He reached out with both hands, gripped her shoulders, and pulled her gently to him.

"I have," he said and bent to kiss her again. In for a penny, in for a pound.

She didn't pull away. She didn't strike him with her fists. She wrapped her arms around his waist as if afraid that he would leave her.

He had no intention of doing that. His thoughts were swirled and jumbled things. All he knew was that he needed to hold her, needed to kiss her, in a way that was elemental. His life depended on it.

Her palms were suddenly flat against his chest and she was pulling away.

He didn't want to let her go, but he dropped his hands. His breathing was erratic, and every thought was centered not on his assignment or his role or even how he would explain to Mount why he'd been summarily dismissed. He was thinking about the pleasure she'd so effortlessly given him.

The image of her in his bed, her hair tousled, her lips swollen from his kisses, wouldn't leave him. He wanted to disrobe her slowly. Were her breasts as large as they felt pressed against his chest? He imagined her long and perfectly formed legs wrapped around his waist.

He wanted to feel her, stroke her skin without

layers of clothing between them. He wanted her hands all over him, her breath against his throat.

Staring down at the carpet was easier than looking at her. He couldn't apologize and was as far from being sorry as he was from respecting the Duke of Marsley. He would be able to recall her in his arms for years, if not forever. That startled catch in her breath when he first kissed her would be something he'd always remember. How could he possibly regret kissing Suzanne?

She took another step back and he wanted to tell her that he wasn't going to ravish her, at least not without her consent. She had nothing to fear from him, never mind that he'd kissed her. That was as far as his efforts of seduction would go. Not because of his assignment. Nor because she would surely dismiss him any second now, but because any relationship they had must be on equal footing. He didn't want to overwhelm her. He didn't want to seduce her. He wanted her, but he also hoped she wanted him.

That night in her bedroom, when he'd looked into her eyes and seen only anguish, the need had been born in him to give her comfort. But this, what he felt now, was different. He ached to lose himself in her, quiet all the memories swirling around in his head. For a few moments, the past had disappeared. When he held Suzanne all he'd been conscious of was her, him, and pleasure.

He thrust his hand into his jacket pocket, retrieved the brooch, and held out his hand, palm up.

"I found your brooch," he said. "It's what you were looking for the other day, wasn't it?"

His voice didn't sound like himself, almost as if it were difficult to speak.

She reached out and took the piece of jewelry, holding it between two fingers.

"It's not a brooch," she said, sounding different as well. Thankfully, however, there was no evidence of tears in her voice. "It's a hair clip. You see?" She turned the brooch on its back and opened a clasp. "It slides onto my hair like that."

"I am somewhat lacking in my knowledge of diamond hairpins, Your Grace."

How effortlessly he had fallen back into his role. He was her servant. She was his employer. They should not forget such things. In addition, he was someone else. Someone she didn't know about.

Standing there, however, he felt closer to his real self than he had for quite some time. Had a single kiss rendered him defenseless? Very well, two kisses. And more if she had allowed him. Perhaps it was a good thing that the portrait of her dead husband watched them.

She was staring at him, her eyes steady. Her color was still high. He concentrated on her lips. Those lips made him want to kiss her again.

"Do you want an apology?" he asked. "Shall I confess to my animalistic nature?"

"Do you have one?"

"Around you, evidently," he said.

"The maids are safe, then?"

"Assuredly, Your Grace."

"And me, Drummond? Am I safe?"

"Honesty compels me to say that I'm not entirely certain."

Her eyebrows rose.

She probably thought he was teasing her, but he was being deadly serious.

"Then I should avoid you at all costs," she said.

"It would probably be the best advice I could give you."

"So if you came upon me in a parlor, for example, I should scream for assistance? If nothing else, I should ring for a maid?"

"Or perhaps you should have a chaperone at all times, Your Grace."

"Strictly to prevent you from demonstrating your animalistic nature, is that correct?"

"Yes."

"Drummond, you can't say such things. I am no great beauty. Surely not someone to inspire a man like you to do wicked things."

"Not wicked, Your Grace. Simply human nature. You have lips I want to kiss. And a form it gives me great pleasure to hold. As to your beauty, if you want compliments, I will endeavor to come up with a few. You should know your own attributes, however."

"Drummond, you are the most extraordinary man and this has been the most extraordinary conversation."

He only smiled at her.

"I don't require an apology," she said.

"Then any time you would wish to duplicate the experience, Your Grace, I stand ready to serve."

They exchanged a very long look. He wasn't entirely certain what she was thinking, but her smile was once more in evidence. If he wasn't mistaken, there was a glint of humor in her eyes.

Good. Marble Marsley needed to be shattered until the woman within was revealed.

She nodded at him, just once, grabbed her skirt

with both hands, and, with chin tilted up slightly, left the library.

She'd given him a bad turn when she'd asked if he was a spy. What kind of man set his daughter's servants to watching her?

The more he learned about Edward Hackney, the more he thought that the ex-director of the East India Company bore watching as well.

He stared at the closed door for several minutes before he, too, left the room.

Chapter Twenty-Three

*H*e'd kissed her.

He'd kissed her and she'd let him.

No, she hadn't lied to him. She'd wholeheartedly participated.

She shouldn't have. She shouldn't have allowed him to touch her. Or hold her. Or kiss her.

If she were a true duchess, she should have dismissed him on the spot. He was her majordomo. He was on the staff of Marsley House. He was her servant. She should have banished him immediately. At the very least she should have been embarrassed and ashamed.

What was she doing?

She was betraying everything she'd been reared to believe was right, proper, and just. She was behaving like a harlot. Yet she felt alive when she was around him. He challenged her, annoyed her, and intrigued her. Plus, he'd protected and defended her.

He'd kissed her.

What was she going to do about Drummond?

She really should avoid him at all costs, but she didn't want to barricade herself in her room with only Ella as company again.

She'd forgotten to ask about the maids. She would have to talk to him soon. If she began to feel the least bit of anticipation about that meeting, she should squelch that feeling immediately. Perhaps it would be better if she acquired another maid as a chaperone. Someone to shadow her as she went from room to room in case she and Drummond encountered each other.

How, though, was she supposed to forget those kisses?

No, she really should have dismissed him this time, but she knew she wasn't going to do anything of the sort.

Maybe she wasn't a true duchess at all.

Suzanne realized she was heading back to her suite and then stopped herself. She didn't want to encounter Ella right now, especially when she was feeling . . . Her thoughts stuttered to a halt. How, exactly, was she feeling?

The hard knot of tension wasn't there in her chest. Nor did she feel like a huge hole existed in her stomach.

She abruptly sat on the bench just past the landing on the second floor. From here she could see part of the staircase and to the end of the corridor.

What exactly was she feeling? A curious excitement, something she hadn't experienced in a great many . . . Her thoughts stopped again. It hadn't been months since she'd felt this way. It had been years.

For a while after Georgie's death, she'd willed herself to die. That's what it had felt like. She hadn't been able to eat or sleep well. It was as if her body was shutting down in stages so that she might be with her son. She hadn't died, though. She'd survived. She'd gotten through those endless months. Somehow, she counted one month, then two, then six, then a year. She'd gotten through that year and more, existing and enduring.

What was it that Mrs. Armbruster had said?

"I know what you're feeling, Your Grace. You think that if you put aside your grief, even for a moment, it means you didn't love him."

She'd wanted to ask Mrs. Armbruster if such wisdom had been acquired through her own loss, but she hadn't.

Learning of someone else's pain didn't ease her grief one whit. All it did was make her feel uncomfortable because she hadn't known.

Had she been that selfish? Yes, for two years she had been.

"Your Grace, you haven't taken your tonic."

She looked up to see Ella standing there. In her hands was a cup no doubt containing the green, noxious brew Suzanne hated. How had she missed the maid's approach? The other woman crept about on cat feet. Sometimes Suzanne thought she did so in order to startle her.

"You didn't take your tonic last night, Your Grace," she said, thrusting the cup at Suzanne. "Nor did you have it this morning."

"I don't want it," she said.

Taking the tonic might render her nights dreamless, but it rendered her days fog-like. More than once she'd found herself sitting in the same chair for hours. Nor could she remember people or events well.

These past two days, when she hadn't taken the tonic, she'd felt more like herself.

"I don't want it," she repeated.

"Your father won't be pleased."

Neither was Ella, if the expression on her face was any indication. The maid's mouth was pinched and the lines at the corners of her eyes were more prevalent this morning, almost as if she had practiced frowning for a good while before coming to find Suzanne.

"He will just have to be displeased with me, Ella," she said. "I'm not taking it. I don't like how I feel when I've had it."

"You know you need it," Ella said, once more thrusting the cup at her. "It's helped you handle your sadness, Your Grace. Without it, I'm certain that life will be so much more difficult for you."

Suzanne pushed the cup away, silenced by surprise. While it was true that she didn't like the other woman, Ella had always behaved properly up until now. The maid had never before talked to her with such contempt in her voice.

She said the words quite carefully, so there would be no misunderstanding. "I'm not going to take the tonic anymore, Ella. I don't care what you tell my father. I'm not taking it."

For the third time, Ella shoved the cup in her face, some of the liquid almost sloshing over the rim. The smell was as bad as it had always been, like grass that had begun to rot.

"Take it, Your Grace."

Suzanne stood, moving a little distance away from the maid.

"Evidently you've forgotten your place, Ella."

"My place is to ensure that you're doing what you should do, Your Grace. That includes taking your tonic. Everyone agrees that it's the best thing for you. You wouldn't want to suffer the effects of not taking it, would you?"

That was a scary question, one she'd not considered. She'd taken the tonic ever since Ella had come to Marsley House six months ago. Was there some sort of deleterious effect if she didn't drink it?

She would just have to find out, wouldn't she?

"No," she said, turning and heading for the staircase.

Ella was undeterred.

She followed Suzanne all the way down to the first floor, talking the entire time.

"You'll be sick, Your Grace. You'll get hideous headaches. You'll be subjected to uncontrollable weeping."

At the base of the stairs, Suzanne turned to face her maid.

"It sounds ghastly, Ella."

The other woman's face was triumphant as she pushed the cup toward Suzanne.

"So ghastly," Suzanne said, grabbing the cup, "that I can assure you I am never going to drink it again."

She marched some distance to the foyer, where Thomas was pretending not to overhear her discussion with Ella. She handed him the cup and he took it, looking somewhat bemused.

"Get rid of this, Thomas," she said.

Ella still didn't cease. "You can't do that, Your Grace. I'm only acting in your best interest."

Suzanne really didn't like being lectured. First by her father and now her maid. Had she always seemed so malleable and desirous of direction? She took a deep breath and, for good measure, said a quick prayer. Surely God would understand her need to do this. God might, but her father wouldn't. Well, she would have to solve that problem as well.

One mountain at a time, however.

"I'm afraid we don't suit, Ella. I think it would be best if you find other employment. I will, of course, give you a letter of recommendation, but I would appreciate it very much if you would leave Marsley House within the hour. We'll be more than happy to send your trunk after you."

She turned and was heading down the corridor when Ella grabbed her by the arm, jerking her so hard that she nearly fell.

"You can't just dismiss me like that," Ella said.

"I can, and I just have." She looked beyond Ella to where Thomas was standing, his eyes wide.

"Go find Drummond," she said.

Ella leaned close.

"If you dismiss me, I'll tell everyone that you've been acting oddly and how worried I am about you. You're inconsolable. Poor thing, you've been made mad by grief."

She tried to free herself from Ella's grip, but the other woman only held her tighter.

"Tell him you changed your mind," Ella said, her tight-lipped smile disconcerting.

Why hadn't she dismissed the woman months ago? The answer shamed her. Perhaps she'd become a little too dependent on Ella's tonic. Perhaps she'd wanted dreamless sleep and formless days. Perhaps she'd even needed the tonic once. She didn't need it now.

"Let me go," Suzanne said.

"You heard her," Adam said, coming up behind the maid.

Suzanne had never been so happy to see anyone.

"The duchess is not herself, Drummond," Ella said without looking at him. "This doesn't concern you."

At least she wasn't the only one being targeted by Ella's venomous rage and contempt.

"I think it does."

Drummond glanced at her and seemed to take in the situation immediately. He frowned when he saw that Ella was still gripping her arm. He came to Suzanne's side, reached out and peeled the other woman's hand away.

"What would you like me to do, Your Grace?"

"Escort Ella to the door, if you would, please. I've dismissed her, but she's refusing to leave."

"The duchess is deranged," Ella said, still standing too close. "She's lost her wits. She's gone mad. You shouldn't listen to anything she says. They're the ramblings of an idiot."

"Let's go," Drummond said, reaching out and grabbing Ella's arm.

"Can't you see she's not in her right mind? The entire staff knows it. They laugh behind her back. The Duchess of Marsley, simpleton."

"Now, Ella," Drummond said.

"How protective you are," Ella said, eyeing Drummond up and down. "What an interesting development. I'm sure her father would want to know."

He didn't say a word, merely took Ella to the door. She truly didn't have a choice, because Drummond was so much larger and more determined.

Suzanne watched as Thomas opened the door and Drummond unceremoniously escorted the woman down the steps before directing the footman to close the door in her face.

It might have been amusing but for the insults

Ella was shouting. She sincerely hoped that the other servants weren't listening, but that was almost too much to hope for. Was the staff really laughing at her behind her back?

Drummond returned to her side, took her arm in a grip that was a great deal gentler than the one he'd used on Ella, and walked her into the closest parlor.

Here George's great-grandfather's acquisitions from Egypt were displayed against sand-colored walls. She'd always liked this room because it seemed to transport her to a different place and time. Unfortunately, she didn't feel that same sensation now, looking at all the canopic jars and intricately carved chests.

She couldn't stop herself from trembling and that both concerned and annoyed her.

Ella had been vicious. She hadn't expected that. Nor had she anticipated seeing herself in the maid's eyes. Had she truly appeared that distraught, insensible, and weak?

Drummond released her to close the door, then turned back to her.

She looked up at him. "Did you tell her? Did you tell her about that night on the roof?"

"No, of course I didn't," he said.

"Did you tell anyone?"

He pulled her into his arms. She really should have stepped away, but she was so cold and she hadn't stopped trembling.

"No, Suzanne, I didn't tell anyone."

"I am not deranged."

"I never thought you were."

"I'm not a simpleton," she said.

"No, you aren't."

She pulled back and looked up into his face. "Do you mean that?"

He nodded.

"Ella told me that I would suffer if I didn't take the tonic. Why would she say that?"

"Would you like me to find out what's in it?"

"Could you do that?"

"I could," he said.

"You are a magical majordomo, Drummond. Is there no lack of things you can do?"

He didn't respond to that comment. Evidently, he was modest as well.

She pressed her forehead against his chest and wished her trembling would stop.

"Are they all laughing at me?"

"No," he said.

She wanted to know what he was thinking. When had she come to value his opinion so much?

"Do you think I'm disordered in my thoughts? Or that my actions have been odd?"

"I think you've been suffering from a great loss," he said. "And that you've been alone with it. You don't have to be alone anymore, Suzanne."

She grabbed his jacket with both her fists, feeling as if he was the only steady person in the universe.

"What happened on the roof was odd behavior, Drummond. Kissing you was odd. Always wanting to talk to you is odd. I have a feeling that most people would see my recent behavior as strange."

"Sometimes you need to ignore what other people say."

He wrapped his arms around her, and rocked slightly from one side to the other, almost as if she were a fractious babe.

"Surround yourself with the right kind of people. Be very selective of who you speak with and who you listen to."

She felt the first stirrings of amusement. "You mean like you, of course."

"Of course," he said, his voice holding a tinge of humor.

She sighed. "I really don't need to be hugged, Drummond."

He only tightened his embrace.

"I should dismiss you, too," she said.

"You can't dismiss me. Just today I approved the purchase of a dozen spoons. And as many bowls for Cook. I am in the process of looking over designs for the expansion of the kitchen garden. I'm much too important to dismiss."

"Is that where you were just now, the kitchen?"

"No. I was in the library."

"On your back again?" she asked, pulling away to look up into his face. "Were you studying the stained glass windows again?"

"I was not. I was actually looking for a book on herbs."

"Herbs? For the kitchen garden?"

He nodded.

"You're always in the library, Drummond."

"I don't always sleep well, Your Grace. It helps to find a book to read."

She stepped back. He dropped his arms, his faint smile fading as he looked at her.

"She won't be allowed inside Marsley House again, Your Grace. You needn't worry about that."

How easily they went from first names back to their proper roles. She preferred to be called Suzanne.

What would Ella say to that? No doubt that she'd lost her mind. Perhaps she had. If so, she preferred this existence to the one she'd been living for so long.

"Where does she keep the tonic?" he asked.

"I don't know," she said. "I've never seen it around my rooms."

"Then, with your permission, I'll go search Ella's."

She nodded.

"Would you like to accompany me?"

She would, but not for reasons she wanted to explain. She didn't want to be alone at the moment and if that made her sound defenseless and weak, she didn't care.

Chapter Twenty-Four

$\mathcal{A}$dam decided that he really needed to finish his assignment and leave Marsley House. More than ever now. He shouldn't have been so honest with her. He shouldn't have kissed Suzanne earlier and comforted her a moment ago. He was almost as much a lecher as Whitcomb. Had she known about her husband's character? Had she cared that the duke hadn't been faithful? A strange thought as he accompanied her up the grand staircase to the third floor.

Placing his hand at the small of her back, he guided her toward the servants' quarters. He caught her glancing to the left, toward the corridor where the nursery was located. Had she been back to the room since they'd talked that night?

He had too much curiosity about Suzanne.

A tendril of her hair had come loose from her severe bun and he wanted to push it back into place. He kept his hands to himself.

"We need to find you another maid," he said. There, a good enough distraction and one that might occupy his thoughts for a few moments.

She only nodded.

"Is there anyone on staff you would like to promote?"

She shook her head.

He wished she would speak and wondered why she was suddenly so silent. Was it due to the proximity of the nursery? Or did it have something to do with the fact that she'd dismissed Ella? Although she was walking with her hands folded in front of her, he could tell that she was still trembling.

"The woman needed to be dismissed," he said, his voice rough.

She glanced over at him.

"You didn't like her," she said.

"No, I didn't."

She didn't say anything to his admission.

"I don't know if any of the maids would like to have Ella's position," she said. "It does come with a significant increase in wages, does it not?"

He nodded. Since he'd recently reviewed the quarterly expenditures he was aware of what was paid to every person. Mrs. Thigpen and the cook earned substantially more than the rest of the staff, but that was because of their positions and their longevity. His salary as majordomo was the equivalent of what was paid to five footmen.

"Do you think Ella told them I was mad?"

He glanced at her. "I don't think Ella communicated with the other maids at all," he said. "She considered herself above them."

"Perhaps Mrs. Thigpen might have a recommendation," she said when he stopped in front of Ella's door. "Someone not like Ella in any way."

"I don't think that's a difficult requirement. Ella was unique in her disagreeableness."

After opening the door, he stepped aside for her to enter first.

Ella's room was larger than a normal maid's quarters, but not as spacious as his rooms or those assigned to Mrs. Thigpen. The hierarchy in the servants' ranks at Marsley House was as pronounced as that of the army. A lady's maid was below the rank of governess or majordomo but higher than those maids assigned to the family quarters. They, in turn, were above the public room maids, who were over the scullery maids. Stable boys figured somewhere in the mix, but Adam was damned if he knew exactly where.

He looked around him, wondering if the duchess had the same impression he was getting. Ella didn't reveal who she was with her personal possessions. The single bed was neatly made; the pillow looked as if it had been fluffed before being placed at the head of the bed in the middle of the mattress. Her clothes were hung on the hooks arranged on the far wall in militaristic precision by color. The only item on the small bedside table was an oil lamp with a gold shade.

A vanity had been provided, topped with a mirror. Here there was only a utilitarian brush, a comb, and a small tortoiseshell-topped box of hairpins.

No perfume scented the room. Instead, there was a curious herbal odor, almost as if Ella had kept plants on the windowsill.

He began opening the drawers of the small bureau below the window. He intensely disliked going through a woman's unmentionables, be it this assignment or another, but he couldn't pick and choose. You couldn't falter in your mission just because you didn't like certain parts of it.

He found the bottle in the bottom drawer, tucked beneath Ella's nightgowns.

Holding up the brown bottle stoppered with a cork, he asked, "Is this it?"

She nodded. "Are the contents green?"

He uncorked the bottle, upended it on the tip of his finger, and nodded. "It's green." He tasted it, immediately identifying the main ingredient. "It's also opium," he said.

"Opium?"

"Did you know?" he asked as he put the cork back in the bottle.

"Of course not," she said.

She still stood at the door, her hands fisted at her waist. The tautness of her demeanor made him think that she could easily explode into anger. Or tears. Of the two, he preferred anger. It was certainly justified.

Why was Ella giving Suzanne opium?

"She always said my father told her to do it."

That didn't make any sense. "Why would your father want you drugged?"

She shrugged, which wasn't an answer, at least one he wanted. He didn't push her to explain, however. Sometimes, it was better to wait until someone was ready to talk.

He closed the drawer, looked around, and decided he'd found everything there was to find.

The duchess still hadn't spoken. He abandoned patience for a more direct approach.

"Suzanne."

She glanced at him wide eyed, but didn't correct him. Nor did she fix an imperious stare on him and demand that he remember her rank. They'd gone beyond that, hadn't they?

"Why would your father want you drugged?"

"Do you know anything about my father?" she asked.

"A little. He was with the East India Company."

"A director," she said. "He's a man who's never seen an obstacle. He doesn't abide them."

That still wasn't an answer.

She sat on the ladder-back chair beside the bed, taking some time to arrange her skirt. She was playing for time and he knew it.

Just as he was at the point of asking again, she looked up at him.

"It's very important for him to be able to dictate the outcome of events. At least those over which he has some control."

He didn't comment. Hackney was a bully, which was a less polite way of saying the same thing.

She looked at the bottle still in his hand and then away, blinking rapidly. If she cried, he'd simply gather her up in his arms and comfort her again.

"He thought he could control you," he said.

"Evidently." Her voice was dull.

He tossed the bottle onto the bed and went to her, drawing her up in his arms. This was getting to be a habit.

"Suzanne," he began, looking down at her face.

He wanted to kiss her again. Yet he wasn't the type of man to be dominated by his impulses. He was disciplined, set on his course, dedicated to his duty. She was a detriment to that, a temptation he couldn't obey. That's what he told himself even as he bent his head to kiss her again.

Ella's room was a strange place for a forbidden embrace. Still, he didn't move even after he lifted his mouth from hers. Instead, he brushed his lips against her heated cheek, then each closed eyelid, tasting her tears.

"You shouldn't cry," he said. "You should be enraged, not sad."

She blinked open her eyes and looked up at him. He stepped back, dropping his arms when all he really wanted to do was keep holding her.

"I have more experience with sorrow than I do with rage, Adam."

"You shouldn't," he said. "Not in this case. You deserve better than to be treated like a puppet, Suzanne. No one has that right."

She didn't answer, merely began moving toward the door. Glancing over her shoulder at him, she said, "At least I don't have to deal with Ella anymore."

He didn't respond. Sooner or later he was going to finish his assignment, and there would be no further reason to remain at Marsley House. No reason whatsoever to try to protect the Duchess of Marsley.

The thought was accompanied by an unsurprising amount of regret.

Chapter Twenty-Five

Suzanne couldn't sleep. Now that she knew what the tonic contained, there wasn't any doubt in her mind why she hadn't had a problem with insomnia since Ella had started in her employ. Opium.

She'd read newspaper accounts of opium dens in the East End. More than once she'd been solicited by various individuals and asked to contribute to campaigns against the opium trade. The most influential group had been represented at one of her father's dinners and it was a cause he purported to espouse.

She had never understood her father and time had not imbued her with any more insight. For some reason he'd thought it necessary for her to take Ella's tonic. Did he mean for it to soften her grief? Or was it just a way to control her? When it came to her father's motives, either was possible.

Adam hadn't told her if she should worry about any ill effects from discontinuing the tonic. Other than being unable to sleep, were there any other symptoms? Or had Ella lied about that? She didn't doubt that Ella used truth like a weapon.

A little after midnight Suzanne gave up the pretense of sleeping, got up, and slipped on her dressing

gown. Of thick, gold-colored quilted flannel, it had
a corded belt with a large tassel at each end. A similar cord, without tassels, tied the neck closed. Most
of her garments were black, but not her nightgowns
and dressing gowns. The dye the laundress used had
not only made her skin itch but the color had bled
onto the sheets, ruining them. When that had happened, she'd decided not to wear mourning to bed.

Her new maid was a young girl Mrs. Thigpen had
recommended. Emily was a sweet person, if a bit
cloying. She'd been promoted from her position as
one of the upstairs maids and was eager to perform
her new duties. Suzanne didn't think that her wardrobe had ever been so assiduously cared for or her
hair done as well.

"Is there anything else I can do for you, Your
Grace?" If Emily had asked her once, she'd done so
five hundred times in the past two days. Suzanne
had assured the girl that she needed nothing further,
that Emily was performing every task perfectly, and
that she was certain the two of them would deal very
well together. Above all, Emily did not try to make
her take opium every morning and every evening.
That alone would make her well disposed toward
the girl.

Suzanne glanced at herself in the pier glass. She'd
plaited her hair for night and now wrapped the plait
around the top of her head, securing it with pins and
a short length of black ribbon. Picking up the atom-
izer, she sprayed a little of her favorite perfume on
her neck, then ridiculed herself for doing so. The
scent lingered in the air, reminiscent of early bloom-
ing roses.

Ella had always spritzed her with the perfume

George had bought her, something spicy that smelled of India, he'd said. After dismissing Ella, she'd taken the bottle and put it in the rubbish, uncaring that only half of it was gone. She'd always disliked it but her wishes had never been consulted.

The fact that her father also liked the perfume brought another issue to the forefront of her mind. She was going to have to handle the matter of Ella but she didn't know quite how right now. She wasn't sure what explanation for Ella's actions her father would give her, if he gave one at all. When she'd confronted him in the past, he'd sometimes answered her questions and just as often blustered that he knew what he was doing and she shouldn't question him. All she had now were questions. She wasn't certain she would be able to believe him regardless of what he said.

She closed the door of the sitting room quietly so as not to alert the footman stationed at the end of the corridor. He sat on a chair she insisted he use. Standing at attention—something George had demanded—seemed ludicrous, especially in the middle of the night. She didn't mind if the footmen dozed. Their presence was to alert the family in case of fire or the unlikely event of a stranger entering Marsley House. Of the two, fire was much more likely.

October was still comfortable during the day although the nights were chilly, making her grateful for the flannel gown. This month the skies would start to become overcast and it seemed to her that they would stay that way throughout the winter, only brightening when spring arrived.

The flame on the enormous gasolier over the

grand staircase was lowered at night, creating pools of shadows that were illuminated only by the newel posts with their gas lamps. She was more familiar with going up the stairs to the third floor and the nursery than going down to the library.

She didn't want to go to Georgie's room right now. She didn't need to sit and look at the array of his toys in order to recall her son. She could feel his body snuggled up against her, his head on her chest. She could still feel her fingers smoothing back his silky blond hair. She could hear his voice, and there were still moments when she swore she heard his laughter. He'd been a happy child, a healthy little boy. She'd been so thankful for that. She'd never anticipated something might happen to him.

She didn't need to be in the nursery in order to remember him. He would live in her heart forever.

What was it Drummond had said? Something about clinging to her grief in order to keep Georgie close. She'd been irritated at his comment, but over the past several days she'd been wondering if he wasn't correct. Perhaps grief could be as addictive as opium.

She got to the bottom of the staircase, then turned and walked down the long corridor to the library. The room had always been George's domain, and she'd avoided it for the most part in the past two years. Adam, however, seemed to gravitate toward it. He'd mentioned that he often found it difficult to sleep and chose a book to read. Would he consider her outrageous for hoping that was the case tonight?

She'd never been around anyone like him. Adam didn't seem to wish anything from her—not influence, or money. In every situation in which they'd been together, he'd acted protectively. She couldn't remember the last time—if ever—that a man had been so solicitous of her or cared about her welfare.

She might have considered him her contemporary but for his faint Scottish accent and his tendency to speak in Gaelic from time to time. He made her think improbable thoughts, such as what her life would have been like if she hadn't married George. Their relationship had been strained from the beginning. After all, he was almost thirty years her senior, a duke her father insisted that she marry simply because he was titled.

She'd always been a docile, obedient daughter, but she didn't feel a bit docile or obedient at the moment.

The sameness of her life and the emptiness of it had stretched out before her, punctuated only by her father's demands. The day she'd banished him from Marsley House had been a turning point. At first she'd thought she was acting unlike herself. In the past few days she realized that she was behaving like the person she'd once been, the courageous young girl who hadn't been beaten down by circumstance and tragedy.

She liked that Suzanne. Once reborn, she hoped that woman wouldn't disappear. She didn't want to be subservient to anyone, a leaf to someone else's wind.

The library doors stood like a barrier before her. She hadn't seen Adam for two days. She'd asked about him a few times, and on each occasion he'd either been with one of the other staff members or in a meeting with the stable master or occupied with some task. It was as if he was avoiding her.

Perhaps he regretted kissing her.

She didn't regret kissing him.

If he admitted that it was unwise for him to do

so, she'd tell him how she felt. If he cautioned her to remember her title, she'd tell him that her title had never brought her happiness, but that the kiss they'd shared had. She would be blunt and daring and truthful.

Perhaps she'd tell him how sorry she was about his wife and how much she wished he hadn't had to go through that type of grief. When you lost someone you loved, it changed you. It made you more conscious that nothing was really permanent. Life was more than sometimes unfair. It could be cruel.

She hoped he had someone to comfort him in that time, but she doubted it. It was sometimes easier to withdraw from the world—like she had—than to confess that she felt like she had to rebuild herself from the inside out. She suspected that Adam had been like her in that respect, both of them isolated in their grief.

She didn't feel so alone now and it was because of him. She wanted to tell him that. They'd talked about everything in the past week. She'd shared stories of her childhood while he talked of Scotland. For the first time in a long time she greeted each day with eagerness. For that she needed to thank him. If that was foolish, it didn't matter. The Suzanne she had once been and wanted to be again was brave enough to say such a thing.

There was a possibility that she was courting scandal. If anyone saw them here together it would mean gossip throughout Marsley House. *Did you hear that the duchess was found in a compromising situation with Drummond? She has no shame. Or she simply doesn't care.*

The latter would be closer to the truth. All her

life she'd been the epitome of everything right and proper and all it had earned her was the privilege of being a hermit in a cold behemoth of a house.

Perhaps she had no shame. Perhaps she should be chastised. How odd that she didn't care.

If she opened the doors and saw that the paraffin lamps were lit, that would mean he was in the library. If the room was dark, he wouldn't be there. All she had to do was to grab the handle of the door and open it. Nothing more than that.

Tonight she didn't want to be the Duchess of Marsley. Tonight she simply wanted to be Suzanne.

She grabbed the handle, then released it and took a few steps back, staring at the door as if it were the yawning maw of a monster from her opium-induced nightmares.

He'd held her. He had kissed her. When he'd drawn back the other day, his hands had trembled the faintest bit as if he were as moved as she. Surely he wouldn't make fun of her for seeking him out. Even if it was after midnight. Even if she did have a title and he was a servant.

She stepped toward the door again, grabbed the handle, and without giving herself time to think, opened one of the doors.

The room was dark. The gas sconce in the corridor allowed her to see well enough to step inside. At first, she thought that the entire library was dark, but then she caught a shadow flickering on the third floor.

The silence constrained her from announcing her presence. How would she explain herself? That she was lonely and of all the people sleeping beneath the roof of Marsley House, he was the only one she sought? Could she possibly be that honest?

Grabbing the skirt of her dressing gown with one hand and the banister with the other, she began to climb the curved iron stairs. Perhaps by the time she got to the third floor, the proper words, the right words would occur to her. Her dressing gown was as thick as a coat and would have been proper to wear to entertain had she been ill. Perhaps, however, she should have changed into a day dress.

At the second floor landing, she looked up. The shadows were no longer flickering. Instead, there was only darkness above her. The faint light from the hallway sconce was not enough to illuminate the steps. Had she been mistaken after all? Had she only seen what she wanted to see?

She was taking a hesitant step upward when she heard a sound. She looked up as a black shape suddenly descended, pushing and shoving against her. She lost her grip on the banister as she tumbled backward. She had the curious thought that the world had been upended. When she landed her head struck something sharp. Her mind registered the pain for one instant and then thought was lost in the nothingness.

Chapter Twenty-Six

Adam had learned a valuable lesson about sleep in the army—take advantage of every opportunity. It might be a while until he got another. That he couldn't sleep tonight annoyed him, but he knew exactly why he couldn't and that irritated him even more.

He sat up, swung his legs over the bed, and lit the lamp on his bedside table. When he reached out for the brooch, he remembered that he'd returned it to Suzanne. When had the damn thing become a talisman? It hadn't looked like something she would choose to wear. She needed a curved bit of gold with one single diamond instead of that gaudy hairpin.

He was like a lovesick boy.

He should remember his mission, the reason he was here at Marsley House, instead of thinking about the duchess.

He dressed but wore only a shirt and trousers, not the uniform of his position. It was nearly two in the morning. The only people who would see him were the footmen assigned to night duty. All good men he trusted. They would ensure the duchess was safe even after he was gone. Not that she knew she was in danger, but if word ever got out that the duke's actions had resulted in the massacre at Manipora, the people of England might well take matters into their own hands. Hell, he'd even given thought to destroying the portrait of the bastard that showed him smugly smiling.

He couldn't imagine any man, especially a peer of the English realm, betraying his own countrymen. According to Roger, that's exactly what had happened. The duke had communicated with the rebel leader, giving him information about the fortifications at Manipora so they could be easily overrun.

He didn't allow himself to think of India very often. There were times, however, when he couldn't help but remember Rebecca. Late at night when he couldn't sleep or when he'd imbibed too much whiskey. Or when he'd been caught up in someone else's conversation and their talk turned to wives. Mostly he tried to avoid situations like those, but there were times when he couldn't.

Their marriage might have been one of convenience, but Rebecca had begun to charm him. She had a delightful laugh and the enthusiasm of a child for new things and experiences. Perhaps he hadn't loved her in the beginning, but he'd given her his loyalty and his growing affection.

He nodded to the footman stationed on the third floor. Instead of heading toward the servants' stairs he walked to the main staircase. His position as majordomo meant that he was in a gray zone: neither truly a servant and definitely not one of the family. However, due to the level of responsibility given him, he was also accorded the great honor of being visible. He did not, unlike the other servants, have to duck into one of the closets accessed through the paneling rather than be seen by the duchess.

He hesitated before descending the staircase, looking down the corridor at the nursery. He couldn't see a light beneath the door. Hopefully, Suzanne was asleep, a more natural sleep now that she wasn't being given opium.

What the hell had Hackney been doing? Why had he conspired with Suzanne's maid?

He hadn't seen Suzanne for days, yet he was conjuring her up from memory, down to the smell of her perfume as he entered the library. That, if nothing else, was a sign that he needed to get the hell away from Marsley House.

After lighting the paraffin lamp closest to the desk, he turned, intent on mounting the stairs to the third level. Only then did he see her.

Suzanne was sprawled on the floor, her dressing gown open, the belt tossed up to her neck, the tassel wicking up the blood beneath her head.

For one frozen second, he couldn't move. His brain didn't function, either. He couldn't think what to do or how to even call for help. Thankfully, his inactivity didn't last. He ran to the base of the steps where Suzanne lay, got to his knees and placed a hand on her neck, his fingers feeling for a pulse. He let out a breath when he found one. Every instance he'd observed in his army career, every single bit of advice he'd gotten on how to treat the injured swirled through his mind. None of it was valuable at the moment.

Her cheek was cold, her face pale. How long had she been like this? Damn it, that was something else he didn't know.

He stood, went to the door, and called for the footman there. When the man arrived, he ordered him to summon Mrs. Thigpen, another footman, and a cot from the storeroom.

"And hurry," he added. The latter wasn't necessary since the young man had taken a look at the figure of the duchess on the floor and blanched.

Mrs. Thigpen, thank God and all the angels, had some experience in wounds. He was sending another one of the footmen to summon the duchess's physician when the housekeeper turned Suzanne's head gently, showing him the blood-matted hair.

"Poor thing must have struck her head on one of those metal steps, Adam. See this gash?"

She parted Suzanne's hair, showing him a two-inch wound still bleeding. He'd never been affected by the sight of blood until this moment. Nor had he ever considered himself a coward, but something clenched in his stomach and it felt too damn much like fear.

He wanted to ask Mrs. Thigpen if Suzanne would be all right, but he remained silent. It wouldn't do for a majordomo to express undue concern about the mistress of the house. Still, he followed the two footmen carrying Suzanne up the stairs on the cot that was doubling as a stretcher. The housekeeper and another maid bearing a large handled basket accompanied them. Evidently, Mrs. Thigpen was prepared for any emergency, including one that made no sense.

What had Suzanne been doing in the library at this hour? None of the lamps had been lit when he entered the room, which meant that she must've been going up the stairs in the darkness.

Most of the books on the second floor dealt with

military history and tactics along with obscure philosophical volumes, and he couldn't see the duchess wanting to read one of those. This side of the third floor was given over to the duke's journals.

Had she been going to the second or the third level? Had she wanted to read one of her husband's journals?

The events of tonight reminded him that he'd allowed himself to take his mind off his assignment. He couldn't afford to feel compassion, empathy, or any other emotion for the Duchess of Marsley.

She was just another person he needed to fool until he found what he needed.

At least, that's what he tried to tell himself.

Chapter Twenty-Seven

Suzanne awoke to find Dr. Gregson poking a needle in her thumb.

"Can you feel that?" he asked, his smile nearly obscured by the gray beard covering his face. He had been a kindly figure to her all her life, at least until this moment.

"Yes!" she said, jerking back her hand.

He pulled out the covers from the bottom of the bed and did the very same thing to her big toe.

"And that?"

"Yes!" she said, drawing her foot away.

He wasn't the only person doing odd things to her. Mrs. Thigpen was placing a wet cloth on her forehead and Emily was standing there looking terrified while fanning her the whole time.

Even Adam was involved, keeping vigil at the door with his arms crossed, looking as fierce as one of those statues in the Egyptian parlor.

"Have you any pain anywhere, my dear?" Dr. Gregson asked. "Any pain at all?"

She couldn't imagine why he was asking her that question. Then it slowly came back to her. She'd gotten out of bed, put on her dressing gown, gone downstairs, and entered the library. How very odd that she couldn't remember anything after that.

"My head hurts," she said, and would've put her hand exactly on that spot except that the back of her head was covered up with a substantial bandage.

"What happened?"

She looked from one to the other, but none of the people in her bedroom seemed to know any more than she did.

"I went into the library," she said. "But that's all I remember."

"Drummond found you at the base of the stairs, Your Grace," Mrs. Thigpen said. "Did you fall?"

She couldn't remember. When she said as much, Dr. Gregson nodded.

"It happens that way sometimes," he said.

"Will she ever remember what happened?"

She looked up at Adam. She had wanted to ask the same question, but he was faster.

Dr. Gregson came and sat on the chair someone had moved beside the bed. Once there, he took her wrist in his hand, felt for her pulse, and then nodded approvingly before speaking.

"Sometimes," he said. "Sometimes not. It all is determined by the circumstances."

She didn't have the slightest idea what he meant, but decided that it would be a waste of time to inquire further. In other words, Dr. Gregson didn't know.

She closed her eyes, tried to remember, but all she got was darkness. She wasn't comfortable with the idea that something had happened and yet she had no inkling of it. Was the memory simply gone forever? Or would it pop up unexpectedly like a word she couldn't recall and that suddenly—when her mind was no longer on it—appeared before her as if it were written on the air?

"We will let you rest," Dr. Gregson said. "I've left a tonic for you with Mrs. Thigpen."

Her eyes flew open. "No tonic. No preparation. No potion. Nothing, Dr. Gregson."

He frowned at her. His beard didn't obscure his disapproval.

"Your head will begin to throb, my dear. You will need something for the pain."

"I will take my mind off it or occupy myself in other ways, Dr. Gregson. I will not be taking anything."

He looked at Mrs. Thigpen. "Nonetheless, my good woman, I will leave the tonic in your hands. Perhaps you can convince my patient to do what is best."

She was not going to take anyone's tonic, a fact that Adam alone seemed to understand. When she glanced at him he nodded. At least she had one ally in the room.

"Emily will sit with you for a while," Mrs. Thigpen said. "I think it best that she have someone with her, do you not agree, Dr. Gregson?"

He nodded emphatically. "That I do. I will return tomorrow. I do not expect you to be out of this bed. I don't expect any further complications, but you must take care not to overdo."

She doubted that anyone would let her do anything. She started to nod, but the throbbing at the base of her neck stopped her.

"Very well, Dr. Gregson, I shall be a model patient."

He shook his head, his way of saying that he strongly doubted that fact, and left the room, followed by Mrs. Thigpen.

"What time is it?" she asked, looking at Adam, who'd moved to the end of the bed.

"Nearly dawn."

Only a few hours had passed since she'd entered the library, then. She suddenly got the impression of darkness, something swooping down on top of her.

"Would it be possible to have some tea?" she asked, turning to Emily.

The young girl jumped up from the chair she'd taken when the physician left the room and nodded.

"Of course, Your Grace. I'll be right back."

"You've remembered something," Adam said the moment the door closed behind Emily.

"I don't know if I have or not."

Before she could say another word, the door opened again. Mrs. Thigpen entered, bearing a brown bottle. They were going to go to war if the woman thought she was going to take another dose of laudanum or opium or anything designed to strip her wits from her. To her surprise, however, the housekeeper merely held up the bottle.

"Will you reconsider, Your Grace?"

Suzanne managed a smile for the woman, who had always been a dear to her and Georgie. She didn't deserve a show of temper.

"No, Mrs. Thigpen, I will not."

The housekeeper nodded and tucked the bottle back into her dressing gown pocket. "I told the physician that you were set in your mind, but he would insist."

"He's a stubborn old goat," Adam said.

Mrs. Thigpen looked like she was biting back a smile.

If they'd been alone, she would have told Adam

what she'd remembered, but she didn't want to speak in front of the housekeeper. There were times when Mrs. Thigpen became a trifle histrionic. She expanded on things and used hyperbole when none was necessary. Several threads of gossip had originated with the housekeeper. If she hadn't been so exemplary at her job, her enjoyment of a good story might have been cause for dismissal.

Consequently, Suzanne remained silent.

Nor did it look like the housekeeper was going to leave, not as long as Adam was standing there.

"Thank you," Suzanne said. "I understand you found me."

He nodded.

He looked straight at her, almost as if he were examining her. Did he know how handsome he was, with his green eyes and freshly shaved face? He didn't wear a mustache or a goatee. She had an inkling that he would be as handsome with both, but she was strangely glad he had gone against fashion.

"A good thing," Mrs. Thigpen said. "Otherwise, it might have been morning until one of the maids discovered you."

Left hanging in the air was the question—what had either of them been doing in the library at that hour?

Adam bowed slightly. "I will say good-night, Your Grace."

She smiled in return. A very cold and frosty smile that she'd perfected in the years of being married to George. It was a reserved expression, one he'd approved of, that gave no hint of true favor toward the recipient.

She watched him leave the room and instantly felt the difference.

Mrs. Thigpen took the chair beside her bed, reached out, and patted the mattress beside Suzanne's hand.

"A most unusual man," the housekeeper said, as if expecting a confidence. "At first all the maids were afraid of him. Now they just act silly around him."

So did she. A thought she was definitely not going to share with the housekeeper.

Chapter Twenty-Eight

Adam wasn't able to see Suzanne again for a few more hours. He did so on the pretense of taking her a luncheon tray, a duty that was not strictly in his list of responsibilities. He needed to see the duchess in order to learn what had happened the night before. That was in keeping with his mission, more important than being a majordomo at Marsley House.

He made his way up the grand staircase with a large tray containing a teapot, a cup and saucer, Suzanne's lunch that was covered with a lid but smelled of roast beef, and a small vase with one of the flowers from the conservatory. This one had a bright yellow center with pink petals. He knew nothing about flowers and couldn't have named it if pressed, but it was a cheerful little thing that bobbed as he went up the stairs.

He set the tray on the table beside the double doors and knocked lightly. When Emily opened the door, he refused to surrender the tray to her. Instead, he asked that she open the second door for him.

"It's very heavy," he said in explanation as he stepped inside the sitting room.

She smiled in thanks and led the way to Suzanne's bedroom, standing aside as he entered.

The duchess was awake, sitting up against both pillows. He wasn't surprised to note that her hair had been artfully arranged around the bandage to conceal it. He wouldn't consider her vain, but she was careful with her appearance.

What did startle him, however, was the fact that she had dark circles beneath her eyes. He wondered if it was the effect of the head wound.

"Are you feeling well, Your Grace?" he asked, genuinely concerned.

"I have a beastly headache, Drummond," she said, smiling. "Other than that, I'm fine."

"Mrs. Thigpen has some karpura." He glanced at Emily and then back at the duchess. "Camphor," he added. "If you massage it into your temples, it should ease your headache."

"That sounds lovely. Emily, would you mind fetching some for me?"

The young maid looked torn at the prospect of leaving the duchess alone with him. Thankfully, Suzanne eased her conflict by saying, "Thank you, Emily," and adding a smile.

Emily finally nodded and excused herself.

Once they heard the sitting room door close, he moved toward the bed. She pushed herself up with both hands. He steadied the tray as she moved the pillow behind her back.

"Are you going to tell me what you remembered?" he asked, sitting beside the bed.

"How did you know?"

He only smiled.

"Very well," she said, somewhat crossly. "I did remember something, but I'm not sure what it was. Or who it was."

He sat beside the bed, knowing he had some time before Emily and Mrs. Thigpen found the camphor where he'd hidden it. He'd taken the metal box containing the white, waxy camphor and hidden it behind the sack of flour in the pantry.

"I was climbing the stairs," she said. "At first I thought something had fallen on me, but then I realized whoever was there was wearing a cloak or something black. They pushed me."

"You're saying someone was in the library?"

"Yes. On the third level. At first I thought it was you."

"Is that why you went to the library? To find me?" That was probably the most improvident question he could have asked and he wanted to immediately call it back.

Her cheeks turned pink as he watched. The metamorphosis from haughty duchess to embarrassed woman fascinated him. He told himself to look away, to give her some privacy, but he didn't.

In the next breath, she turned the tables on him.

"Tell me about your wife, Adam. Has she been gone long?"

No one asked about his wife. No one who knew about India ever spoke about it. Suzanne's ignorance was a shield, yet her curiosity was a spear.

"Seven years," he said.

"Have you had no desire to remarry in all that time?"

"No."

He could only give her that one-word answer and

nothing further. However, he had the feeling that his monosyllabic response would not be enough for the Duchess of Marsley. He was beginning to think that she was her father's daughter, as stubborn and determined as Hackney.

"Did you love her very much?"

He reached for the teapot, their fingers meeting. He didn't remove his hand immediately and neither did she. Their eyes met and something seemed to flow between them, an emotion he didn't want to analyze at the moment. She finally pulled her hand away.

"I thought her smile engaging," he said. "And she was very kindhearted."

She didn't say anything for a moment.

"It sounds like you're describing a woman you've just met. Or maybe a friend about which you wish to say nothing detrimental."

He couldn't fault her insight.

"Rebecca needed to be married. It was suggested that I should marry as well. She was killed at Manipora."

The words were spoken with infinite calm, almost as if they carried little import. Still, they lingered in the air between them.

He never spoke about Rebecca. Until that night in the nursery, he hadn't said her name aloud for a good year, maybe more.

"India," she said. "George told the story often. It was an example, he said, of the treachery of the people."

He didn't say anything. He couldn't talk about the Duke of Marsley without wanting to add a few profanities and she didn't deserve that.

"Did you know my husband?"

"I knew him. I served under him."

"You never said."

"The topic did not come up, Your Grace."

"I much prefer it when you call me Suzanne."

He looked away, unwilling to let her see his confusion. Ever since the night on the roof she'd befuddled him. She was unlike any of the peerage he'd met. She didn't hold herself above others. She didn't consider herself better than her servants. If she had been perceived as distant, he suspected it had been because of her grief. Now, tucked up in bed, with her pink cheeks and her troubled eyes, she wanted him to call her Suzanne.

It would be so much better if he remembered his place, his role, and his mission. Everything else was ancillary and unimportant.

The confusion he felt was his problem, not hers.

"Did you wear a kilt in the army?"

He shook his head, grateful that she had changed the subject.

"I don't even own one anymore," he said. But he didn't tell her what he thought, that it wasn't the clothes that made the Scot. Nor was it the accent. Instead, it was his heart, his mind, and his soul. He was a creature of independence, someone who had willingly yoked himself to the British Army first and now to the Silent Service. Neither organization should ever take his loyalty for granted and so far neither had.

"You didn't like my husband, did you, Adam?"

He looked at her, wondering if he should tell her the truth. In the end, he didn't have a choice. The truth donned wings and flew from his mouth.

"I despised him, Suzanne."

"Why?"

"Because he was responsible for the death of my wife."

She looked stricken. The moment he'd spoken the words he wanted to call them back. Not because they were untrue. He believed the Duke of Marsley was guilty of treason.

Yet Suzanne was innocent of her husband's sins. At this exact moment, however, she looked as if he'd accused her.

Reaching out, he poured her some of the tea Mrs. Thigpen had brewed. The smell of it, something strong and spicy, reminded him of India. That's probably why the floodgates had opened up on his memory, and emotions spilled out.

"Forgive me," he said.

"Why?" she asked again. "For saying what you felt?"

"Yes. Some things should not be given voice."

She didn't say anything for a long moment, merely took the cup and saucer from him, careful not to let her hand touch his.

"Tell me about it," she said. "Tell me about Manipora."

That was the very last thing he wanted to do. He glanced at her and then away. How could anyone refuse to grant Suzanne whatever she wished when her eyes were filled with such compassion?

Chapter Twenty-Nine

"We lived at Manipora," he said, then cleared his throat.

She should have interrupted and told him it wasn't necessary that he tell her the story, but the truth was that she very much wanted to know. Everything about him incited her curiosity.

"By June the rebellion had spread, getting closer to Manipora. General Wheeler, however, thought the locals would remain loyal. After all, he'd married an Indian woman and he'd learned the local language. He was so convinced of that fact that he sent most of the soldiers assigned to Manipora to help Lucknow."

"Leaving Manipora without defenses?" she asked.

"Not entirely," he said. "Some military men were left as well as a significant number of businessmen." He stared at the far wall for a moment, almost as if he was viewing Manipora seven years ago.

"The rebels attacked the entrenchment. Their forces numbered over twelve thousand men, but we held on for three weeks."

She asked the next question softly, wondering if she should. "Your wife was at Manipora. Were you there, too?"

He nodded, leaving Suzanne to wonder if she should stop him now. There was an expression on his face that wasn't hard to interpret. The tale of Manipora wouldn't be easy for him to relate.

"On June twenty-six," Adam continued, "we were overrun. Somehow, the rebels learned of our defenses and entered the entrenchment. Wheeler surrendered and accepted the offer of safe passage to Allahabad. The next day we headed for the Ganges and the forty boats arranged to take us there. Safe passage evidently didn't mean the same to the rebels as it did to Wheeler because we were shot at after we boarded the boats and left the dock. Two boats got away. I was in one of them. The boats holding the women and children were brought by the Indians back to Manipora."

Her meal forgotten, she was caught up in Adam's story, relayed in such a calm tone that it might seem, to a casual listener, that he felt nothing about the circumstances. Yet emotion was there in the timbre of his voice, in the way he kept having to stop as if to guard his words, and the deep breaths he took. She couldn't help but wonder if it was the first time he'd ever discussed Manipora with anyone.

"The women and children were moved from the entrenchment to another house in the city," he said. "The plan was to use them for bargaining with the East India Company. Unfortunately, that didn't happen." He took another deep breath.

"Where were you?"

"I'd been assigned to General Wheeler's boat. We led a charge against the rebel soldiers and were able to get away. We decided to take refuge in a shrine, but we were overrun by a crowd of villagers with clubs. We finally reached the river again and began swimming downstream. I didn't realize, until much later, that the women had been taken prisoner."

"How much later?"

"Several weeks," he said in that same dull voice. "I'd been shot. We were rescued by men who worked for Raja Singh, who was still loyal to the British, but by the time I was able to make it back to Manipora, word had already come of what had happened."

George had told her about Manipora and she'd read the horrible details in the newspaper. The rebels had been alerted that British troops were headed for Manipora to rescue the women and children. In those last days, one hundred twenty-four children and seventy-three women had been killed, their bodies thrown down a well. Soldiers had reached Manipora the day after the killings. Incensed by what they saw, they'd retaliated with violence against the population of the city.

She didn't know what to say or what kind of comfort to offer Adam. Words were just noise that echoed against the wall you'd built around yourself.

What people said sometimes didn't make any sense. *Time heals all wounds. God never gives us anything we can't handle.* One intrepid soul had the temerity to tell her, "God evidently wanted Georgie to be one of his angels." Someone—and she couldn't remember who—had stepped between her and that woman as if afraid that Suzanne would say something cutting. They needn't have worried. She'd been so shocked by that announcement that she'd been unable to speak.

Now she had nothing to say to Adam. All she had to offer him was her empathy, compassion, and tears.

None of those things, however, were worthwhile in the face of his loss.

She stretched out her hand, kept it in the air until he clasped it and brought their joined hands down to the mattress.

Her other hand wiped her tears away from her cheeks.

"I've made you cry. I'm sorry."

"Don't be. It's a daily occurrence. I've gotten quite used to it."

She smiled at him and he surprised her by returning the expression.

They didn't have the opportunity to speak further because the door to the sitting room opened. Adam dropped her hand and stood as Emily rushed into the room, breathless.

"I'm so sorry, Your Grace. I apologize. We couldn't find the camphor so I had to go to the stables and get some from the stable master."

"That was very responsible of you, Emily. Thank you. And thank you, Drummond," she said. "For bringing me my tray."

He only bowed slightly, his faint smile still in evidence.

When he was gone, she explained to Emily that her tears were due to the pain in her head, no doubt leaving the young maid thinking that she was weak and infirm. Better that than what she was truly feeling, anguish for Adam. For the first time in a very long time she was not immersed in her own pain. She was not the only one to have suffered a loss. At least she'd not had to fight for her life on top of everything else.

In the newspaper accounts of Manipora she'd

learned that only four men had survived the attack. Evidently, Adam was one of the four.

Her majordomo was a hero. A survivor who'd managed to escape being killed not once but countless times under monumental odds. Upon his return to England he'd avoided the attention the press would have lavished on him. Now here he was, at Marsley House.

George thankfully rarely spoke about India because his command there had happened before their marriage. On one occasion, however, he'd talked about General Wheeler and his idiocy in not guarding his magazine.

She'd listened attentively, said something supportive when George hesitated, and tried to be a good wife. All in all, her husband's account of Manipora had been remarkably different from Adam's.

The more she knew of Adam, the more she admired him. Yet in addition to that admiration was another emotion, one that startled her. She liked him. She liked the way he looked at the world.

She'd become frozen in time while Adam had kept moving through his life. She'd never heard him say anything that would make her think he was mired in sadness. Instead, he struck her as a man who had his eyes focused on the future, not the past.

She liked him and even more. He attracted her, intrigued her, and charmed her down to her toes.

He hadn't asked her why she had been in the library. Would she have told him the truth?

I wanted a kiss, Adam.

No, perhaps that wouldn't have been the wisest course.

Chapter Thirty

$\mathcal{F}$or the next week, Adam stayed close to Suzanne. He didn't care if the maids gave him quick glances as he prowled the corridor outside the duchess's suite. Or if the footmen looked as if they wanted to ask questions when he assigned two of them to guard her door.

Every morning he checked on her without a single coherent reason for doing so. He didn't even bother coming up with a pretense.

His greeting to the duchess was the same in case anyone was within earshot.

"Everything was calm last night, Your Grace. How are you feeling?"

She would answer in the same manner, her voice holding that tone he'd come to expect of the peerage: haughty, almost cold. However, she always had a twinkle in her eyes.

"I'm feeling well, Drummond. Thank you for asking."

Each morning he would simply nod and leave, relieved.

Every afternoon he would bring her tea. Emily would join him in setting up the tray for the duchess, offering her a selection of tarts or biscuits Grace had made. Conscious of the maid's presence, he would tell Suzanne what was happening in the house, including any repairs that were ongoing. He found himself discussing matters pertaining to the staff, none of which he'd ever communicated to her.

She, in turn, asked questions about Scotland. He found himself telling her stories of his childhood and she reciprocated, making him think that the two children they'd been weren't that far apart in their dreams and wishes.

She even asked about Wals, which made Emily's cheeks turn a bright red. Evidently the footman had made inroads there. Adam was torn between wanting to warn Emily that the young footman had no sense of decorum and wasn't loyal to one female and simply allowing nature to take its course.

Suzanne was the one who cautioned her maid, surprising him again.

"Wals is a reprobate." She glanced at Adam and said, "I've met him once. He was exceedingly charming. Too much so for my peace of mind." Her attention turned to Emily again. "I do hope that you don't allow your heart to be involved. If he isn't yet, he's well on his way to becoming a lecher, a despoiler of innocents. I'd be truly concerned if you were involved with him."

Emily only curtsied, mumbled something in agreement, and left the room.

He and Suzanne looked at each other. Unspoken was the certainty that Emily had already been wooed by Wals.

In the evening, after Emily was dismissed for the night, he visited the duchess again. Their conversations were always more personal at that hour. He found himself anticipating their nightly talks, learning a great deal about Suzanne Hackney and her life as a wealthy man's daughter.

It was an upbringing that, strangely enough, mirrored his in some ways. She didn't have to worry about where her next meal was coming from, but with her father so often in India, she was essentially an orphan for most of the time. Without any siblings, Suzanne had learned to be comfortable with being alone, just as he had.

The drawback with that kind of attitude was that he didn't make friends easily. Neither did she. When he came to see her on Wednesday afternoon, she was entertaining Mrs. Armbruster. The older woman was telling a tale that made Suzanne laugh. He'd left the room annoyed and it wasn't difficult for him to figure out why.

He had made her smile, but he'd never made the duchess laugh. Mrs. Armbruster had. In addition, she'd stolen his time with Suzanne.

Thursday morning was the same familiar regimen, but by the afternoon Suzanne had been given permission to leave her bed for the sitting room. Sunday she was pronounced healthy enough to go anywhere in the house, which meant that it would have looked odd for him to call on her in her suite.

He'd spent a great many hours in the past week trying to figure out who the other operative was at Marsley House. The minute Suzanne had said something, he'd known that the second man had also been given the task of finding the duke's journal. There was no other reason for him to be on the third floor of the library.

With the help of two footmen, Adam had checked the locks on all the windows. Three of them were found to be broken, with the entrance point being the laundry.

He added lookouts, stationing two stable boys at the rear, between the kitchen garden and the stables. Two footmen were added to the front, assigned to the gate area. Any of the men were to report to him if they saw something amiss. For a week nothing had happened which, paired with Suzanne's recuperation, allowed him to concentrate on other matters: namely, confronting Roger Mount.

On Monday Adam decided it was time to pay a call on Roger. He wasn't going to send advance notice of his arrival. If the other man was busy, then Roger would need to rearrange his schedule. If he was gone, Adam would wait for Roger to return. They were going to talk and this time the conversation was going to provide Adam the information he needed.

Traffic through London was congested as it always was. He tapped impatiently on the fabric below the window, grateful that it was only an overcast day and not raining.

He'd rarely allowed himself the luxury of rage, but he felt it now. He wanted to throttle Roger.

It was one thing to put a man in danger if he knew the odds and the risk. Suzanne didn't deserve to be treated that way. She'd done nothing other than bow to her father's pressure and marry the Duke of Marsley.

He wished he'd known her back then, but she probably would have had nothing to do with him. He hadn't smoothed all his rough edges. Not that he lacked his share of them now. Put him in a fancy dinner party—and thankfully he'd only one experience with all those forks and knives and spoons—and he was out of his element. He'd much rather be given a sword and be in hand-to-hand combat with an enraged Sepoy.

What the hell had Roger been thinking? What would make him pit two operatives against each other? It wasn't as if Adam hadn't proven his worth to the Crown. He'd received commendations on more than one assignment.

Whoever had been installed at Marsley House had made a tactical error. The man should not have endangered Suzanne. Roger had been an idiot not to make that perfectly clear. He had to pull Adam's shadow out of Marsley House. Today.

When the carriage finally reached the War Office, Adam told the driver that he wouldn't be long. He bounded up the steps two at a time and made his way to Roger's office.

He'd forgotten Oliver's aversion to loud noises, and the man reacted to the slamming of the outer door by jumping nearly a foot. Adam waved Oliver back into his chair.

"Is he here?"

"He is, but he can't be disturbed."

He strode across the room, surprised when Oliver sprang up from his chair, rounded the desk, and put out an arm. As if that would stop him.

In India, Oliver had been pale and sweating almost continually. It wasn't just the heat and the humidity that had affected him. Oliver had spent the majority of his time in India genuinely frightened.

The man looked the same now.

"Step away," Adam told him. "I don't care how busy he is. I'm going to see him now."

"He has someone with him, Drummond. You can't interrupt. It's a very important meeting."

"Then he's just going to have to reschedule it," he said. He didn't care if the Queen was in Roger's office.

Oliver was no match for him and he pushed the secretary out of the way and opened the door, only to stand there speechless.

Edward Hackney sat in the comfortable chair in front of Roger's desk, his feet up on a needlepoint stool, a cup of tea in his right hand, the saucer in his left. Roger's pose was as indolent, slumped back in his chair, an affable smile on his face.

Thoughts cascaded into Adam's mind like a fusillade of bullets. This was a meeting of men who knew each other well. Roger had never mentioned that he was acquainted with Suzanne's father. What the hell was Hackney doing at the War Office? Did he know of Adam's assignment? If he didn't, the man wouldn't lose any time informing his daughter of the fact that he'd seen Adam here, a thought that was reinforced by Hackney's expression as he turned.

The two of them exchanged a look.

Roger stood, his smile fading into a frown. "What are you doing here?"

He had too many questions and absolutely no answers, so Adam didn't even try to respond. Instead, he turned on his heel and left Roger's office, intent on getting back to Marsley House at all possible speed.

SUZANNE WAS READING in the Grecian Parlor, a restful place due to its colors of beige and tan and the fact that it was away from most of the activities midday. None of the maids came here after eleven and the footmen weren't stationed in this corridor until after dark. Consequently, few people interrupted her unless she rang.

"Suzanne."

She was startled to hear Adam call her name. She looked up to find him framed in the doorway. He wasn't wearing his usual majordomo attire. Instead, he was dressed only in a white shirt and black trousers beneath a long topcoat. In his hands he held her cloak.

"Will you come with me?" he said.

"Will I come with you?"

He nodded. "Will you come with me?"

What a silly conversation they were having, but Adam evidently didn't feel that way. There was a look in his eyes, the same expression that had been there when he was talking about India. Serious and somber, with another emotion she couldn't decipher.

"Where?" she asked.

"Somewhere safe," he said. "Where we can talk."

She should have countered that Marsley House was safe. That there were hundreds of rooms they could occupy that would be private enough, but something in his voice or in his eyes kept her silent.

"Yes," she said, surprising herself.

She stood, placed her book on the sofa cushion beside her, and approached him.

Instead of offering his arm, he grabbed her hand. He walked quickly down the corridor of the north wing, and turned left and then right to a rear door that was not often used.

"Adam? Is something wrong?"

"Yes," he said. "But I can't talk about it until we're away from here."

She stopped and when he would have pulled her to him, she shook her head.

"Is it my father?" she asked. "Has he been hurt? Has there been another accident?"

He put his arm around her shoulders, drew her close, and looked down into her face. "Your father is fine, Suzanne. I promise you that. There is something wrong, but give me a few minutes and I will explain everything."

There were dozens and dozens of servants around Marsley House, but they only encountered one maid. She glanced at their joined hands and then away, trying to hide her smile but being unable to do so successfully.

Suzanne realized she was probably going to be the subject of gossip in the servants' quarters. Why wasn't she more concerned?

She would think about that later.

Perhaps she was wrong to trust Adam. She, who had lost trust in nearly everything. Yet for some reason she did. Perhaps it was because they'd each known anguish. Adam knew how she felt, what she'd gone through, and he was possibly the only person she'd met who did. They'd each experienced the worst of what life could deliver. Or maybe she trusted him because he'd always sought to protect her.

She squeezed his hand and nodded, assent in a gesture.

He helped her with her cloak, and together they left Marsley House.

Chapter Thirty-One

*A*dam didn't know why he was doing what he was doing. Or, rather, he knew exactly why he was doing it. He just couldn't believe he was actually going through with it.

His duty was to the Crown. The army had saved him, had fed him, had trained him. He'd transferred his allegiance from the army to the War Office and it was as strong as ever.

Yet he was skirting dangerously close to violating his duty at the moment.

He wasn't sure that he had a clear picture about anything, and that lack of understanding made him both frustrated and angry. It wasn't just seeing Hackney at the War Office. It was Roger putting a second operative at Marsley House. It was the sensation he'd always had that he was being manipulated.

What the hell had Hackney been doing in Roger's office? Why had Roger been entertaining a wealthy former East India Company director?

Had Hackney always known who Adam was? The look on the older man's face had been one of surprise, so it was possible he hadn't.

The one thing Adam was certain of in this entire

fiasco was that he wanted to tell Suzanne who he was before Hackney had a chance to mention their encounter this morning. He didn't want her to think that he'd violated her trust or taken advantage of her. Although how she could think anything else, he didn't know.

The truth was always best. He would just have to tell her who he was and let fate decide what happened after that.

He gave the driver the address to his lodgings, normally twenty minutes away in good traffic. It took them twice as long to reach the house he'd considered home for the past six and a half years.

He and Suzanne talked of inconsequential things, like the weather or the new maids at Marsley House. Both of them were settling in well and performing their tasks admirably. In fact, Mrs. Thigpen had asked if there was any way that the two girls could come back to work after the birth of their children.

"What do you think?" he asked now, desperate for any subject other than why he was taking her away from Marsley House. If he began his explanation too soon, she could easily command the driver to turn the carriage around and take her home.

"I think it would be a wonderful idea. And the babies can come and stay, too."

He glanced at her in surprise.

"We've all those rooms, Adam. It seems to me that the infants would be better there than at the Institute or the Foundling Hospital. The girls don't seem willing to abandon their children, thank heavens. Their babies need to be somewhere safe, just like them."

She stared up at the ceiling of the carriage. "We could turn one of the rooms on the third floor into a nursery. Maybe Mrs. Armbruster knows of a young girl who could come and watch the babies during the day."

"You realize that the girls are unwed?"

For the first time since he'd spirited her away from Marsley House, she looked annoyed.

"And they're women of ill repute, little more than prostitutes, isn't that what people say? Harlots." She shook her head. "If you ask either of them, Adam, they were in love. They made a mistake, true, but must they be severely punished for it?"

She stared out at the street a moment before returning her gaze to him. "And another thing. Where are the men? Where are the men that they fell in love with? Have you noticed that they're nowhere around? Nor does the law compel them to provide for their children."

Only one time had he seen her so fierce and that's when she'd fired Ella.

"Tell me about the Foundling Hospital," he said. "And the Institute."

She frowned at him. "Are you really interested?"

He nodded.

"It's Mrs. Armbruster's project. Hers and her husband. She didn't say, but I suspect that their efforts began in the church. A great many charities are run by the church for sinners. Only you can't be too much of a sinner."

That comment surprised him, but he didn't speak.

"You can be a fallen woman, but if you also have an illegitimate child, there aren't many places where you can get help. People like the Armbrusters step in and offer a solution. Otherwise, these poor girls would have nowhere to go. They would be living on the streets with their children." She leaned back against the seat. "It's not an ideal situation," she added, describing the layout of the Institute and the Foundling Hospital. "But at least those poor babies aren't doomed to die a terrible death."

He suddenly understood why she was more than willing to open up Marsley House to the two girls and their infants. Her need to help, to rescue those girls, had at its roots her inability to have prevented Georgie's death.

The carriage slowed. A glance out the window showed him that they were in Pimlico and nearing his lodgings.

He hadn't seen Mrs. Ross since he'd brought the kitten to her. The kitten, strangely enough, was the first to greet him when he jumped down from the carriage and held out his hand to help Suzanne.

The kitten jumped from an overhanging branch to land on the top of the carriage roof. He gave Adam a quick once-over, then calmly settled in to wash himself.

Adam chuckled.

"A friend of yours?" Suzanne asked, smiling up at the kitten.

"I'd say he was a friend of yours," he corrected her. "I found him at Marsley House. Outside your bedroom window, as a matter of fact."

"And you brought him here?" she asked, looking up and down the avenue.

"It's where I live."

On one side, terraced houses lined the street, the hedges pruned to militaristic precision in front of each home. Steeply pitched slate roofs sheltered each identical-looking house, the bay windows acting like eyes on their neighbors. On the other side of the street sat detached houses, one of which belonged to Mrs. Ross. The white stucco structure had been built only twenty years ago when her husband died.

"I lost a husband and gained a house," she was fond of saying.

The residence, with its four classical columns, was a sprawling structure consisting of four floors and a substantial basement. His lodgings opened up to the garden, an overgrown hodgepodge of colorful blooms and out-of-control greenery. When he'd first seen it, Adam had smiled, realizing that Mrs. Ross's garden represented England to him. An England that had remained the same for centuries and would likely resist change.

He offered Suzanne his arm and they proceeded up the curved walk. Mrs. Ross, who had acute hearing, opened the front door, smiling a greeting.

"Mr. Drummond, how lovely to see you again."

She looked from him to Suzanne, an expectant expression on her face and curiosity in her eyes. He glanced at Suzanne, then at his landlady.

"Mrs. Ross, I'd like you to meet Suzanne Hackney. My cousin."

Both women looked at him.

"Your cousin?" Mrs. Ross said. "I thought you had no family in London, Mr. Drummond."

"I've only recently returned," Suzanne said. "I was living in Sussex."

At least she'd managed not to lie on that point, which was more than he could say for himself.

He'd known that he'd have to appease Mrs. Ross. He hadn't planned on lying to her, but at the last moment he hadn't been willing to divulge Suzanne's identity. Mrs. Ross was not above a little gossip over the hedges. What he didn't want was for Suzanne to be the topic of the week.

"Then welcome, Miss Hackney. Any family member of Mr. Drummond's is welcome here," Mrs. Ross said, turning and holding the door open.

"Actually, it's Mrs.," Suzanne said as Adam stepped aside and let Suzanne precede him inside the house.

As usual, it smelled of cinnamon and oranges and something else that reminded him of pepper. He'd rarely tasted Mrs. Ross's cooking, preferring to do for himself, but occasionally he'd shared meals with the other two lodgers. After the first experience, he'd learned to decline a meal whenever Mrs. Ross was making something fancy. She was good with roasts and fish but tended to odd flavors in her stews and casseroles.

"I noticed the kitten outside," he said.

"The best mouser I've ever seen," Mrs. Ross replied, straightening her apron. "Can I do anything for you, Mr. Drummond? Or your cousin?"

"We don't require anything, Mrs. Ross, but thank you."

"You'll let me know?"

He smiled. "Indeed I will."

He led the way down the hallway, turned to the left, and inserted his key in the lock. Mrs. Ross stood behind them, even as he put his hand on the small of Suzanne's back and urged her inside.

Once more he turned to his landlady and smiled. "Thank you, Mrs. Ross."

"Mr. Drummond," she said, nodding.

She glanced once more at Suzanne, taking in her black silk dress.

He closed the door in his landlady's face, wondering how long she was going to remain in the hall.

Moving into the sitting room he stood in front of the now cold fireplace. The day wasn't chilly enough to build a fire. Yet it would have given him something to do rather than stand here and wonder how to begin this conversation.

"Why did you lie?" he asked, removing his coat and tossing it onto the back of the chair.

"Why did you?" she said when he took her cloak from her and placed it beside his coat.

Time had run out. He needed to tell her the truth now.

Suzanne walked slowly into the room, looking around. The rebels had burned everything they'd owned at Manipora. There was nothing of his life with Rebecca here. No traces of his life in India or anything to indicate that he'd spent a substantial amount of his life there.

Instead, the room was furnished with Mrs. Ross's castoffs: a comfortable sofa upholstered in a faded blue fabric, a chair with a flower print beside the fire, two tables, each equipped with a lamp. A few bits of statuary, a faded blue-and-red carpet on the wood floor. Shabby yet welcoming. Nothing pretentious or costing a fortune, just a few places to sit and talk or read.

He had arrived back in England with a valise and two changes of clothing. That's all. He'd acquired some additional clothes, but he hadn't made any substantial purchases for his rooms. Without much effort he could walk out the door and leave little trace of himself behind.

He glanced toward her, then away. The moment

the words were spoken, things would change between them. The friendship that had grown in the past few weeks, the easy camaraderie they enjoyed, all that would vanish.

He'd be left only with the longing.

Chapter Thirty-Two

*E*ver since leaving Marsley House, Suzanne felt as if she were living a different life. She wasn't the Duchess of Marsley at the moment, but someone else. Perhaps she was just Suzanne Hackney, the girl she'd wondered about a few days earlier.

No noise penetrated the heavy door to the corridor. She couldn't hear anyone else in the house. It was as if the world faded away.

Adam didn't answer her, but strode through the sitting room, leaving her to follow.

The room she entered was flooded by light from the six windows facing a garden. She watched as Adam opened two of the windows on either side of a door. The day was chilly, but the air was fresh, laden with the scent of flowers.

A rectangular table was against the far wall with a stool beneath it. A large metal-rimmed bowl for washing up was stacked next to a few dishes and cups. The opposite wall held a fireplace with a curious stove in the middle of it, something that looked as if it could be used not only to heat the room but also to cook.

The closest she could come to labeling this space was to think of it as half kitchen, half conservatory.

Granted, the plants were on the outside, but it would be difficult to ignore the blowsy beauty of the late-blooming flowers. The yellow wallpaper, in a geometric pattern, brightened the space even more.

"These are your lodgings?" she asked as he went to the round table in the middle of the room and pulled out a chair for her.

"They are."

"Yet you live at Marsley House."

"Only recently," he said.

"But you felt it necessary to keep lodgings elsewhere?"

"There's something I have to tell you, Your Grace."

He called her that—Your Grace—when he wanted to distance himself from her. She got the hint, but it annoyed her nonetheless.

"What is it, Adam?"

Her use of his first name was deliberate. He might want to distance himself from her, but she had kissed him. More than once. Their kisses had been wondrous, something she'd never before experienced.

She'd confided in him. He had confided in her. Did he think their conversations were everyday occurrences? She'd never shared her pain with anyone else and now he was calling her Your Grace?

She sat, placing her hands atop the table. She hadn't worn her hat or her gloves. Or brought her reticule. No wonder Mrs. Ross had looked at her oddly. What kind of woman went somewhere without being properly dressed?

Someone flooded with curiosity. Someone fascinated and interested and too emotional right at the moment.

He sat opposite her, and stretched out his hands. For

a moment she didn't understand, but then he grabbed her hands and held them beneath his. She wanted to pull free, but she didn't. She wanted the ache in her chest to disappear, but that didn't happen, either.

"Why do you live here, Adam, when you should be living at Marsley House?" She wished her voice didn't sound so plaintive. She cleared her throat. "I think I deserve an explanation, don't you?"

He nodded, but didn't speak for a moment.

"Would you like some tea?" he asked.

"No."

One of his eyebrows arched. "Brandy?"

"No."

"Is there anything you'd like?"

"An explanation. Why did you tell Mrs. Ross I was your cousin?"

"I couldn't very well come out and tell her that I'd spirited the Duchess of Marsley to my rooms."

She moved her gaze from their hands to his face. His cheeks were bronzed.

"I saw your father this morning," he said.

She hadn't expected that.

"Did you?"

He nodded. "At the War Office."

She frowned at him. "That isn't unusual. He has several political protégés who work in the government."

"Does he? Do you know their names?" he asked.

She knew them very well since she'd attended every event to introduce the three men to potential campaign donors. "Harry Taylor, Roger Mount, and James Parker. Those are the ones he's working with this year."

"Roger Mount?"

She nodded. "What were you doing at the War Office, Adam?"

"Meeting with the man who sent me to Marsley House."

She held herself very still. For some reason it was important for her to remain calm and composed.

"I don't understand," she said. There, her voice didn't sound plaintive at all.

"I'm not a majordomo, Suzanne."

"Then why are you working at Marsley House?"

"Being at Marsley House is one of my assignments," he said.

"One of your assignments." She pulled her hands free.

How odd that she'd become a magpie in the past few minutes. She could only repeat what he was saying, which didn't aid in curing her confusion.

"Yes."

"You're not a majordomo. But you took the position."

"For another reason," he said.

"Another reason? Are you telling me that you are spying for my father?"

"No."

"Is your name really Adam Drummond?"

"Yes."

"And Rebecca? Was she real?"

"I wouldn't lie about her."

"Were you really in the army?"

"Yes."

"What other reason, Adam?"

He didn't say anything, only stood and walked to the door leading to the garden. For a moment he remained there, staring out at the plants and flowers, his back to her.

"Would you be content to know that it was important?" he finally asked.

"No."

He turned and came back to the table, taking a seat opposite her. This time he didn't grab her hands. She had the feeling he was not only physically distancing himself from her but emotionally as well.

"I was spying, but not for your father. I'm a member of a group of men who work for the government," he said. "We find and keep secrets. We protect and guard."

"That sounds very patriotic," she said. "And as clear as London fog."

His smile was rueful; his glance quick and shuttered.

"The Duke of Marsley was a traitor," he said. "My mission was to find evidence to prove it."

She stared at him, shocked. "You can't be serious."

"I've never had a mission that was more serious, Suzanne."

She shook her head. "My husband was a great many things, Adam—a libertine, grossly unfaithful—but no one could fault his loyalty to the army or the Crown."

"I have it on good authority that he wasn't all that loyal."

"Then whoever your authority was, he's lying to you."

"And my own experiences, Suzanne? Are they false, too?"

She felt cold in a way that had nothing to do with the weather. "What do you mean?"

"There were rumors at Manipora that someone betrayed us. One of the reasons the rebels didn't overpower us at first is that we commanded cannon to the east side of our barricade. They also thought we had trenches filled with explosives surrounding the entrenchment. Someone let the rebel leader know that it had been a carefully planted lie. Someone gave him the plans of the entrenchment. Someone intimately familiar with Manipora."

"He was no traitor, Adam. George always said that his time in the army, in India, was among his favorite memories. Men who used to serve under him would visit Marsley House every month. They seemed to love him."

"Or they were looking for financial help," Adam said, his tone dry.

"What kind of evidence were you searching for?"

"A journal," he said. "Specifically from his time in India."

She stared at him, suddenly understanding. "That's why you're always in the library," she said.

Her voice had taken on a sharp tone, the same one she'd used with Ella. She didn't try to soften it or ease her words in any way. He'd betrayed her and yet he would probably never understand why.

She hadn't opened her heart since Georgie. She hadn't stretched out a hand to another person. Even her faint attempts with Mrs. Armbruster were just that, attempts. With Adam—Drummond—she'd revealed herself completely. She'd hidden nothing from him, and all this time he'd been as transparent as a piece of slate.

He'd lied to her.

It wasn't disappointment she felt. No, it was more than that. Something crucial and necessary had broken inside her.

Chapter Thirty-Three

Suzanne moved her hands to her lap and clasped them together. She felt sick, but it wasn't a physical feeling as much as a soul-deep one. No wonder he had brought her here, someplace where she was stranded, cut off from everything she knew as familiar. She couldn't summon one of the footmen to take him away. She couldn't ring for a maid or send for her solicitor. Instead, she was trapped here, forced to listen to his notions about George.

"I will be the first to admit that George was a horrible husband. Or at least, the kind of husband I didn't want. But he took great pride in his duties for the army."

"I will wager that he enjoyed putting on his pretty red uniform jacket with all its polished metals and looking like a general."

She would not gaze up at him or in any way acknowledge that his words were unfortunately correct. Sometimes she'd caught George standing in front of his portrait in the library, his chest puffed out and his chin lifted, almost as if he were inspecting the man portrayed in his finery.

"Did your father know your husband in India?"

She nodded. "They never discussed India, at least in my presence."

But, then, they didn't talk about much around her. Their last argument, two nights before George's death, had been so loud that she could hear them from the second-floor sitting room.

"Spend your money on my daughter or my grandson. Not your mistresses and bastards."

For his part, George had hated the fact that her father didn't have to worry about money and had enough to finance the careers of various young men who craved power.

A thought occurred to her and it was so discomfiting that she pushed it away for a moment, but it kept returning. Would George have engaged in treason if it would have profited him to do so? If the rebel leader—and she wasn't sure exactly who Adam had been speaking about—had promised him a king's ransom, would George have succumbed? Surely not. He was the Duke of Marsley, the tenth in a long line of distinguished men.

Unfortunately, those same men had done what they could to dissipate the family coffers.

Yet if George had engaged in treason, why would he have agreed to marry her? Or had the lure of even more money been too much to ignore?

Wasn't it telling that she didn't know the exact nature of George's character despite having been married to him for six years?

Another thought occurred to her, one that was just as unsettling. She could guarantee that Adam would never have betrayed his men or his country.

"As horrible as George was, Drummond, I didn't hate him. But I want, very much, to hate you."

If she hadn't been watching him so closely, she wouldn't have seen the way his eyes changed, became flat and expressionless.

"And do you?"

His question was a whip, a cat of nine tails against her raw and bleeding emotions.

It would have been easier if she could have hated Adam instead of understanding. He wanted to be able to blame his wife's death on someone and George was an available scapegoat. She would have felt the same if it could be proved that someone was culpable for Georgie's death.

She pounded her fist on the table, just once. Adam's eyes widened. Good. She wanted to startle him. Let him feel just a portion of what she was experiencing right now.

"How dare you do that to me. How dare you come into Marsley House and be charming and comforting and protective? How dare you make me think certain things, Drummond. How dare you kiss me." That last was said in a lower voice. She should have been ashamed, not him. He had only ventured to kiss her. She had allowed it. No, she had gone on to encourage it. That night in the library, she'd sought it.

"Were you the one who pushed me down the stairs? In the library, was it you?"

His face changed again, became set in stone. "You would think that of me?" Even his voice was rough.

"I wish I did," she said, shaking her head. "I truly do."

They were exchanging too many truths. Honesty was causing a bloodletting. During those six years with George, she'd craved an end to the lies. Why, then, was she feeling the opposite now?

Adam confused her. He had from the very beginning.

"The fool mourns an idiot."

"What does that mean?"

"You wanted to know what I said to you that night on the roof. That's what it was. In Gaelic."

"So even then you were warning me about George, is that it?"

"No," he said. "Even then I was calling you an idiot for grieving for him. *Gabh mo leisgeul.* I hadn't gotten to know you."

"Did you kiss me because it was part of your assignment?" she asked, surprised at her own daring. Was she truly brave enough to hear the truth? Wasn't it better, though, than always wondering?

"I kissed you because I wanted to," he said. "It wasn't the wisest thing to do and it was definitely in violation of my assignment. You weren't the only fool in this, Suzanne."

"Kissing me was acting the fool?"

"Yes," he said. "Because I wanted to do it again, constantly. Or take you to my bed and keep you there for a day or two."

She was no longer cold. In fact, her body was becoming strangely heated. Her heart, however, felt like it was breaking. She needn't have worried about causing any scandal. The Duchess of Marsley and her majordomo. Not true. The Duchess of Marsley and a man of mystery. Suzanne and a fraud, a liar, and a spy.

She tried, she really did, but the tears couldn't be stopped. She hadn't brought her reticule, either, which meant that now she had no handkerchief, nothing.

"Suzanne."

"Go away," she said.

"I can't."

"You have to. I insist upon it. I demand it."

"How like a duchess you sound," he said. "Quite like Marble Marsley."

"What?" She glanced over at him to find him holding out a pristine white handkerchief.

"That's what they called you. The staff at Marsley House. At least, they did. I haven't heard that name for a while now."

"Marble?" she asked, dabbing at her tears.

"As in cold, unaffected."

"Or like a crypt," she said. "Like the crypt at Fairhaven."

He looked startled.

She didn't expect the knock on the outer door.

Adam strode through the room. She followed him, just in case it was her driver asking for instructions. If it was, she'd tell him that she very much wanted to return to Marsley House. Now, please.

"I brought you some biscuits," Mrs. Ross said, extending a tray toward Adam. "I remember how much you liked my Scotch shortbread. You said it was just like what you could find in Glasgow."

She shot a quick look toward Suzanne. "Are you from Scotland, too?"

Suzanne shook her head.

Mrs. Ross gave her a once-over, the look not so much rude as it was comprehensive.

"You've been crying," the older woman said. She glanced at Adam for confirmation, but he didn't say anything, leaving it to Suzanne to explain as best she could.

"We have just been talking about my poor dead George," she said. "My husband."

"It's sorry I am," Mrs. Ross said. "It's a hard thing we widows face, doing without the men we love."

Suzanne nodded.

Mrs. Ross startled her by entering the room, reaching out, and patting Suzanne on the upper arm, a gesture of comfort and one she'd never before received. Had that been because she was a duchess? Most people were intimidated by her title. Or had she appeared cold and unaffected, like marble?

"Thank you, Mrs. Ross."

The two of them looked at each other and nodded, a wordless communication that had nothing to do with Adam, who still stood there with a tray of biscuits, glancing from one to the other.

In the next moment, the landlady turned and left the sitting room. Adam closed the door behind her and retreated to the kitchen, placing the tray of biscuits in the middle of the circular table before going to a cupboard against the far wall. A minute later he returned with a bottle of wine that he uncorked and sat beside the biscuits.

"Mrs. Ross really does make excellent shortbread," he said.

"It's the middle of the afternoon," she said. "Surely tea would be better."

"I might not ever have you in my rooms again, Your Grace. I think it's a momentous occasion and needs to be celebrated."

Perhaps he was right. Besides, she'd followed rules all her life, all the ones laid down by her governesses, her father, George, plus all the ones that society decreed. On this one occasion, on this singular day, with a man who wasn't a majordomo after all, but a hero and a spy, she would defy every convention. It was better than her tears. Or her anger. She'd drink a glass of wine and have a piece of Scottish shortbread and try to hate him.

"Why now?" she asked. "Why tell me the truth now?"

He didn't meet her eyes, a clue she'd noticed when Adam didn't want to answer. He also blew out a breath from time to time, as if the effort to hold back his words was too much.

She'd evidently been studying him assiduously to notice those traits. Or the fact that he could sometimes hold his face just so, as if refusing to reveal any of his thoughts or emotions.

She was content to wait for an answer as she sipped her wine. She hadn't had any spirits since attending her father's dinner weeks ago. At least now she wasn't taking that hideous tonic. If she did something improvident it would be difficult to blame it on anything else other than her own wishes and wants.

He took a sip of his wine and placed the glass on the table before meeting her gaze.

"Because I thought it was possible that your father would tell you first."

That was a surprise.

"Why did you care? Is that the only reason for your honesty, Adam? Because you thought you'd be found out?"

He looked away and she had a feeling that he wasn't going to answer.

She sipped at her wine and waited.

Chapter Thirty-Four

"Being at Marsley House was my duty," he said.

"Do you always do your duty, Adam?"

"Yes."

He was determined to give her the truth, even if it was harsh or difficult to hear.

She nodded and that simple gesture had the effect of disturbing him greatly. He wanted to know her thoughts, but Suzanne was like an ornate puzzle box. Brute force would not open it. Instead you needed to use a deft touch and patience.

He topped off his glass then held it aloft.

"*Firinn*," he said. "To truth."

She finally raised her own glass and clinked it with his.

Her look was directing and unflinching. He could get lost in her eyes.

Marble Marsley. He'd never considered that the staff might have been talking about her grief, and he should have. The appellation wasn't an unkind one as much as one of understanding.

"To truth," she finally said.

They each took a sip of wine.

"Why do you think George was responsible for the massacre at Manipora?" she asked.

She had mastered the art of ensuring that her voice gave nothing away. She sounded perfectly calm, entirely reasonable. If he hadn't seen her fingers trembling, he would have thought her unmoved by the question.

"Because he was the most logical person. He met with the rebel leader twice. He knew Manipora well. He'd made foolish decisions in the past that had resulted in casualties. He might have thought that trying to end the siege was wise. Or he might have given out the information accidentally."

"Do you think him that much of an idiot?"

"Yes," he said, making no apologies for his bluntness.

She took another sip of her wine, then carefully placed the glass down on the table. She stared at the crystal pattern for a moment before asking, "Did you take these goblets from Marsley House?"

He sat back in his chair, his gaze not veering from her. He was beginning to understand Suzanne Hackney Whitcomb. She used words as bricks, not only to pummel her opponent, but to build a wall between her and anyone else. Insinuating that he'd stolen something was one way to anger him. Added to that was the hint that he couldn't have afforded his own crystal goblets. Or that he was too much a member of the hoi polloi to drink his wine from a glass.

"You know I didn't," he finally said.

She glanced at him and then away.

"Yes. No, I mean—" She looked at him again. "No, of course you wouldn't have. Forgive me."

"Anything."

She took a deep breath then released it. "It makes no sense, Adam. Let's say you're right and that George did have something to do with what happened at Manipora. Why would he make a record of it? Why would he write anything down? He had a secretary who was privy to everything George did. Why put a secret like that into words so Sankara could read it? Or anyone else, for that matter?"

"For the same reason that anyone writes about his triumphs and his tribulations. To be heard. To let someone else know what he did. To be praised or lauded, perhaps. To be judged in future years. I don't know, Suzanne, but then, I don't know why Whitcomb kept journals since he was twelve."

He took another sip of his wine. "Answer a question for me. Why demonstrate such loyalty to him now?"

Her faint smile surprised him, as did her next words. "George considered himself a great shot, but he was abysmal at hunting. He thought he was a marvelous equestrian, but he had a very poor seat. He believed himself quite well versed in the amatory arts, as he called it, but the truth was . . ." Her voice trailed off and her blush intensified. "I had thought that being in the army, commanding men, was the one skill he possessed in truth. I never heard different from anyone. I thought in this thing, alone, he might have been adept."

Standing, she went to one of the windows overlooking the garden, taking the same pose Adam had earlier.

The wind had calmed, preparing for nightfall. The glow cast by the setting sun made the plants appear touched by gold. The sky was indigo, that shade just before darkness.

The air was sweet here in this secluded garden in the middle of London. Instead of a hint of the odiferous Thames, there was the scent of grass and soon-to-go-dormant riotous plants. He always felt at peace looking at Mrs. Ross's garden.

"After Georgie died, I hated this time of day," she said. "It always reminded me of when I joined Georgie's nurse and we'd ready him for bed." She took a deep breath. "He fussed about it. I used to sit in his room and rock him until he fell asleep." She placed her fingertips on the window as if wanting to touch the plants in the garden before the shadows obscured them. "I can still feel the linen of his nightshirt against my fingers."

He understood, perhaps more than she knew.

"My roughest time was morning. Rebecca was an early riser and loved to greet the dawn. I hated mornings for a long time."

"How did the feeling go away?" she asked, turning.

"It's been replaced. I deliberately changed my life so that I wouldn't be reminded of things I couldn't alter. I came back to England. I became a member of the Silent Service. I obtained new lodgings." He met her gaze. "You live in the same house. You see the same people you used to see when Georgie was alive. You visit his room. No wonder you're still in pain."

She looked taken aback, almost as if he'd insulted her.

"Do you think going to Georgie's nursery is a terrible thing for me to do?"

He thought about the best way to say the words. "I think that we hold on to pain as a way of keeping those we lost close. If we suffer it means we care more. That isn't really true, but it's what we feel."

She didn't say anything for a moment, merely studied him in that way of hers.

"So you think I should raze Marsley House," she said. "And dismiss all the staff."

He shook his head. "I think you should move from Marsley House," he said. "Take the staff with you, but find a new home."

She looked startled.

"Or, if you won't do that, get rid of Georgie's nursery. It serves him no purpose and it only keeps your heart bleeding. You don't need physical things around you to remind you of your son."

She blinked several times, and he was prepared for her tears. When they came, he reached for the handkerchief she'd left on the table and took it to her.

"You are forever doing things like that, Drummond."

"Yes, I know, Your Grace."

"I do dislike you intensely at times."

"The feeling has been mutual, Your Grace."

She surprised him by smiling through her tears. All he could do was answer her smile with one of his own.

"Do you hate me?" he asked.

She sighed. "No."

"Do you still want to?"

"No."

He stood close, too close for propriety, but when had that ever mattered to him, especially around her?

He smoothed his fingers over her cheek, feeling the warm softness of her skin. A blush followed his touch, almost as if he had the power to summon her embarrassment. Tenderness was not something he felt often, but Suzanne had always drawn emotion from him in ways that no other woman had, even Rebecca.

In the next moments it felt as if his heart slowed, each beat important, profound in a way he couldn't explain.

They were united in loss. With each other they'd shared both their greatest sorrows and their most touching recollections.

Grief, however strong, however powerful, was not their foundation. Life connected him to Suzanne. He knew her as he'd known no other person. He accepted her, expecting her to be nothing more than what she was, because that was enough.

He bent down, brushed a kiss against her forehead, ridiculing himself as he did so. He was acting like he'd never touched a woman or kissed one. She was not a saint and yet he didn't feel unlike a supplicant. The room was silent, only the breeze outside blowing the green fronds of one of Mrs. Ross's plants against the window. A gentle tap, then another, as if to recall him to himself.

He felt more himself than he had for years.

He grinned at her. "If the cat is away, the mice play."

She looked startled. He only gave her a second to think about what he said before he took her hand and led her into his bedroom.

Chapter Thirty-Five

Adam held her hand as they entered his bedroom. She could have easily pulled away. When he dropped her hand to close the door behind them, she could have turned and demanded that he let her out. At any moment she could have demurred, claiming propriety, or a fear of scandal, or a half dozen other excuses.

She didn't have to stand there mute and still.

The room was shadowed, the pieces of furniture gray squares or rectangles except for the bed with its pale spread.

He came to stand in front of her and unfastened the cameo at her neck. When he was done he handed it to her, almost as if it were a gesture of sorts. The brooch represented her status, her title, perhaps even her persona, the Duchess of Marsley, the role she'd held for the past six years.

By handing it to her it felt almost as if he was giving her a choice, a final option. She walked a few feet away to the table beside his bed and gently placed it there before returning once more to him.

If she were castigated for this moment then let it be for the truth of it. She had not been overpowered.

Nor had she been convinced. She was in his bedroom of her own free will. It was her choice fueled by the emotions racing through her. This was passion. This was desire. This was tenderness. This heat that felt like hot oil flowing through her body was caused by the way he touched her and kissed her and looked at her.

She reached out and flattened her hands against his chest. Not to push him away, but simply to feel him. He placed his hands on her upper arms, drawing her closer. Time crawled, slowing almost to a stop. Each separate movement they made felt as if it had happened before, that they had practiced on endless occasions for just this moment. How else could he so perfectly unfasten all the buttons on her bodice, help her to remove her dress, her hoop, the corset, until she stood there in front of him attired in only her shift and stockings?

She stripped him of his shirt, pushing it off his shoulders, before unbuttoning the placket of his trousers. Never before had she thought to undress a man and yet her fingers worked with expert precision.

Pressing her palms against his skin she marveled at the feel of him. Everything was firm and warm. Her fingers stroked over his chest, through the hair and down to the open waistband of his trousers. The heels of her hands measured the shape of the muscles of his stomach.

"Suzanne."

She even liked his voice, low and holding the first hint of urgency.

The rhythm of her breathing increased as if to keep pace.

She had never felt like this before, growing heated

with a heavy feeling deep in the core of her, as if her body knew that something wonderful, different, and amazing was about to happen. If they stopped right now, if she donned all her clothes and escaped from this lovely home, she would still not forget this day or the promise of this night. Or the sheer joy of this moment standing before him exposed and vulnerable yet not feeling either.

She had the curious notion that she was supposed to be here. In this exact spot with her hands exploring the body of a man who'd touched her heart. It was right and fitting that she offered her body to him not in sacrifice, but in wonder.

He toed off his shoes and then his trousers. In seconds, the rest of his clothing was gone and he stood before her, naked in the gray shadows. What a pity there wasn't sunlight to see him.

He lifted the hem of her shift. She stood silently as he pulled the garment up and off. He surprised her by kneeling, helping her remove her shoes and then rolling down her stockings one by one.

A voice that sounded too much like her governess made its way to the forefront of her mind. *You should be embarrassed. Or ashamed. Or certainly you should be feeling fear. What would the world say to see you here, Suzanne Hackney Whitcomb?*

The world would be scandalized. No doubt everyone she knew would be horrified. She would certainly be pilloried. Why should she listen to anyone? She was strong enough and brave enough to choose her own path, even if the world decried it. And the path she chose at the moment was to be with Adam, the one man who could break her heart, spur her to rage, and then drive her to passion.

He stood, dropping her stockings on the same chair where the rest of her clothing lay.

Wordlessly, he put his hands on her waist and gently pulled her forward until her breasts grazed his chest, her nipples sensitive against the soft hair there, the rigid part of him insistent and startlingly impressive against her.

"I want to light a lamp to see you," he said, mirroring her earlier thought. "Or maybe study you by firelight. I knew you would be as beautiful as you are."

She was filled with so much happiness, almost as if she were a sparkling wine. She wound her arms up and around his neck.

"How can you tell?" she asked, a smile in her voice.

"I can feel you," he said.

Both his hands palmed her breasts, his thumbs gently flicking her nipples. He bent his head and mouthed one, sucking gently. She could feel the sensation deep inside her.

Her hands cupped the back of his head as he lifted her, carrying her to his bed.

At another time she might've felt the chill in the air, but not now. His body warmed her, covered her, and sheltered her. His hands stroked over her skin, memorizing the shape of her legs, the curve of her hips, the indentation of her waist. Then they were back at her breasts, measuring them, holding them for his lips. His fingers were teasing and tender, gentle and exploring. One hand went to cup her derriere, turning her slightly toward him. He inserted a leg between both of hers, his thigh pressing up against her. She responded by undulating against him, wanting the touch.

His fingers were suddenly there, stroking through

the moisture. He made a sound in the back of his throat. A hungry growl that echoed her own sudden ferocious need.

The serenity she'd felt earlier was abruptly gone, replaced by her body's dictates. Sliding out from under him she rose up, demanding in a way she had never been. She wanted to feel him. Her abdomen rode against his hip, slid down to his upper thigh and over the rigid tumescence jutting out like a sword.

A friendly sword, one that responded to her hand. She had never touched a man there, never felt curiosity or compulsion. Never wanted to make him groan as Adam did when her fingers slid over that intriguing shaft.

When had she become so adventurous? When had this act become so imbued with joy?

She didn't have time to wonder because she was suddenly tumbled onto her back.

Chapter Thirty-Six

Adam entered her slowly, conscious of the fact that it had been a while for her, as well as for him.

He didn't want completion as much as he wanted to indulge in the act of love with Suzanne. He wanted to feel her around him and to bring her pleasure. Above all, he wanted to ensure that she would remember this, remember them, of all the memories she held in her heart.

His movements were slow, deliberate, elongating the seconds as he gently pulled out of her.

He propped himself up on his arms, brushed light kisses across her mouth until her hands reached out, locked at the back of his head, and pulled him down for a deeper kiss.

If he was mutely counseling himself to slow the moments, she was doing the exact opposite. Her heart beat so rapidly it was like a frightened bird's.

His lips traced a path between her breasts and to each nipple in turn. Her hands slid to his neck and then to his shoulders, her nails gripping him, commanding without words.

He smiled as he sucked on a nipple. A moment later he kissed his way down to her abdomen. Her indrawn breath gave him a clue that she'd never been touched like this before.

He'd learned some things in India and he was all for using his education.

Sitting in front of her, he pulled her up to her knees and then moved her so that she sat on his lap. Her eyes were wide, her mouth curved.

"Adam?"

"You're not a duchess here. Not in my bed."

She only shook her head. He wished he had lit the lamp to see her.

He sat cross-legged, placed each of her legs on either side of his waist and then lifted her derriere into position. Her eyes widened even further as he entered her again.

Passion could be fun and experimental, engrossing and stirring. Passion could make you feel as if you were turned inside out, like you had never truly lived until that moment of bliss. He had the feeling that Suzanne had never felt that, never been powerless and adrift in wonder.

He bent his head and bit at her neck where it joined her shoulder. She gasped.

"Drummond."

"How very duchess-like you sound," he said. "If I were truly your servant I would be quivering in my boots."

"If you were truly my servant I would dismiss you right now."

"Would you?"

He moved one of his hands from her bottom to her breast, his thumb flicking an erect nipple, then lifting it for his mouth. He paid attention to that one nipple, and when he raised his eyes to her, Suzanne's head was back, her eyes were closed, and she was biting her lip.

"I am so very sorry, Your Grace. I will never do it again."

Her eyes flew open. "Now that's a pity, Drummond."

"I wouldn't want to be dismissed."

"I shall take your employment under advisement," she said, her voice trembling slightly. "I may reconsider, but only if you promise to be very, very good. But it shall be on a probationary basis only."

"How can I possibly convince you of my rehabilitation?" he asked, returning both hands to her derriere, lifting her up a little and then letting her slide back down on him.

She was biting her lip again.

He reached out and with his thumb pulled her lip free. If anyone was going to bite her mouth, it was going to be him. He matched the action to the thought, and would have smiled at the sound she made, helpless and needy, had he not been caught up in the same sensation.

It felt as if they were in the middle of a vortex, some wild waterspout of feeling. He wanted to laugh and bring her pleasure right then and there. He wanted to end it yet elongate the moments. His breath was harsh and fast. His heart was beating like he was running a race, and perhaps he was.

He put his hands on her waist, placed his cheek against hers and forced himself to take several deep breaths.

It didn't work. He still wanted her. He still wanted to feel her shudder around him. He wanted to taste her and mouth her and teach her all those things he knew, but he hadn't counted on his own weakness and need.

"Adam."

When had his name become an aphrodisiac? Or was it her voice, soft and tremulous?

He lowered his mouth over hers.

"Suzanne," he said softly. Had anyone ever felt free enough to call her something different? A derivative of Suzanne or some sweet nickname?

He wanted to light the lamp again to see her. Was her face rosy? Did her eyes glitter with passion? Were the centers of them black and deep like an ocean whirlpool?

He lifted her up again and lowered her once more before placing one hand on the small of her back and the other behind him to give him leverage. He raised his hips.

"Oh, Adam."

"Am I doing something wrong again?"

This time she didn't answer him, only moaned.

He couldn't wait. He wanted her to come in his arms. He wanted to feel her gripping him.

Moving his hand, he trailed his fingers through her soft folds, down to where they joined. She gasped again and the sound spurred him on.

He wanted her. He didn't think he'd ever desired anything more than Suzanne finding pleasure in his arms. He lifted her up and when she opened her eyes and would've protested further, he merely kissed her silent.

"In a moment," he said, rolling her to her stomach and pulling her up to her knees.

He entered her quickly, so deep inside he almost came right at that moment. She gripped the sheets

with both hands. She might have been unfamiliar
with this position, but she acclimated herself in mere
seconds, pushing back against him with her beautiful derriere.

He slid his hands up to her waist then to her breasts.

She pushed back against him again, impatient and
autocratic once more.

"In a moment, duchess," he said, his voice sounding harsh.

"Now, Drummond."

The one thing bad about this position was that he
couldn't kiss her, couldn't nibble on those full lips.

He pulled back until he was nearly out of her and
then slid back in again, slowly. She pushed back
against him as if encouraging him or demanding
him to finish.

"In good time, duchess," he said.

He pulled at her nipples, then trapped each one
between his fingers, palming her breasts.

Once more he withdrew. Suzanne arched her back.

She was perfect in every way, from her breasts,
to her derriere, to her long legs, to the curve of her
waist. He would not have changed one single thing
about her. The fact that she was eager and impatient
was just one more delight.

She leaned forward, bracing herself on her forearms, her cheek against the mattress. Each time he
slid forward she moaned, a soft appeal that had the
effect of making him even harder, even more desperate for completion. He moved his hands from her
breasts to her hips, pulling her tighter against him
even as he felt her begin to shudder.

Her body trapped him, cradled him, imprisoned
him in a demanding grip. He was powerless to con-

trol himself. No words on earth, no will, nothing could have stopped him from joining her in that next moment. Bliss overcame him, nearly felled him, and for long minutes he was in the center of a maelstrom, awash in a storm of sensation.

When it was over, with aftershocks still thundering through his frame, he collapsed on the bed, holding her. His rational mind surfaced, told him to release her and move away. Instead, he wrapped his arms around Suzanne's waist, his lips against her neck, needing her as much now as he had a moment earlier.

Reason enough, perhaps, to feel the dagger points of warning.

Chapter Thirty-Seven

Suzanne lay awake, listening to the wind howling around Mrs. Ross's house. Nature had brought them a storm overnight. Perhaps she'd been aware of the thunder and the lightning in a vague way. Adam had interested her more.

The rain came down in a thunderous volley and then seemed to stop for a little while, a curiously calming rhythm.

Her arm was extended toward Adam, who was still asleep. Her hand was curled, her knuckles resting against his bare chest. For some reason, it was important to her that they touch and maintain a connection.

He'd loved her again in the predawn hours before the world woke. This had been a silent joining, one without a word spoken. Their dance had been perfectly choreographed from the beginning of time. A strong and muscular male paired with a curvy, soft female. The only sounds they'd made were those of pleasure. The only requests were done with a kiss or a tender touch.

They had probably scandalized Mrs. Ross. Had their driver waited outside all night? Was Michael sitting, even now, in the rain? Adam had left his rooms for a few minutes last night. Had it been to make arrangements?

How very irresponsible of her not to have thought of Michael before now. She was not like George in that regard. He'd thought anyone in his employ should endure any sort of ill treatment. The privilege of working for the Duke of Marsley was enough, in his mind, to make up for any discomfort.

Yet she'd acted as selfishly last night, hadn't she? She'd forgotten about anything but Adam.

If Michael had returned to Marsley House, had it been with a tale that he couldn't wait to share with the rest of the staff? Surely she should be more concerned about her reputation? How very odd that it didn't matter to her one whit. She just didn't care.

The wind howled at the window as if to chastise her.

What did she care about the opinions of others? They hadn't sat with her during the long, dark, endless nights. Not one of them had inquired as to her pain. None of them had even mentioned Georgie in all this time. As if the loss of her child was something unmentionable like her corset or shift.

She turned her head toward the window. Dawn had been overpowered by the storm, the rainbow of colors on the eastern sky muted by black clouds. Shadows lingered in this bedroom, draped Adam, and shielded both of them.

They would whisper about her behavior, that she wasn't acting the role of duchess but one of a strumpet. What did she care about her title? It had never brought her happiness or belonging or a true home. If Georgie had lived she would have tolerated George without a word spoken in protest. If her son hadn't perished, she would have endured her life, grateful for the gift of being a mother. Now?

She stared at the shadowed ceiling.

A thought was beginning to penetrate the haze of grief surrounding her for the past two years. Living didn't mean that she loved Georgie any less. In the back of sadness, pushing forward inexorably was another emotion: hope. It had no actual reason for being. It wasn't tied to anything tangible. It simply existed like the sunrise and the sunset, ephemeral and constant.

Georgie's death had taught her that her world, the world that was familiar and normal, would be forever different. Nothing would be the same. Yet her life needn't be over. She could still feel. Last night had proven that.

Adam's hand touched her cheek gently before he rose up and kissed her softly.

"Have you been awake long?"

"Only a few minutes," she said, rolling over to face him. She was naked beneath the sheet, but she didn't feel awkward or self-conscious. Instead, she felt free in ways she never had before. The Daring Duchess. She much preferred that to Marble Marsley.

His fingers pushed the hair behind her ear. She was going to have a terrible time brushing it later. She would have to borrow his brush because she hadn't left Marsley House with her reticule and didn't have a comb.

When she returned home, everyone would know what she'd been doing. She hadn't taken a great deal of care with her clothing last night. No doubt it was wrinkled, but the black silk didn't show much abuse. Perhaps she could get away with it.

"What excuse shall we give when we return to Marsley House?" she asked.

"Why must we return?"

Now that was an idea, one she hadn't considered. Perhaps she could run away completely from her role and that enormous house. Georgie had been the only bright light in an otherwise dull and dark existence.

She reached out, her fingers trailing over Adam's bristly cheek and then tracing the shape of his lips. What a truly handsome man he was. Her hero. Her man of mystery. What had he called it? Not the War Office, but something else. The Silent Service.

She placed her hand gently over the scar on his shoulder. "How did you get this?" she asked.

"I was shot."

"At Manipora," she said.

He nodded.

Horrified, she stared at that small mark. A few inches lower and it would have struck his heart. He would have died in India and she would never have known him.

She pressed both hands against his chest.

"Oh, Adam," she said, unable to tell him what she felt. She was both terrified and grateful. He must take greater care. He could still be injured.

What would she do without him?

The question shocked her. He wasn't her major-domo. He wasn't her servant. He owed her no loyalty or devotion. After today she would probably never see him again.

"Sankara," she said, the name suddenly occurring to her.

"The duke's secretary?"

She nodded. "He came home from India with

George. I sometimes think Sankara was George's only friend. If anyone would know where that journal is, it's Sankara."

"He left after your husband died, didn't he?"

"I was all for him staying on, but I think he was lost without George."

He leaned over to kiss her again.

"Fair enough," he said, several delightful moments later. "I'll send word to him."

She shook her head. "Sankara won't come. He's a man of great pride, Adam."

"Then I'll go see him."

She curved her palm against his cheek. "Not without me. I absolutely insist upon it."

"Are you back to being a duchess, Your Grace?"

"I am, Drummond, and I also insist that you kiss me again. Consider it a command."

"Very well, but only because I always do my duty."

And much more than that.

Chapter Thirty-Eight

$\mathcal{A}$ few hours later they dressed. He was more fortunate than Suzanne. What wardrobe he kept at his lodgings was assiduously cared for by Mrs. Ross. He had a snowy-white recently laundered and ironed shirt, and trousers to wear. He considered suggesting that Mrs. Ross might be willing to put an iron to Suzanne's wrinkled dress, then immediately thought better of the idea.

Like it or not, his landlady was protective of him. You might even say that she was possessive to a certain degree. He had not, up until now, done anything to dissuade her. It had been pleasant to have someone fuss over him.

However, now it might prove to be a problem.

He shaved and finished dressing, then entered the kitchen to find the windows misted over. The day was a wet one, the view of the sky promising even more rain. After having lived in India for so many years, he liked the smell of an English rainy day. Something in the air tingled his nose and made his lungs want to expand even farther. Rain cleansed and wiped the dust off nature.

"However do you make tea?" Suzanne asked.

He turned from his examination of the garden to see her standing there barefoot in her wrinkled black dress.

He smiled and wondered how long it had been since amusement had cut through his thoughts and lightened his heart.

"Is the duchess about to be a serving girl?" he asked.

She sent him a look over her shoulder. "I've been known to do some extraordinary things from time to time," she said, contemplating the small stove set into the room's fireplace with a frown.

"Normally, Mrs. Ross brings me tea."

She sent him another look. "I don't think that's a good idea, Drummond."

"Neither do I, Your Grace."

They smiled at each other in perfect accord.

He hadn't been able to get the sight of her out of his mind. He'd always remember her in his bed, the down pillows behind her, her rosy and flushed skin against the backdrop of his sheets. The covers had been rumpled, the counterpane fanned to the bottom of the bed.

He walked to the table, grabbed the neck of the wine bottle and held it aloft.

"'A jug of wine, a loaf of bread, and thou beside me singing in the wilderness.'"

"Are you quoting, Drummond?"

"Indeed I am," he said. "I, too, have been known to do some extraordinary things from time to time. It's from the *Rubáiyát of Omar Khayyám.* A Persian poet."

"Must I sing?" she asked with a smile. "And where is this loaf of bread you claim? I'm starving."

"Regretfully, I don't have any bread, either."

"Only wine," she said. "I'll get silly at breakfast."

"Something I should very much like to encourage," he said. "I'll get silly along with you."

She tilted her head slightly, regarding him in the same manner he used to inspect the footmen.

"I cannot think of anyone else with whom I'd rather be silly, Drummond."

"Nor I, Your Grace."

She walked to him, took the bottle, and startled him by uncorking it and taking a swig. Then she stood on tiptoe and kissed him.

Kissing Suzanne's wine-flavored lips was a treat, one he duplicated often in the next few minutes.

He was about to suggest that they adjourn to the bedroom once again. Or, if she preferred, he could easily throw down a blanket on the floor and they could make love in view of the rain-tossed garden. The only problem was that Mrs. Ross was almost as protective of her plants as she was of him. He wouldn't be surprised to see her peering in the window with her umbrella in one hand and her flower basket in another.

"Where is our driver?" Suzanne asked, banishing his thought of making love for the whole of the morning.

"I sent Michael back to Marsley House last night."

She nodded, as if she'd expected that information.

"And you asked him to come back this morning, didn't you?"

It was his turn to nod.

"We are so very scandalous, Drummond."

"No, we aren't, Your Grace. You were visited by a violent headache. Mrs. Ross, who, incidentally, is an old friend of yours, settled you into a guest bedroom. I slept on a downstairs sofa."

"You're doing it again," she said. "You're protecting me when no one asked you to do so."

Her words rankled him. "A man should not have to be asked to protect the woman he . . ." His words trailed off. What the hell was he about to say?

They stared at each other.

"I apologize, Suzanne," he finally said. "It's a natural response to want to care for someone."

She still didn't say anything, and it was probably the first time in his life when silence was acutely disturbing. Should he tell her that he hadn't known the words he was about to utter until he heard them? That made him sound like a simpleton, didn't it? Unfortunately, it was the truth.

"I'll go and check if Michael is here," he said.

Anything but stand there and try to figure out what, exactly, he was feeling. He didn't have any problems analyzing obscure patterns, deciphering codes, or understanding the people he'd been assigned to watch. But emotions? That was entirely different and out of his range of expertise. Could anyone claim to be an expert? God knew he couldn't, especially now.

Michael was in the carriage in front of the house. Adam spoke with him for a few minutes.

"Begging your pardon, Mr. Drummond, but is Her Grace all right?"

"She's fine," he said. "Her headache seems much better this morning."

Michael nodded, evidently satisfied.

An hour later he and Suzanne managed to exit the house without encountering Mrs. Ross. No doubt she was watching them from one of her many windows. He didn't turn and look.

Mrs. Ross had, up until now, showed a remarkable lack of curiosity as to his movements. He couldn't help but wonder if she was part of the growing network of War Office operatives. He tried to remember how he'd first learned of her all those years ago, but he couldn't recall. For some reason, however, he thought she'd been recommended to him by someone at the War Office.

If that was true, it made him uncomfortable. The woman's caring and concern could mask an assignment—to keep an eye on him.

When had he become so watchful and questioning of everyone around him? Since he learned that Roger had put another operative at Marsley House. Since he'd started examining every single one of Roger's motivations.

Reaching out, he placed his hand on the small of Suzanne's back, walking with her to the carriage. Once he'd given Michael their destination, they arranged themselves inside the vehicle.

He had an idea and it wasn't sitting well with him. Instead of Hackney supporting Roger in his ambitious run for Parliament, maybe their relationship was more complex.

Was Roger working on Hackney's behalf? Was this whole assignment merely to hide the fact that Hackney had something to do with Manipora? After all, Hackney had been in India at the time. In return for Roger's protecting Hackney—and in gratitude—Hackney would be Roger's financial backer during his run for Parliament.

Another thing that had been bothering him ever since that first meeting with Roger—how had the man come by his knowledge of the journal? He'd mentioned that someone—an informant—had been close to the duke. Was it his former secretary?

Adam's suspicions of Hackney, coupled with Suzanne's vehement denials of the duke's treason, were making him seriously question his conclusions, something he'd never before done.

"What's wrong, Adam?"

He glanced at Suzanne. Her eyes were filled with worry. Not grief. Not pain. Only worry, but he wanted to see her as she was this morning with a grin on her face and amusement in her eyes. She deserved to be happy.

He was determined to give that to her.

"Nothing," he said, smiling at her.

He wouldn't say anything to her yet. Not until his ideas were more fully formed.

Chapter Thirty-Nine

Sankara Bora lived in a detached house in a fashionable part of London, exactly opposite from where Adam had thought he would live. Evidently, being the secretary to the Duke of Marsley had been a profitable venture.

"Sankara married after George died," Suzanne said, almost as if she'd heard his thoughts. "She is the daughter of a prince, I'm told."

There had been stranger pairings. That of a War Office operative and a duchess, for example.

The double bay windows looked like eyes staring at them. The black wrought iron fence contained two green squares intersected by a pathway leading to a red painted front door. He had the impression, as they walked up to the house, that they were being watched. It could just be that his senses were on high alert and he was seeing enemies where there were none. After the events of the past weeks, he could be excused for eyeing the world around him somewhat skeptically.

He used the brass knocker in the shape of a lotus blossom and waited.

"I don't have my reticule," Suzanne said. "Or my calling cards."

He wasn't familiar with the niceties of society, so he couldn't offer any suggestions. Surely you could call on someone without announcing yourself? Whether or not it was proper, it was what they were going to have to do.

The door was opened by a young maid in a black uniform with a spotless white apron. He shouldn't have been surprised by the fact that she was Indian. No doubt the rest of Sankara's staff was of his nationality. In the same fashion, English servants had been highly desired by English families in India.

"I should very much like to see Mr. Bora, if he's available," Suzanne said, before he could speak. "If you would, please, tell him that the Duchess of Marsley is calling."

The young girl's eyes widened, she hurriedly curtsied, and she stepped aside for them to enter the house.

Being with a duchess could be helpful.

They were led into a formal parlor, one that could rival Marsley House for the richness of its decor. The room was crowded with furniture, all of it overstuffed, fringed, and dark brown in color. Even the draperies hanging at the bay window were brown. Adam immediately felt as if he was entombed in a trench. Even the air smelled dusty, but that was no doubt from the collection of stuffed birds in their glass domes. Six ferns hung in front of the window, further darkening the space.

He preferred the congestion of the London streets to this room.

After Suzanne sat at the end of one of the uncomfortable-looking sofas he took up a position in one of the wing chairs opposite. Neither he nor Suzanne said a word. Even conversation was choked to death in this parlor.

Thankfully, they didn't have long to wait until the duke's secretary made his appearance.

Sankara Bora was a tall, stick figure of a man, with an elongated neck and a prominent Adam's apple. His hawk-like nose looked as if it had been stretched to match the length of his face. His large mouth, now smiling, was his only softening feature. Even his brown eyes were hard, like clods of earth in a drought.

"Sankara," Suzanne said, smiling. "Thank you for seeing us."

"On the contrary, Your Grace. Thank you for coming to see me. I have few visitors these days and none who bring me memories of happier times."

"I would like you to meet a friend of mine. Adam is from the War Office, and he has some questions about George."

Her words surprised him, but they shouldn't have. She wouldn't have continued with his masquerade, although he wasn't quite ready to give it up. They needed Sankara, however, and perhaps the best way to approach him was with directness and honesty.

The two men sat in the matching wing chairs opposite Suzanne.

"You are the majordomo at Marsley House," Sankara finally said. "Or you have pretended to be."

Again, Adam shouldn't have been surprised, but he was.

"You have friends on the staff," he said.

Sankara nodded. "I bring Mrs. Thigpen some spices for her cook from time to time as well."

He couldn't remember having seen such a distinctive man before. When he said as much, Sankara smiled once more.

"I have found that it is better to be unnoticed than it is to be singled out."

The secretary struck him as the type of man who would avoid a direct answer and use words as a wall. Therefore, Adam used a frontal attack.

"I was the majordomo," he said. "I was placed there by people who believed that the Duke of Marsley acted contrary to England's interests when he was in India. Do you have any knowledge of that?"

"You have come here to prove that the duke has done such a thing?" Sankara asked, looking at Suzanne.

"On the contrary," she said. "I've come to have you help me prove George was not a traitor."

They were silenced by the arrival of a maid carrying a heavily laden tray. Adam wanted answers, not tea, but he buried his impatience after Suzanne's quick look. Refusing Sankara's offer of refreshments would be an insult.

There were more rules on how to treat people socially than all the regulations in the army.

After Suzanne had been served, he accepted the cup of tea as well as two sugary biscuits. They would have to suffice for breakfast and maybe lunch if he couldn't speed this meeting along.

For a few minutes, Suzanne and Sankara discussed matters of mutual interest: the cook's new curry recipe, Mrs. Thigpen's interest in the stable master at Fairhaven, the contents of the kitchen garden. Adam ate another two biscuits, drank the tea that smelled and tasted of citrus and cinnamon, and listened to them talk.

Finally, during a lull in their conversation, he turned to the former secretary. "I believe that the duke gave information to the rebels about Manipora," he said. If he didn't get to the heart of the matter, they would be here all day, being polite and oh, so proper.

"Who has given you this information?" Sankara asked.

He was violating all sorts of rules and had, ever since yesterday. But seeing Hackney in Roger's office had also alerted him that he might have gotten everything wrong.

"An undersecretary at the War Office," he said. "His name is Roger Mount. He says that the Duke was a traitor and the information is in a journal that the duke kept."

Sankara didn't say anything for a long moment. "You have looked for this journal?"

Adam nodded. He decided to tell the other man the truth. "I'm not the only one," he said. "I believe there's another operative at Marsley House, someone who injured the duchess the other night."

He sent a quick glance to Suzanne, hoping she understood why he hadn't mentioned his suspicions to her earlier.

She gave him a look that made him certain they were going to discuss this omission later.

"I have seen his journals," Sankara said. "Before the duke's death, he required me to write in them." He gave Suzanne an apologetic look. "Forgive me, Your Grace, for speaking of such personal things, but the duke was not well."

"In what way?" Suzanne asked, sounding surprised. "He never mentioned his ill health to me, Sankara."

"This I can understand," the secretary said. "His Grace was a proud man, but his vision was not what it had been. He was finding it difficult to read."

Adam exchanged a glance with Sankara. If the duke had been as much of a lecher as he'd written about for years, it was entirely possible he had been suffering from the end stages of syphilis. Adam knew the signs only because some men in his regiment had been unwise in their choice of partners.

"An *aadmi* came to see the duke not long before his death."

"I don't know what that means, Sankara," Suzanne said.

"A man," Adam translated.

"You speak Hindi?" Sankara asked.

He nodded. "I lived in India for a number of years. It's a fascinating country."

"That it is. Almost as intriguing as your England. And Scotland, if I do not mistake your accent."

Adam inclined his head.

"You say a man," Adam said. "Who was he?"

"A soldier. One from a native regiment that reported to His Grace."

A Sepoy, in other words. Nearly eighty percent of the Sepoys had participated in the rebellion of 1857. Those who hadn't had proved invaluable to understanding what had started the open resistance to British rule.

Had the one who'd visited the duke also come bearing information?

Sankara was a man comfortable with formalities.

Being direct with him hadn't helped. Adam had a feeling they would continue to circle the issue until the man felt more at ease. Either that, or he needed something to cut through to Sankara, some knowledge that would jolt the man. It was entirely possible that the secretary had been privy to the duke's secrets. Whether he would reveal any of them was the question.

"I lost my wife at Manipora," Adam said. It was a story he didn't often tell, yet here he was divulging it again.

The secretary looked at him, his eyes intent.

"You have my deepest condolences, Mr. Drummond. Is it vengeance you seek?"

"In a sense," Adam said, giving the other man the truth. "I want the person who betrayed us punished."

"Vengeance does not restore our loved ones to us, however."

"No, it doesn't. But perhaps it allows those of us left behind a little peace, knowing that justice has been served."

Sankara contemplated the contents of his teacup. Adam bit back his irritation.

"I can understand why you would want to protect his memory, Sankara," Suzanne said. "Especially if he was guilty of such a terrible deed. But if he was not, if he is innocent, will you help me prove that?"

"Silence is a shroud we should wrap around our heroes," Sankara said.

Adam could feel his temper ratchet up a few notches. Hero? What the hell had the Duke of Marsley ever done to deserve that label?

"Not if it conceals the truth," Suzanne said. "What is the truth, Sankara?"

He lifted his eyes and exchanged a glance with Suzanne. "You do not know what you are asking me, Your Grace. I was the duke's faithful servant. I was his confidant, if you wish."

"I don't care about his women, Sankara. If you think to keep that knowledge from me, then you're too late. I know and I've always known."

"And I don't care about his personal life," Adam said. "All I care about is whether he betrayed us. Did he?"

He and Sankara exchanged a long look.

"If I give you proof of his innocence, will you use it to ensure His Grace isn't portrayed as a traitor?"

"If it's really proof," Adam said.

The secretary abruptly stood and left the room. He and Suzanne glanced at each other. What proof was Sankara going to bring them?

Chapter Forty

"Do you think he's coming back?" Suzanne asked.

She hoped Sankara was, for Adam's sake. He looked as if he wanted to pummel the absent secretary.

She couldn't blame him. Were she Adam, she'd probably feel the same way. If the person who was responsible for the bridge's collapse was before her now, she doubted if she would be understanding. Instead, she'd want some kind of justice for Georgie.

The problem was that she honestly didn't believe George had been a traitor. From what he said, nothing else in his life had meant as much to him as his position in the army. He loved his medals and being able to inspect the troops. He loved being thought of as a general. She assumed it was because he hadn't done anything to be the Duke of Marsley. Being awarded a position of leadership had required that he convince others he was worthy of the honor.

It was the one thing he'd done on his own.

Granted, he might have been as inept at command as he had been other things. But a traitor? He was related, albeit by some distance, to the Queen. The relationship mattered to him and she couldn't see him betraying the crown.

However, Sankara's reluctance bothered her.

Who decreed that nothing bad should ever be said about the dead? Was it just one of those rules in society that everyone agreed to obey? The minute you died a halo surrounded you or, as Sankara said, a shroud of silence.

She would hate if George's honor was tainted and his reputation suffered, but if he was guilty of what Adam believed, then it would be the price he needed to pay for his treason even posthumously.

Standing, she smoothed down her skirt. She'd worn her at-home hoop only the day before, and the dress was one of her favorites with lace on the shoulders and down the bodice. Still, she was in no condition to be calling on anyone.

She'd worked diligently on her hair using Adam's military brushes, but she'd been missing a few of her pins and the style was more casual than she normally wore.

Nor was she going to think about the fact that her lips still looked swollen and there was a pink spot on her chin—a mark from Adam's night beard.

What had Sankara thought of her appearance? The secretary had always been a proper individual and it was quite obvious that she hadn't been all that proper recently. Surely she should be feeling more ashamed of her behavior? At the very least she should be chastising herself.

How very odd that she wasn't.

In fact, and it was a confession that she didn't feel comfortable saying aloud, she didn't want to return to Marsley House all that much. The house had become a prison of sorts. While she was within it, she was expected to act in a certain way, to be a certain person. She couldn't be the Suzanne of her youth, but must always be the Duchess of Marsley.

"I never wanted to be a duchess," she said, moving to the window.

The room was quite oppressive and all these ferns in front of the glass blocked the view.

She hadn't meant to say that, but now that she had, she turned and faced Adam.

"My father was all for having a title in the family. What was a great deal of wealth, after all, if you couldn't buy your way into the peerage?"

He didn't say anything, but his look wasn't condemnatory. Instead, she saw warmth in his eyes, the same look he'd had this morning in his bed. She smiled at him, suddenly absurdly happy despite the seriousness of their errand.

"The Whitcombs were on the edge of poverty. They had an ancient family name. They had enormous credit, which they used to live on. By the time George came around, the credit was used up and the money was gone. So my father bought me a duke and George got a fortune in return."

Adam still hadn't said anything.

"It's the way of the world, I was told. The law of supply and demand. There aren't that many dukes, all in all. They cost a pretty penny. I don't know how much my father paid George, but it was evidently enough."

"Do you think it was worth it for him?"

"For my father or for George?" she asked.

"Either or both," he said, smiling.

"I don't think George cared all that much. I think he was content enough to have his second cousin assume the title at his death. When Georgie came along, everything changed. He was devoted to Georgie. As for my father, his investment hasn't ended. George might be dead, but he still has a duchess for a daughter. I'm a commodity he trots out whenever he can. I think he was annoyed the first year of my mourning because he couldn't present me at his dinner parties and gatherings. It would've shocked society. But it's been two years now and he's all for getting me out of black and parading me around." She shook her head.

"What if you had fallen in love?" Adam asked. "Would he have allowed you to marry the man of your choice?"

"Only if the union could benefit him in some way." She turned back to the window, fingering one of the fern leaves. "My father is desperate to be accepted," she said. "I never realized that when I was a child. Or even when I married George. It was only in the last few years that I've become aware of it."

He didn't say anything in response. How tactful Adam could be at times.

"As for love, I don't think I'm that brave."

"Is love something you need courage for?"

She nodded. "I think that when you love someone, you also invite pain into your heart. You tell it to come in, but sit in the back, because it isn't needed right now. Then one day, maybe sooner, maybe later, you summon it forward and you tell it, 'It's your turn.'"

"That doesn't always happen, Suzanne," he said.

"It has for the two of us."

He stood and walked to her, grabbing one of her hands and holding it between his.

"That doesn't mean it would happen again."

"What about you, Adam? Are you ready to marry? To fall in love again?"

He didn't get a chance to answer, because Sankara entered the room, hesitating at the doorway.

They turned to face him.

Suddenly, Suzanne felt a sense of dread that she had to keep swallowing down.

In his arms he cradled a large volume, one of the journals that George had used to chronicle his days. She'd never known why he had documented everything so assiduously, especially since some of his actions had not been especially laudable. She'd never read any of the journals, unwilling to be privy to his intimate thoughts, especially those dating from the years of their marriage. There were some things she didn't need—or want—to know.

"I have guarded the duke's secrets as if they were my own," Sankara said. "Some of which are detailed here. Even more important, however, there is proof of his innocence."

Adam strode toward him, but Sankara shook his head. Instead, he approached her and extended the journal with both hands.

"Your Grace, I know you to be an honorable woman. For the friendship and affection I held for His Grace, I beg you to read this with kindness. Do not fault him for his failings. He was, after all, no greater than the rest of us."

She didn't quite know what Sankara wanted from her, but she took the journal, and said, "He was my husband and Georgie's father. For that alone, he gets my loyalty, Sankara. I will leave it up to God to judge George."

He relinquished the book and stepped back, bowing slightly. "That is as much as I can expect, Your Grace."

"Why did you take it?" Adam asked.

"To protect George," Suzanne said. "Did he have another mistress, Sankara?"

The secretary bowed his head before meeting her eyes. "And another child, Your Grace."

Her stomach clenched. "What does that make? Eight?"

"I believe so, Your Grace."

She wrapped her arms around the oversized journal, nodded to Sankara, and looked at Adam.

He startled her by addressing Sankara again.

"Did you speak to anyone at the War Office, Sankara?"

Sankara didn't answer him, merely regarded Adam as if he'd suddenly sprouted a horn in the middle of his forehead.

"I was told that their informant was someone close to the duke, someone who was disturbed by learning of the duke's treachery."

"I know of no treachery, sir. His Grace was not a perfect man, but he was no traitor."

Adam didn't answer, only nodded once.

Soon enough, they said their thanks and their farewells, hopefully masking the fact that she was desperate to leave Sankara's home as quickly as possible. Once they were in the carriage, she clutched George's journal to her chest and sat back against the seat.

Reason enough, perhaps, to succumb to tears.

Chapter Forty-One

Adam decided that he could go for a very long time without seeing Suzanne in tears again. At least this time, he had not caused them. Or perhaps he had, by insisting that the Duke of Marsley was guilty of treason.

He pulled the journal from her grasp, placed it on the seat, and moved to sit beside her. Putting his arm around her, he encouraged her to place her head on his shoulder. When she finally did, he held her as she wept, thinking that he would rather face a hundred rebelling Sepoys than her tears.

Her crying affected him in an odd way. A cavernous space opened up in his chest, almost as if he had been shot. Right at the moment it was preferable to this.

He wished he had the capacity to take the pain from her.

Some part of himself, probably more intuitive and less practical, understood that what he was feeling was something he hadn't expected. It was part of that moment at his lodgings when he'd been about to confess emotions he'd not yet admitted to himself.

His other hand went to her far shoulder, cocooning

her in his embrace. He heard himself say things he'd rarely said, bits of Gaelic he'd once spoken. Words from his childhood when his mother was well and Mary existed only to bedevil him.

The vibration of the carriage wheels over the cobblestones was jarring and he wanted to spare Suzanne that, also. Did he want to wrap her in cotton bunting and protect her from the world?

Yes. The answer was so fast that he startled himself. Yes. He wanted to ensure that she was never injured, that no one ever said anything unkind to her. He wanted to take away her grief, even though that was something he couldn't do, any more than she could strip him of his. Instead, perhaps, they could ease each other, mitigate the anguish when it emerged from time to time, coax it to shrink again. Perhaps they could learn to live with the holes in their hearts and patch them up with other, better, sweeter memories.

Yes, he did want to smooth her way, make her laugh, and hear her indrawn breath of wonder like he had last night. He wanted to repeat that over and over again on as many days as God granted him.

That's what he'd started to say this morning.

"He isn't worth your tears," he said. "Or your loyalty."

She placed her hand on his jacket before sliding it against his shirt. He could feel the warmth of her fingers on his skin just as he had last night.

"I'm not crying for George," she said. A moment later she shook her head. "Oh, maybe I am. I'm crying for everything, Adam. Everything and nothing. Doesn't that make me sound foolish?"

"No," he said. "Just human."

Too soon they entered the gates of Marsley House. Adam withdrew his arms, moving to sit on the opposite seat. He blessed the fact that he'd grabbed two handkerchiefs this morning and passed one to Suzanne.

She blotted at her face, then shook her head.

"I must look a fright," she said, her voice low.

"If I didn't know better, I would think you were soliciting for compliments. Some women do not cry well. With some, tears only seem to increase their allure."

She smiled. "If I didn't know better, Drummond, I would think you were hinting at an increase in salary."

He was glad she'd brought it up.

"I need to retain my role of majordomo for a little while," he said. "At least until I find out who was in the library that night."

She nodded, then looked away at the sight of Marsley House growing nearer.

"Do you think it was your father?" he asked, a question he'd been considering for a while. Hackney had acted like a bully with Suzanne. Had he deliberately injured his daughter?

She glanced at him. "I don't know. How would he have gotten in?"

"Perhaps he had a contact within the staff."

She reached over and grabbed the journal, holding it close to her chest.

"I have the feeling that things are happening around me. Things I need to know."

"I have the same feeling," he said.

She didn't say anything. Nor did he speak further. What could he say, after all?

The door opened, but before she exited the carriage, Suzanne handed him the journal.

"Perhaps I'm a coward, Adam, but I don't want to read George's words. My life was almost idyllic back then. I concentrated on Georgie and that was all. Perhaps it wasn't fair to George, but I don't think he wanted it any other way."

He took the book from her. "If you're sure."

She nodded. "Keep what you learn about me to yourself, if you would. Or about any of George's women. I don't want to learn about his children, either. I do not wish them ill, Adam, but neither do I want to know that they're well and happy and have bright futures. I'm not that much of an angel."

"And if I discover that he is a traitor? Do you want to know that?"

She nodded.

He was prevented from saying anything else by the opening of the carriage door.

THEY HAD BEEN gone a day and a half with no explanation. The story Adam had concocted had been received by Olivia with no indication that she disbelieved him. After all, he was in the company of the Duchess of Marsley, whose reputation was heretofore sacrosanct. He trusted the housekeeper to disseminate the tale as well as she did most gossip. He would continue on with the premise that he had nothing to hide.

In other words, bluster worked when all else failed.

As for Suzanne, her new maid was so awed by working for a duchess that she'd never question her.

He tended to those details that couldn't wait due to

his absence before returning to his office. He brought himself a pot of tea, to the surprise of one of the upstairs maids. He was not supposed to serve himself, but allow the staff to do for him. Under normal conditions he would've agreed. It was important to keep boundaries as they were and traditions as they always had been. His role as majordomo would end soon and he didn't want to upset the status quo.

However, these were not normal conditions. He didn't want to be alone with a maid. She might ask him questions about their absence from Marsley House. He didn't want to talk about Suzanne. First of all, she didn't deserve being an object of gossip. Second, he was afraid that what he felt for her might inadvertently be revealed.

Not that it mattered. Nothing could come of their relationship, such as it was.

He placed the journal on the surface of the desk, lit the lamp, poured himself a cup of tea, and settled in to read. Within a few minutes he began to understand why Sankara had been so reluctant to turn over the journal.

While it was true that the duke had a mistress and she had delivered him another child, somewhere along the way the man had become more and more intrigued with the woman under his own roof. Whole chapters of the journal were devoted to Suzanne. How she walked and spoke, the way she tended to Georgie, refusing to give over the whole of his care to his nurse. Everything about her seemed to fascinate the duke, and it was all too obvious what was happening. The Duke of Marsley was falling in love with his wife.

Four hours later he stopped and stared. There, in

Sankara's distinctive flowing handwriting, was the information he'd been looking for all these months.

> *I was visited on April 13th by a soldier from India who recounted a story I found disheartening to believe. It seemed that there was a traitor in our midst, someone who traded with the Sepoy rebels.*

He moved on to the second page, impatient with the duke's flowery explanation of how his visitor looked, what he wore, and the refreshments he'd been served. It wasn't until the fourth page that the secret was finally revealed.

When the name *Manipora* was mentioned he hesitated, forcing himself to read slowly. When he finished, he stared at the far wall for a few minutes, unwilling, or perhaps even unable, to believe what he had read.

His forearms rested on the desk, on either side of the ledger. His hands clenched into fists. He forced them to relax, splayed his fingers on the wood of the desk. If he concentrated on anything other than the words, he could allow himself to process what they truly meant.

Everything he'd believed had been a lie.

Rebecca's face came into his mind, the memory of the last time he'd seen her perfectly etched in his memory. Her eyes had been filled with fear as he'd tried to reassure her.

"They've given us safe passage," he'd said. "We'll be together soon enough."

"Are you certain?" she'd asked, her voice thin.

He'd hugged her then, taking a minute from his duties to comfort his wife. He'd seen her into the boat with the other women and children before heading for the barge carrying the rest of the garrison.

Standing, he circled the desk, unable to calm his sudden restlessness. His mind was racing, his thoughts first jumbled and then arranging themselves into an almost militaristic order.

Someone had betrayed them. That's why they'd been forced to negotiate with the rebel leader. The information of the compound and all their fortifications could only have come from someone who'd either lived at Manipora or had knowledge of the defenses.

That's why he'd always thought the Duke of Marsley culpable. The man had a command role. It was to him that the head of the entrenchment had pleaded for reinforcements. It was the duke who'd sent half their garrison to Lucknow to help stifle the rebellion there.

That was another mistake Adam had made—not seeing the intent behind the massacre. It hadn't been stupidity. Instead, it had been greed.

He'd never entertained the idea that the Duke of Marsley might be innocent. Instead, he'd been intent on finding proof that the man was guilty of treason. He'd had tunnel vision and that was never a good trait to possess in the War Office. He'd believed everything he'd been told like a gullible puppet. All along, his instincts had been shouting at him to pay attention, and it wasn't until he'd seen Edward Hackney in Roger's office that he'd listened.

He rang for Thomas and when the footman appeared, he apologized for the lateness of the hour.

"It's a sensitive errand I'm sending you on, Thomas, and I'd appreciate your tact."

The younger man nodded. "Of course, sir," he said, as proper as an English sergeant.

He gave the senior footman the envelope with instructions. "You must wait for an answer," he said.

Inside the envelope were two questions: *Did the Duke of Marsley confront the traitor with the truth? Did he tell him about the journal?*

Chapter Forty-Two

When Suzanne returned to her room, she bathed and then changed into another dress, black silk with ruffles on the bodice and sleeves. Now she quickly surveyed herself in the mirror, put on her mourning ring, and forced a smile to her face for Emily's sake.

"Are you sure you're feeling well, Your Grace?" Emily asked. "I was so sad to hear that you were ill. I should have been with you. Was it because of the accident, do you think?"

Suzanne met her maid's eyes in the mirror and held up another hairpin. Emily was exceedingly talented at doing her hair. The girl was skilled in a great many things, plus she was much more amenable than Ella.

"You mustn't worry, Emily," she said. "I'm feeling much better, thank you. Mrs. Ross is very kind."

No one was to know that Adam maintained lodgings outside of his role as majordomo. That would require too much explanation. Thankfully, Emily didn't continue to question her. Nor did anyone look at her, point their finger, and declare that she was now a fallen woman, one of those despicable creatures who engaged in sin.

Not that it felt like sin. She could still remember every bit of last night. She couldn't get over how wonderful making love was with Adam. Despite his many women, it was entirely possible that George had been bad at that skill, too. Or it could be that she and George hadn't suited at all, in any way.

She and Adam certainly did. She liked talking to him. Or discussing things, even arguing with him.

". . . told him that I'm certain you would be fine."

She met Emily's eyes in the mirror. Whatever had her maid been talking about? She could feel her face warm. She'd been thinking of other things.

"Oh, I am," she said. "I'm feeling absolutely wonderful," she added, so brightly that Emily's eyes widened in surprise.

Had she never sounded happy before? Evidently not. She'd not only been grieving, but in the past six months she'd been drugged, too. She must have been like a gray cloud moving through Marsley House, ready to rain on anyone who said a word to her.

"How long have you been working here, Emily?"

"Since I was fourteen, Your Grace. It's been six years now."

Six years. Six years and she couldn't remember seeing Emily in the past. In fact, she'd thought that Emily had been recently hired. What did that say about her?

"So you knew Georgie," she said.

"Oh, yes, Your Grace. Such a beautiful little boy and such a tragedy. We were so sad about him. And for you, too."

Another thing that she hadn't noticed. She'd been so immersed in her own anguish that she hadn't seen anything beyond her own pain.

Don't neglect today in your longing for yesterday. Had Adam said that?

She had given up today, hadn't she? She'd been determined to be a martyr to grief. Perhaps she'd been Marble Marsley after all. A creature who was cold and hard and entombed in her own emotional grave.

Could she be as strong as Adam? He'd remade his life. No, she didn't have his strength. Yet the minute she had that thought, something within her rebelled. She'd endured being married to George. She'd never let anyone know how much she'd disliked her husband. She'd also recently stood up to her father.

Maybe she was stronger than she once believed herself to be. Maybe even strong enough to live in the present.

"There, Your Grace," Emily said.

The maid stepped back as Suzanne looked at herself in the mirror again. "You've given me a new hairstyle," she said.

"I thought it would favor your face, Your Grace. But I can change it back if you don't like it."

"I do like it," she said, surprised.

She looked a little different. Her hair was drawn up on both sides, pinned back and tucked up into an assortment of curls.

"I really do. How did you become so skilled?"

"I used to practice, Your Grace. With the other maids."

She could almost imagine those nightly events, a few girls in one room giggling and talking.

"I think your practicing paid off well. Thank you, Emily."

The young girl looked surprised again. Had she not thanked members of the staff before now? Surely that wasn't right. She had the horrible thought that that was exactly what she'd done. She couldn't blame her actions on Ella's potion. For five out of the six months she hadn't fought against taking it. Had she wanted to escape the grayness of her life? Or had she wanted to escape herself?

"Oh, Your Grace, I forgot." Emily rushed into the sitting room and returned a moment later holding an envelope. "This came for you yesterday by messenger."

She recognized the handwriting of one of her father's two secretaries and wanted to refuse to take the envelope. Emily didn't deserve her sudden irritation so she opened it, reading the invitation that was a barely masked summons to her father's next luncheon.

She abruptly stood, stuffing the invitation into her skirt pocket.

"Thank you, Emily," she said, leaving her bedroom for the sitting room. If she followed her usual routine, she would go down to dinner, taken in the family dining room. Her meal would be attended by a plethora of people, from the footman stationed behind her chair to the maids who would offer her a selection of courses.

Most of the time she motioned for all of them to leave. She remained at the foot of the long mahogany table in the room designed to show off the lineage of generations of Whitcombs. The walls were adorned with a portrait gallery of previous dukes, all of them looking prosperous and more than a little portly. They stared down at her from their framed perches in studied disapproval. A lone woman dining in stately and aloof elegance.

She wished she was free enough to seek Adam

out. They would talk as they had today. Or last night cuddled together in bed. She'd told him secrets she'd never divulged to another soul and he had reassured her that she wasn't terrible for hating the life foisted upon her. Or that it was natural to think that she sometimes heard Georgie call her name.

So much had happened in the past four weeks that her head whirled when she thought of it. She had changed since that night on the roof. Perhaps she hadn't grown or altered her life until now because there had been no impetus to do so. All it had taken was a man of mystery. Someone who'd dared to question her actions, give her advice, and challenge her.

She'd taken him as her lover. *Her lover.* Even the words were scandalous.

Rather than worry Mrs. Thigpen and Grace, she went ahead and ate a quick dinner, but instead of dismissing the staff, she conversed with them. She learned that one of the girls had been born in Wales, another had a married sister due to make her an aunt any day, and one of the footmen had a talent for mimicry. Afterward, she thanked Grace for a lovely meal before finally going in search of Adam.

She couldn't go to his rooms. Marsley House was settling down for the night. Half of the staff was retiring to the third floor and would see her. Nor could she send a footman to him with a note. Her only hope was that he would come to the library. If he didn't she'd simply brazen it out and go to him.

She hadn't wanted to read George's journal, but she needed to know the answer to the mystery. That was not, however, the only reason she wanted to see Adam. She liked being around him. She liked herself when she was with him. Besides, she missed him.

Even a few hours without him made her want to seek him out, speak to him for a moment or two.

She loved him.

Love made her feel silly and foolish and youthful and filled with joy, all at the same time.

She needed to tell him. He would no doubt counter with reasons why they couldn't be together. He would say that she was the Duchess of Marsley, the chatelaine of one of the largest houses in London. She would just have to marshal her arguments, explain that she would gladly trade having a title for being with him.

He wasn't exactly her servant. She wasn't exactly his employer. Those were just roles they had to play for a little while. When it was over he would be Adam Drummond and she would be Suzanne Whitcomb.

Titles didn't matter one little bit. Hers certainly hadn't made her life easier. Nor had it bestowed on her great happiness.

They would be free to spend as much time together as they wanted. They could discuss anything they wished for as long as they wished without worry as to appearance or staff gossip. She could share her life with him and he could confide in her. They would laugh about silly things and counter the sadness that had enveloped both of them for so long.

She could hold him and tell him how sorry she was about Rebecca. She would tell him that her death wasn't his fault. He'd never said, but she knew he felt that way. People like Adam took on the responsibility that others sometimes shirked.

Adam, with his military background, had been pressed into a mold as rigid as the one used to form her. If they stepped outside of the person they had been reared and trained to be, would the world collapse? Would society take a deep breath and suddenly vanish? Would London crumble around them?

No one would notice. No one had noted the death of an innocent child and an unwise duke. The world had gone on as if nothing had happened, as if there hadn't been a rending in the fabric of her life. The world had barely noticed when hundreds of women and children had been killed in a senseless massacre.

Now she pressed her hand against the library door. The last time she'd entered this room she'd encountered someone who wished her harm. Perhaps it had been a stranger. Or even worse, it had been someone living at Marsley House.

Until now she'd never been all that brave. Or perhaps she'd never been in circumstances in which she needed courage. The double library doors loomed as a test.

Pushing open one of the doors, she stepped inside. The moonlit night was the only illumination as she made her way to the desk and lit the hanging lamp. The silence surrounding her should have been absolute, but it was accompanied by memories.

She could almost hear George pontificating on some subject, correcting a member of the staff guilty of an infraction, or commanding the servants as if they were a battalion. Georgie's laughter sounded faintly from those times when she'd brought him to see his father. George had always spared the time to hold his son, bounce him on one knee, and admire how fast Georgie was growing.

The faint light from the lamp illuminated only the surface of the desk. She glanced up to the third floor. Again, her courage was being tested. All her life she'd been protected, guarded, and cosseted. Even her grief had been sheltered.

Until Adam. Until she was forced to realize that her loss wasn't special or unique, that there were other people who had suffered in their lives, too.

She took one step up the curved iron staircase and then another, her hand clamped to the banister. At the second floor landing she hesitated. The shadows were deeper here, the darkness absolute. The faint light from the desk surrendered to the moonlight for dominance.

One more flight and she was on the third floor. She couldn't remember the last time she'd been here. If she recalled correctly, a small reading nook was at the end of this row of shelves. Beside the love seat was a table and lamp. She reached out with her right hand against the books, her breath shallow as she made her way even farther into the darkness.

When she lit the lamp, she blew out a breath filled with relief. Nothing greeted her but rows and rows of books. No, not books. Journals. George's journals that he'd kept since he was a child. She walked to the end of the row. Each one was marked with a notation, but it wasn't a date. She selected one of the journals at random and took it with her to the love seat.

Did she really want to read George's words? She never had before. Even this afternoon she'd given Adam the journal, unwilling to learn about George's children.

Courage again, that's what she needed.

Sitting, she opened the journal to the first page, beginning to read.

Chapter Forty-Three

"What are you doing here?" Adam asked, his head appearing as he climbed the circular iron stairs.

Suzanne looked up. A month ago she would have responded with a very cold and rather autocratic remark. *Who are you to question me, Drummond?* However, a great deal had happened since then, and Adam had been involved in most of it. He'd kissed her, held her while she cried, saved her life, and been her lover.

For that reason and even a greater one—that she wished to be a better person than she had been—she gave him the truth.

"I came looking for you," she said. "Then I dared myself to come up here. I don't like feeling afraid and I didn't want to feel that way every time I came into the library."

She was prepared for him to lecture her, but he didn't. Instead, he came to her side and sat down on the love seat beside her. Only then did she realize that he carried the journal Sankara had given them.

"We were both reading George's journals," she said, glancing down at the book on her lap. "I was reading about the time before he was sent to India. It was startling to see his handwriting."

Adam held her hand and squeezed it gently.

She opened the journal to the part that had almost made her cry.

"'I am hoping to be given a commission, one that will allow me to place the Whitcomb name in glory again. I have not done a good job of it to date and would have shamed my father and grandfather by my inaction. Yet I believe I am destined for greatness, a feeling that has been in my heart since my boyhood. As duke I will lead men to valor and be the epitome of all that is good and right and just about England.'"

She slowly closed the book and put it on the table.

"But he didn't, did he? I think he knew what a failure he was. I think he didn't want to come out and say the words, but I think he knew."

Adam only squeezed her hand again.

"Perhaps he was a traitor, after all," she said. "If he thought it might bring him glory or respect or fame, it's possible that he might have done something terrible for a good reason."

"He wasn't a traitor, Suzanne," he said.

She turned her head to look at him. "Did you find something?"

He nodded.

"What?"

He looked like he was debating with himself.

"Do you know who it was?" she asked.

He nodded.

If he thought she was content to remain in ignorance, he was badly mistaken.

"Who is it, Adam?"

"Roger," he said. "Roger Mount."

"Your friend at the War Office?"

"Hardly that," he said dryly. "Roger doesn't have any friends, just people he uses."

"And he's the traitor?"

He nodded.

"Why?"

"Why does anyone betray his country? Maybe money, for one. The rebel leader was the adopted son of a prince. He had a fortune at his disposal. Enough to pay any amount of money for information. Revenge? Roger was sent to Lucknow because he didn't get along with the commander at Manipora. He always thought rules and regulations applied to everyone else, but not him."

He handed her the journal. "I think you should read it."

She took the book but didn't open it. "I really don't want to read about George's women," she said. She tried to give him back the journal, but he wouldn't take it.

"That's not what he wrote. You need to read it, Suzanne."

She studied him for a moment. He didn't look away.

Biting back a sigh, she opened the book.

FROM TIME TO time he glanced over at Suzanne. He knew what she was reading. Part of him wanted to spare her any hurt those pages might cause. Yet it wouldn't have been right to hide the information from her.

He wanted to ask her forgiveness for a great many

things, none of which she'd had any part in, but for which he'd judged her. She hadn't known that his sister had been taken advantage of by a young lord who'd only laughed at her excited announcement that she was going to have his child. Adam hadn't bothered to let the man know that Mary had died in childbirth and that his son had perished as well. At least the Duke of Marsley had cared for his bastards. Mary's lover hadn't been interested in anything beyond taking her innocence.

Nor did Suzanne know that the tenement in which he'd been born and reared was a slapdash of three-story buildings leaning against each other, owned by a peer who'd raised the rents every year with careless disregard for any of his tenants.

Whatever contempt he felt for the aristocracy, it was not fair to visit it upon Suzanne.

She turned the pages quickly, evidently more familiar with Sankara's formal handwriting than he had been.

He glanced toward the rows of journals. Something didn't look right. He knew these books well since he'd haunted the library in the past months.

"Did you mix up the journals?" he asked.

"No. Why?"

"The middle section is out of place," he said.

He went and stood in front of the bookcase in question, fingering the volumes that had been moved. He'd come to the library after Suzanne had been injured. The books weren't out of place then. Nor were they out of order two days ago.

"Someone was in the library last night," he said.

"How do you know?"

"Because this book," he said, pulling it out, "should

be in that section." He pointed to the journals on the next shelf.

"It might've been one of the maids," she said.

"No. I think it was the same person who pushed you down the stairs." He glanced at her. "You should go back to your suite, Suzanne."

"Why?"

"Because I think someone is going to come to the library tonight to look for the journal."

She folded her arms and frowned at him, an expression he'd seen on Edward Hackney's face. He had a feeling he was about to encounter the same obstinacy in his daughter.

"I'm not moving, Adam. I should very much like to push him down the stairs myself and see how he likes it."

He bit back his smile. The situation wasn't amusing.

"I'm going to sit in the dark and wait for him, Suzanne. I assure you it will be exceedingly boring."

"I have nothing more pressing to do, Adam. I shall enjoy the experience."

From the look on her face, lips tight, eyes narrowed, it didn't seem that she was going to descend the stairs and leave the library.

"Then I'm going to extinguish the light," he said. "I don't want our visitor to know that we're here."

He went down the stairs, turning the key on the lamp before making his way back up to the third floor. Once he sat beside her again he blew out the lamp on the table next to the love seat, plunging them into darkness.

"Do you really think someone is still looking for this journal?" she asked.

He turned to her. "If we're lying in wait for someone, it's important that we're quiet."

"Not until you tell me who you think it is."

Yes, she was most definitely stubborn.

"I haven't the slightest idea," he said. "Only that he was assigned here by Roger."

He sat in the darkness holding her hand. A month ago, no more than that, he'd been a different person. His world had narrowed to become his work and only that. When he thought about those things that mattered in his life there was a huge black spot where the smiling faces of loved ones used to be. His mother, Mary, Rebecca, and long lost friends. Whatever the reason, he'd been left alone and he'd adjusted in his way.

He hadn't expected Suzanne. Nor had he anticipated that she'd make him feel whole again.

Passion linked them, true. He desired her right at the moment. Something else, however, formed a bridge between them. Not mutual loss as much as trust, a growing friendship, and more. He knew that he could tell her almost anything and she would accept it. If she judged him it would be fairly. She was also loyal, somewhat to a fault in the case of the Duke of Marsley.

The fact was that their time together was coming to an end. Now that he had the journal, there was no need for him to remain at Marsley House. His assignment was over. He didn't even need to discover the identity of the second operative. The man would be recalled to the War Office soon enough, but Adam wanted the pleasure of punching the idiot in the nose first for hurting Suzanne.

Reaching over, he put his arm behind her back. She leaned against him, placing her head on his shoulder.

She would never be the Duchess of Marsley to him again. Instead, when he allowed himself to think of Suzanne, it would be with a surprising amount of regret. Not for what had happened between them, but for a future that would never be theirs.

Chapter Forty-Four

*T*he minutes ticked by uneventfully. About an hour later, from Adam's estimation, he heard a noise, a muffled click. He knew that sound. He'd made it himself, entering the library in the darkest hours of the night. He withdrew his arm from Suzanne, his body tensing.

He stood and walked halfway to the stairs, then pressed himself back against the bookcases. None of the lamps were lit, which made Adam think that the intruder was familiar with the library. No doubt he knew there was another lamp next to the love seat.

He could hear steps on the metal stairs.

A black shape appeared at the landing. Adam forced himself to wait. The shadow began walking toward the bookcase.

Suzanne gasped, the sound faint but enough to stop the man in his tracks.

So much for the element of surprise. Adam launched himself, only to encounter a softer form than he'd expected, one that felt pillowy.

"What the . . . ?"

He didn't have a chance to say anything further before he was bitten on the wrist. It was one thing to restrain a man, but he'd never encountered one who used his teeth as a weapon.

Suddenly, the light blazed in the corner. He stared at the person he'd pinned to the shelf.

Ella glared back at him. The hood of the black cloak she wore tumbled from her head, revealing hair frizzing about her face.

He stared at her uncomprehendingly for a moment before all the pieces of the puzzle fit into place.

He'd been right in thinking that Roger had placed an operative at Marsley House before him. He hadn't gone back far enough. Ella had been here four months before he arrived. Another mistake he'd made and one he wouldn't make again—not considering that Roger would use a woman. Female agents were new to the War Office.

"What are you doing here?" Suzanne said, standing and approaching them.

"She's Roger's other operative," he said. "And the person who threw you down the stairs."

"That was an accident," Ella said, spitting the words out.

"You failed," he said. "We found the journal."

She stopped struggling in his grip. "Then I haven't failed," she said. "The assignment was to find the journal. It didn't matter who accomplished it."

He would've thought the same thing a while ago, at least until he'd discovered the identity of the traitor.

"How did you get in?" Suzanne asked.

Ella didn't answer. If the look she sent Suzanne was any indication, Ella detested her former employer.

"I believe Ella is playing coy, Your Grace," he said, smiling at Suzanne. "If you would precede me down the stairs, and inform the footman on duty to summon the authorities, we'll rid ourselves of her."

"You can't do that," Ella said when Suzanne edged past them for the stairs. "You know I was working for the War Office."

"I know that you're guilty of burglary. Not to mention bodily harm."

She twisted in his grasp. "You can't do this, Drummond."

Her face was contorted with barely controlled rage. Perhaps in another circumstance he could have ignored her actions, knowing that she was a member of the Silent Service. But she'd harmed Suzanne and for that she needed to be held accountable. Let the War Office explain her actions. He wasn't going to shield her.

Ella tried to free herself again. It must have infuriated her that he could keep her pinned with his hands. Just in case, he kept himself carefully out of range of her teeth.

He held her wrists tight as they descended the steps. If she fell it would be because of her own behavior. She seemed to realize that, and didn't try to pull away from him.

"Roger isn't going to be happy," she said.

"Strangely enough, that isn't one of my concerns."

By the time he and Ella got to the front door, a crowd had gathered. Thomas had evidently not retired for the night, and as the head footman he'd summoned an additional man. Mrs. Thigpen was there, attired in a dressing gown with her hair done up in rags. The night maid stood beside her, eyes wide as she looked at him holding Ella. He didn't doubt that stories would fly around Marsley House by morning.

Suzanne stood apart from the rest, the duke's journal clutched to her chest.

He wanted to go to her. Instead, he spoke to Thomas, explaining that Ella had entered Marsley House in order to steal. She'd been here before, at least twice, he suspected, after she'd been dismissed. When the authorities arrived, she was to be surrendered to them.

Thomas nodded, looking as fierce as a young man could. "Yes, Mr. Drummond. I'll see that it's done."

He didn't have any doubt that Thomas would do exactly as he said. "I would take the precaution of tying her hands and perhaps her feet," he added.

Although Thomas looked surprised, he nodded. The footman glanced over at Mrs. Thigpen, who immediately sent the night maid after some sturdy rope.

"Roger will hear about this," Ella said.

He didn't bother telling her that Roger was going to face his own justice shortly.

"He's not a fancy majordomo," Ella said, addressing Thomas, then glancing at the housekeeper. "He's not a servant at all. He's a member of the Silent Service. A spy."

Mrs. Thigpen glanced at him, but instead of wearing an expression of shock on her face, she looked pleased. Almost satisfied, as if Ella had proven her right about something.

He walked to where Suzanne stood.

"Your Grace, thank you for your assistance this evening."

They had an audience of curious people who were not trying to hide their interest. Anything he said at this moment would be enhanced and speculated on by the entire staff, especially since Ella had divulged his identity. Tonight would be his last night at Marsley House.

He didn't want to leave Suzanne yet. Above all, he didn't want her to be standing there alone. She needed to be surrounded, not by servants, but by people who cared about her, who loved her. People who admired her for who she was, not the title she bore.

She nodded to him, a gesture that was definitely duchess-like.

"Thank you, Drummond. We wouldn't have discovered the identity of the burglar without your investigation."

He bowed slightly and left them. The sheer fact that he hadn't countered Ella's words was an admission. Perhaps they would ask for clarification from Suzanne. Or perhaps he would be confronted before he left tomorrow morning.

At least he had lodgings, even though he was certain that he was going to have to soothe Mrs. Ross's feathers when he returned. Suzanne's perfume would still be in his rooms. Her scent would be on his sheets.

He climbed the stairs slowly, entered the shadowed office he would leave tomorrow, and lit the lamp. He sat heavily, staring off into space, filled with a sudden and surprising feeling of hopelessness.

That wasn't like him.

He pushed the feeling away and concentrated on examining each of the ledgers that were his responsibility. He entered the rest of the expenses that had been furnished to him, made notes about the staff, and finalized the entries that would be sent to the solicitor. He wanted everything to be perfect for the next majordomo. He might have been playing a part, but he didn't want anyone to say that he had neglected the job.

A few hours later he put away the books for the last time and locked the drawer, putting the key on the top of the desk.

When someone knocked he stood and walked to the door, expecting it to be Thomas. Instead, Suzanne stood there, the journal clutched in her arms.

Chapter Forty-Five

Suzanne didn't say anything, only went to his desk and put the journal on it, opening the book to the pages revealing the traitor.

"You and I really should not be here alone," he said. "It was one thing in my lodgings, but here gossip spreads quickly."

"I don't care."

"Well, I do, for your sake. Don't be foolish, Suzanne."

She looked at him. "We have more important things to discuss, Adam, than whether the staff is talking about us."

He motioned her to the chair in front of his desk and closed the door. She sat, staring at the journal. She'd read it straight through.

Adam finally sat and faced her.

"You've been crying," he said.

"How do you know?" She'd examined herself in the mirror before leaving her sitting room.

"Your eyes look luminous when you've been crying."

She didn't admit to her tears, but he was right.

"I didn't love George, but I could have dealt well with him for the rest of my life. He was my husband, after all. But I think he was lonely, and for that I'm sorry I didn't feel more for him. I've known what it was like to be lonely surrounded by dozens of people. It's not an emotion I would wish on anyone." She looked down at the journal. "All he had to do was to give me a little notion of what he was feeling and everything could have changed. But he didn't."

"Some men can't," he said. "They're content to worship from afar. Or they're afraid that their affections will be rebuffed. I read a poet not too long ago and the last lines were, 'For of all sad words of tongue and pen, the saddest are these: it might have been!'"

"Do you ever wonder what your life would have been like if Rebecca had lived?"

"Not anymore. In the first year I did, but I think it was partly because I refused to believe that Manipora had really happened. Time gives you a finality as nothing else can."

He reached over and placed his hand on hers.

She cleared her throat before speaking. "What are you going to do about Roger? And don't tell me it's War Office business, please."

She'd been shocked at the words she'd read, but probably not as much as Adam.

There was no doubt, in my mind at least, that what my visitor said was the truth. It made perfect sense that Roger Mount might be the one who conspired with the rebels to overrun Manipora. He had been familiar with the rebel leader, having done business with him in the past. A sorrowful thing, but one that must be addressed.

She was certain he was about to speak when there was a knock on the door. She quickly stood.

He pointed toward his bedroom and she nodded, slipping into the room and pressing herself close to the door, listening.

"Mr. Bora didn't look surprised to see me, sir," Thomas said. "In fact, it was like he was expecting me."

"Did you get the answer?"

"He wrote it down right away, sir, and sealed it up."

Adam thanked Thomas. A moment later she heard the door close.

She peered into the room to see Adam tearing open an envelope. She opened the door fully and he turned to her, his face a mask.

"What is it, Adam?"

He handed her the envelope. There, in Sankara's swooping handwriting, were the words: *His Grace visited the War Office.*

Adam's face was expressionless, but there was a look in his eyes that she'd seen in her own mirror: disbelief mixed with a feeling of betrayal. The same look she'd worn when first learning that her husband was not interested in maintaining his marriage vows.

"You didn't want George to be right, did you?" she asked.

He smiled faintly. "No, I didn't."

She understood that feeling—when everything you'd based your life on crumbled into dust. Or when you realized that you'd been hopelessly ignorant until that moment.

"What does it mean, Adam?"

Hopefully he wouldn't treat her like George had,

preferring to put his thoughts and feelings on paper instead of voicing them.

"Evidently, the duke visited Roger, no doubt to let him know what he'd learned."

She stared at him. "Why would he do something like that?"

Adam looked at her. In his eyes was an expression she'd seen before, something close to pity but warmer.

"Perhaps he thought that Roger would confess to his actions and that he'd be lauded for capturing a traitor. It's a bit naive, if not dangerous. Any man who was willing to sacrifice the people of Manipora wouldn't hesitate to silence your husband. The duke probably told Roger that he'd written it all down, thinking that would keep him safe."

She turned and walked, stiff-legged, back into Adam's bedroom.

He was very neat, no doubt a result of his army background. The coverlet on the narrow bed was squared. The sheets were pulled tight. Even the pillow was aligned just so on the mattress. A bowl of potpourri smelling of sage sat next to two silver-backed brushes atop the dresser. The wardrobe was closed, but even from here she could smell the cedar shavings in the bottom. He was probably very organized there, too, his shirts and jackets in militaristic order.

She sat heavily, staring at the painting on the wall. She'd seen it before. It had hung in the hallway in the north wing once. Nothing was ever lost at Marsley House. They circulated furniture and artwork throughout the rooms. Up until this moment she hadn't known that some of the works found their way to the third floor. She was glad, though. Someone else should enjoy the depiction of rust-colored flowers against a brighter background.

All she had to do was keep looking at the porcelain vase in the painting and she would be able to keep her emotions together. That's all. A simple task, really.

"Suzanne?"

No, not now. She really couldn't answer any questions right now. That would shatter her. Speaking would ruin this false poise.

"Suzanne."

He was determined, wasn't he? The same persistence had no doubt made him a hero after Manipora. Yet he hadn't been able to save all those women and children. All those young, innocent lives. His determination hadn't meant anything then, had it? Was that why he'd pursued George with such insistence?

He came and picked her up as if she weighed no more than a feather, then sat again, with her on his lap. She'd never sat on anyone's lap in her entire life. At another time, it would have been a novel experience. Right at the moment she couldn't concentrate on anything but the refrain repeating in her mind.

She was so cold that it felt like January in this third-floor room. January without a fire going in the nearby grate. January and she was standing atop the roof again.

"The accident. The bridge. It wasn't an accident, was it? Is it because of what George knew?"

"I don't know." But the knowledge was there in the tone of his voice and the fact that the pity in his eyes had warmed to something else.

She felt like her insides were being crushed by a weight heavier than anything she'd ever known.

He pressed her cheek against his chest. His heart was beating loudly, proof that he was alive. She needed life at the moment, especially when she felt so cold and nearly dead.

Survival and stubbornness, that was Adam. He'd fought her and challenged her and now at this, another dark hour, he was with her, warming her, holding her when she felt like she was going to split into a thousand pieces.

"We may never know, Suzanne. I doubt it's something that Roger will admit to doing."

She nodded. "Would it be something he'd do to protect himself?"

For the longest time she didn't think he would answer her, but finally he did, the one word so soft and low and so horrible that she almost asked him to repeat it.

"Yes."

She closed her eyes and concentrated on breathing. It shouldn't matter if it had been an accident that had taken Georgie's life or an intentional act. The result was the same. Her darling son had died. But it did matter. When she said as much to Adam, he nodded.

"What are you going to do?" she asked.

"Confront him. We have the journal as proof and Sankara might be willing to give a sworn statement as well."

"Would that be enough?"

"Yes." This time the word was strong and assertive.

"I want to go with you."

"I don't think that would be a good idea, Suzanne."

"I'm the Duchess of Marsley," she said. "The title opens some doors, Adam. Even at the War Office."

"I'm certain that you're right, but I don't think it's going to matter in this case. Besides, it might be dangerous. He's not a man to underestimate."

"Please."

She couldn't remember the last time she'd begged someone for something. It might have been as a child. She'd learned that it was better to keep silent than to allow herself to appear vulnerable or needy. Now, however, she had no qualms about letting Adam see exactly how she felt.

"I want to see his face when you ask him about the bridge."

"Suzanne."

"I'll know," she said. She pressed her hand against his chest. "I'll know if he's lying."

He didn't say anything, but she wasn't foolish enough to think she'd won this battle. Adam was capable of simply leaving Marsley House without any notice and carrying out his mission without her.

She pulled back and looked at him. "I have to do this. For Georgie. For George. Just like you had to come after George for your wife. Not vindication, Adam. Justice."

"There's every possibility that Roger would look you in the face and lie."

"I'd know if he was lying," she said again, feeling a certainty she couldn't explain.

"All right."

She nodded, allowed herself to sink back into his embrace, putting her head on his shoulder.

Tomorrow, then. All she had to do was get through the night.

Chapter Forty-Six

"*I*t's late, Suzanne."

One of his hands was at her hip, the other smoothed from her shoulder to her elbow and back again.

"You should return to your suite," he said.

"I should."

"Emily will be waiting for you."

"I dismissed her for the night," she said.

He didn't say anything for a moment. She wanted to ask him what he was thinking but decided that it would probably be more prudent to keep her curiosity to herself.

"I don't want to leave," she said. There, a little more honesty for him. "I could always invite you to my bed, but then it would be difficult to hide you from Emily. Or pretend that I've been virtuous."

"Suzanne."

There was a note in his voice she couldn't identify. Did he object to her staying?

"Do you lie?"

"What?"

"You intimated that Roger was skilled in lying. Is that a function of being in the Silent Service? Have you ever lied to me?"

The seconds ticked along ponderously.

"I don't think so," he said.

She pulled back to look at him. "Why do you sound so surprised?"

There was an expression in his beautiful green eyes she couldn't decipher. Bemusement, perhaps.

"It never felt right to lie to you, Suzanne."

She sank back against his chest, feeling a lightness streaming through her like sunlight. It didn't banish the darkness completely, but made it gray more than black.

"I don't want to leave," she said, giving him the truth. "I don't want to."

He said something half under his breath, a word that was so startling she rose up to look at him again.

"Do you truly want me to leave, Adam?" Did he know how difficult a question that was to ask?

She was so worried about his response that she didn't anticipate the kiss. Was it possible for the top of your head to simply float off and vanish? Every part of her body welcomed him, wanted his touch and the magic that he brought her. She'd never before considered herself a sensual person or one motivated by her baser instincts. Such things were for people who were lax in their morals or hadn't been trained to be proper. At least, that's what she'd always been taught. But what if everything she'd learned up until now was wrong? What if you could be entirely decorous and yet love with abandon?

She sat up, never losing contact with Adam's lips, and wound her arms around his neck.

He breathed her name against her mouth. No doubt it was an admonition of some sort.

Was he cautioning her about her own behavior?

Or was it his lack of control he was warning her about? Either way, she didn't care. Let them both be profligate and unwise and wild.

She thought she heard him say her name again, but she was concentrating on kissing her way across his face and down his throat. He had a beautiful neck. She had never noticed a man's neck until now.

His hands were holding her shoulders in a tight grip, but she noticed he didn't push her away. If she wanted to leave, now was the time.

Why would she choose lying in her solitary bed, staring up at the ceiling, in exchange for being with Adam? Kissing him and anticipating what they would do together? She might have been foolish at times in her life, but she learned from her mistakes quite quickly.

She was not leaving.

Delight was threading through her body, making her aware of muscles and nerves and sensations she had never truly noticed until this moment.

She nibbled on his ear, smiling when he muttered something under his breath.

"I'm not leaving," she said. "I don't want to."

"Heaven forbid I make you do something you don't want, Your Grace."

She leaned back, smiling at him, happiness rushing through her. She shouldn't have been so filled with joy at that moment. He was teasing her again and no one ever had. His eyes were intent as they studied her, and there was something in the depths of them that made her heart soar.

"Thank you, Drummond."

He frowned. "What for?"

"For liking me," she said.

He shook his head. "Sometimes, Suzanne, you say the most ridiculous things. Who wouldn't like you? Who wouldn't cherish you? And love you?"

She was going to cry again and it had nothing to do with grief or sorrow. Her heart was so full that she couldn't bear it.

All she could do was frame his face with her hands and kiss him gently and tenderly. "And you, Adam? Who wouldn't love you? And cherish you? And admire you and respect you?"

He abruptly stood and carried her to the end of his bed. It was smaller than hers, the mattress thinner and the sheets not the quality designed for a duchess. Yet she wouldn't be anywhere else, because it didn't matter. Nothing mattered but the look in his eyes as he slowly unbuttoned her bodice, giving her time to protest or refuse or stay his hands.

Instead, she reached up and began to unbutton his shirt, freeing him from his clothes with sudden talented fingers. When had she become so adept at undressing a man?

He had been her tutor in passion, and now the pupil was impatient to demonstrate everything she'd learned from him.

"You are wearing entirely too many clothes," he said a moment later.

"I would say the same about you." They smiled at each other.

Fingers flew as well as buttons. Laces were loosened and then a corset was tossed across the room. She stood to rid herself of her dress. Her cameo was placed on his bedside table, but she had no idea where one stocking had gone. Its mate was draped over the chair where they had earlier sat. And her shift? It was the last garment to be dispensed with and she stood there before him, naked and as vulnerable as she had ever been in her life.

She should have covered herself with her hands. She should have grabbed the blanket at the end of his bed and draped it over herself. She should have done something other than just stand there and let him look his fill. The light on the desk in the other room was sufficient to expose her. Unlike last night, she had no shield of darkness. Nor did she want one.

He was bare-chested and had removed his shoes, but his trousers were still on. She approached him and began to unfasten the placket.

He reached out and smoothed his hands down her arms, and then he pressed his palms to her nipples and cupped her breasts. She had never realized how sensitive her breasts were until Adam touched her. She closed her eyes at the sensation.

She blocked out the past and the future and concentrated only on this, the present with him.

He bent to kiss her, but she shook her head.

"Not until you're undressed. It's only fair. If I'm naked, you should be naked."

She'd always been modest. She hadn't liked being completely naked even in front of her maid. Why was she being so brazen now? She thought it was because of the look in his eyes again, that same intensity that warmed her from the inside out.

Or could it be that desire was heating her body, turning her into someone else? The Suzanne she'd always wanted to be. The girl who reveled in her freedom. Being naked in front of him, unafraid, untouched by modesty was the greatest demonstration of freedom she could imagine.

They tumbled onto the bed, the mattress sinking in the middle, almost creating a well around them and causing her to laugh. They didn't wait. Instead, he entered her and she widened her legs, first wrapping her feet around his calves and then his waist. They were so close, so wound together that their heartbeats seemed to match, their breathing in tandem.

This was different from before. Before when he'd loved her, it had been sensual and erotic, then gentle and sweet. This was a maelstrom, fury and fire. She'd wanted wildness and abandon and he gave it to her and demanded, with each movement, that she come with him and experience the wholeness of passion with him.

It was Adam, so she put her trust in him, wrapping her arms around his neck, lost in his kisses. His thrusts and withdrawal teased and pleasured her at the same time. His mouth left hers to gently bite at the base of her neck, a gesture of capture, a demand for surrender. Then his lips were pulling at her nipples, saying her name against her breasts.

Her body shuddered, clamped around him with a demand of its own. She saw darkness and sparkles behind her eyelids as if the heavens had exploded in a black night sky.

For a moment, she wasn't Suzanne. She was simply a being, a creature of pleasure insensate but for bliss. Her hips thrust up to implore him to return. Her arms clung to him as his back arched.

Her body responded so perfectly to him, with him, as if they were destined to love each other. Nor was it simply her physical body that was involved, but her mind as well. She'd given him trust and he'd returned it. They'd revealed secrets to each other. With him she didn't have to be anybody but herself. Not a woman with a title. Not the daughter of the fantastically wealthy Edward Hackney.

She held him as he shuddered in her arms a few minutes later, his body reaching completion. She realized that in this, too, they were alike. Each needed the other, not only for pleasure but for holding in the aftermath, to treasure that small window of time when it was acceptable to be so open and vulnerable, to be weak.

She didn't try to hide her tears. She doubted she could have if she'd wanted to. This weeping came from another place entirely. Not grief exactly, but something similar. Anticipatory loss, perhaps. Seeing something troubling ahead and being unable to stop it.

He collapsed beside her, the sound of her name now coated with wonder.

She wanted him to stay, to remain with her. Sometimes being a duchess didn't matter at all.

Tomorrow they would go and label a man a traitor.

Yet tonight was hers and she wasn't going to give a second back to the world.

Chapter Forty-Seven

Suzanne woke at dawn, stretched, and ran the ball of her foot down a masculine, hairy leg. What a delightful pleasure it was to wake up with someone beside you. You began your morning feeling as if you weren't alone, that whatever happened during the day, their thoughts would occasionally be on you, that they would smile in remembrance. Or that they would hurry to be back in your company.

"I have to leave," he said.

That simple comment was like a spear to her chest. For a little while she'd pretended that reality wasn't real, that he didn't have to assume his rightful place in the world. As did she.

She would miss him. She would miss him much more than she should. But then, she didn't wake up in the bed of just any man. He was the only man. George's visits to her bed had been perfunctory things, a few hours here and there and then gone. He'd never slept beside her. She had never awakened with a smile on her face at the sound of his snoring. Not once in the middle of the night had she ever placed her hand on his naked back just to touch him.

"I will have to replace you," she said, her eyes still

closed. There, her voice sounded quite calm, didn't it? "As the senior footman, Thomas would be next in line for your position, wouldn't he? Is he up to it?"

"I would take him rather than bringing someone else in, someone new."

"I think I shall dismiss my solicitor," she said, blinking open her eyes. "After all, he was the one who recommended you. He did the same with Ella. What do you think his relationship is with your Mr. Mount?"

"He's not my Mr. Mount," Adam said, rising up on his forearms. He reached out one hand and trailed a finger down her nose, then pressed it against her lips just once. "I think there is some cooperation going on between them, but I'm not sure why just yet."

"You're going to find out, aren't you?"

"I hate a mystery that hasn't been solved," he said.

"That sounds like you still have questions."

He smiled. "Let's just say I have a certain degree of curiosity."

"And a sense of justice," she said. "I think it's probably your quest for justice that fuels most of your actions, Adam."

"You make me sound much more virtuous than I am."

"Must you leave?" she asked, even though she knew the answer.

What she was really asking—and she couldn't help but wonder if he knew—was, *Must you leave me?*

Yesterday, she'd wondered if she was brave enough to love again. Now she knew it didn't matter what she decided or if she was courageous enough. Love had come to her without her participation, without inviting it into her heart. He might cause her pain.

He might grant her anguish. She had no choice in the matter. She loved him and would do anything for him. And to keep him with her she might even beg.

She swung her legs over the side of the bed, the sheet still draped in front of her. She didn't want to seem needy or weepy. She wanted to be strong and resolute, someone like Mrs. Armbruster, perhaps. A woman who knew exactly what she wanted from life and had no qualms about demanding it.

Perhaps she should emulate that determined lady.

She stood and gathered up her clothing, wishing she had the courage to ask him not to watch her so closely. Did he expect her to dress in front of him? Evidently, because when she glanced at him he didn't look away.

Very well, if she was going to be strong and resolute she would begin right this moment. She dropped the sheet and reached for her shift, standing and pulling it on, hoping to appear nonchalant. The truth was she was acutely conscious of his gaze on her.

"You will be dressing in front of me, won't you?" she asked. "It's only fair."

"I'm not nearly as beautiful as you are."

She pulled the shift into place, pushed her hair back, and looked at him. "You underestimate yourself, Drummond. You're quite the most beautiful man I've ever seen."

If she'd had the time she would have sat on his chair and watched him for long moments, absolutely fascinated by the fact that his cheeks were turning bronze. Had she embarrassed him? The idea was both charming and amusing.

She pulled on her pantaloons and then her corset, fastening the busk with a little more difficulty than she'd anticipated. Since she had to go down only one flight of stairs to reach her suite, she decided that it was not sufficiently important to put on her stockings. She slipped her feet inside her shoes and tied the laces before putting on her dress. She was not in any way properly attired, but it would be enough to get to her rooms and slip beneath the covers before Emily arrived.

"You haven't forgotten, have you?" she asked, standing and grabbing her stockings. "You will let me go with you when you confront him?"

"I'm afraid that will have to wait," he said. "He won't be at work today and I don't think it wise to confront him at his house. I'll go and see Sir Richard first."

"No," she said, reaching into her pocket for the invitation Emily had given her, now a little worse for wear, and handed it to him. "He'll be at my father's house."

One of his eyebrows arched as he read.

"It's one of my father's political luncheons."

"Honoring his protégés?" he asked.

She nodded.

"Your father isn't going to be pleased if we make a scene. Does that bother you?"

"Not in the least," she said.

"I've never been to a political luncheon. What's it like?"

"A great many important people commenting on the food and the wine," she said. "And talking about and over each other. Sometimes they want to be overheard. At other times, not."

"It sounds like any War Office gathering. Or any social function after I became lieutenant."

She studied him. "I'll bet you were exceedingly handsome in your uniform," she said.

"It was less complicated than what I had to wear as your majordomo."

"I've noticed that you don't wear a hat, though."

"I detest them," he said. "I only wear them when I have to, which isn't often, thank heavens."

"I should very much like to dispense with hats. And corsets. And stockings."

He chuckled. "Why stockings?"

"They're never seen. You only wear them because of your shoes. But sometimes they are bothersome. If you don't tie the garter tight enough, they slip down. If you tie the garter too tight, they chafe."

"But they're delightful to remove," he said, smiling.

She hesitated at his door, wanting to say something else but uncertain what it should be. If she said thank you it wouldn't be just for the pleasure he'd given her last night, but for his kindness and concern, his tenderness and gentleness, as well as the laughter he'd summoned from some dark place. He had been like sunlight in the dark cave in which she'd lived for so long, and she would never forget that. She'd never forget him, either. But she didn't want to have to remember him. She didn't want to have to summon memories. She didn't want him to leave.

How could she say all that in just a few words in parting? She couldn't. Her plea would have to wait until later. She did have one last question, though.

"Why?" she asked. "Why try to prove that the traitor was George, even after his death? The War Office couldn't punish him. All that you could do was harm his reputation."

"I was told that the Foreign Office was trying to

make amends in India, making up for the mistakes made during those years, and that they didn't want any further embarrassments to surface now." He swung his legs to the side of the bed. "That's the story I was given. And I took it in, every lying word. The truth? A traitor didn't want to be discovered."

They shared a long look before she finally nodded.

"Until noon," she said before opening the door, looking both ways and slipping out of his room.

Suzanne reached her chambers without being seen—at least, she hoped so. There was a possibility that the footman stationed at the end of the corridor saw her, but he'd been chosen for that duty not only because of his trustworthiness, but his devotion to tact. If he'd seen her, she doubted he would tell the tale of the duchess who crept through Marsley House before dawn with her hair askew and clutching her stockings in one hand.

She opened her sitting room door and, relieved, leaned back against it.

At least until Emily stood, scaring her into a gasp.

"Begging your pardon, Your Grace, but I was worried about you and decided to check on you early."

How very commendable of Emily. Unfortunately, she couldn't think of a thing to say to her maid.

"He's a very attractive man, Your Grace," Emily said.

There was no unkindness in the remark. No cruelty in Emily's eyes. Instead, there was only a slight bit of humor, if she wasn't mistaken. All in all, it seemed as if she had an ally in her maid.

Suzanne didn't quite know how to respond. She could, of course, retreat behind the icy demeanor that kept people away. They didn't bother her when she was being the Duchess of Marsley. They didn't intrude. They wouldn't even think of asking her a personal question or being brash.

Emily was new to the position and no doubt would understand being chastised for her impudence. Yet something stopped Suzanne. The younger her, the person she longed to be, stepped forward and said, "Emily, I have been very sinful. I know I should feel terrible, but I don't. Is that horrible?"

Emily waved one hand in the air. "The minister would say yes, Your Grace, but the rest of us would understand. I guess that's why sin is sin, if you'll pardon me for saying so. If it didn't feel good, why would we do it?"

She couldn't help but laugh. Emily was going to be good for her, she could tell.

"Then if you don't mind," she said, "it will be our secret."

"I'll paint my lips blue if I say something bad about you."

Suzanne smiled. "What's that from?"

"It's what my brothers and sisters say. It's almost a family vow."

She found herself interested in Emily's family, questioning how many brothers and sisters she had— five—where they lived and what her parents were like. From the girl's conversation, it was evident that Emily had been one of the fortunate ones, growing up in a family that truly loved each other, even as adults.

"Help me dress," she said striding toward the bedroom and one of her two armoires. "I need to look very much like a duchess today," she added, glancing at Emily over her shoulder. "And I will need your talents with my hair."

Neither of them mentioned that she hadn't worn a braid the night before and that it would take some time to brush her hair free of tangles and tame it into shape.

That was the price one paid for love and perhaps even lust.

But, oh, it was worth it.

Chapter Forty-Eight

They didn't speak for long moments after leaving Marsley House. Adam's two valises were in the back of the carriage. He'd said his goodbyes to those friends he'd made, a little surprised at how many there were. Even those members of staff with whom he'd had disagreements or issues came to wish him well and see him off.

Mrs. Thigpen—Olivia—had been the more difficult of partings. He'd wanted to explain to her why he'd engaged in deception, but found that the words wouldn't come. He hadn't wanted to take advantage of her. He had genuinely appreciated their friendship. At least he got that part out.

"I understand, Adam. Truly I do. It's the rest that flummoxes me."

"The rest?"

"It's Her Grace, Adam. She's not the type to trifle with, and it's sad I am that you've taken advantage of her."

He hadn't said anything in response. Not one word had come to mind.

"You aren't wearing mourning," he said to Suzanne now.

He'd never seen Suzanne wearing anything but black. The color had suited her, but this lavender shade was even more attractive. It made her blue-gray eyes appear more piercing, and enhanced her creamy complexion. He admitted to himself that he could spend a great deal of time simply looking at Suzanne. Her beauty was understated, elegant, and everything about her made you want to study her more.

"It's half mourning," she said.

There was something about her voice, too. Low-pitched, it seemed to travel up and down his spine. It was a hell of a thing to find himself aroused by the sound of her voice. She could recite the list of the scullery maids' duties and he'd still find himself captivated.

He wanted to ask her if there was a reason why she had gone to half mourning now. He wasn't all that versed on society and every one of its rules, especially the ones about grieving. Had she done it because of him? The arrogance of that thought kept him silent.

"Does it matter what color clothing you wear?" she asked after a moment. "You don't wear a black armband, but it doesn't dictate your thoughts or the feelings in your heart."

He'd never talked about how he felt about Rebecca. Yet he found himself doing so often with Suzanne. It was a strange catharsis, discussing his lost wife with a woman who'd gone through her own anguish. Another point of comparison: she'd made no secret of the fact that she hadn't loved George. Nor had he been reticent about telling her that Rebecca had become his wife more out of convenience than emotion.

"No," he said. "It doesn't matter what you wear. Nothing will change what you think or feel. Time numbs the pain a little, but it never changes the facts."

"Do you ever get used to that? Or the bitterness?"

He smiled at her. "Bitterness is only anger unvoiced, I think. You can rid yourself of anger by expressing it in some way."

"Most people don't want to hear what you feel," she said.

He nodded. "You can tell me, Suzanne."

How long had he lived without love? Seven years? He could manage as long as he had a task, a goal, something to accomplish. He'd kept frenetically busy, one of the few operatives who could be put to work without regard to family obligations, holidays, or a personal life, for that matter. He didn't have people pulling on him, demanding that he share his attention with them. Damn it.

He didn't want to live that life any longer, a realization only weeks old, ever since meeting Suzanne.

She'd taught him, without words, that it was important to care about someone. To feel that his day was complete if he shared his life with her. To worry about someone else more than he did himself. He wanted to ask her thoughts, protect her from being hurt, and help her heal. He wanted to ask her opinion, share laughter with her, kiss her until they both lost the idea of time or place. He wanted to hold her when grief overwhelmed her, share his own sorrows with her and let her soothe him. He wanted the two of them to face the world together as a couple, a pair.

Yet that simple wish was a ludicrous and insane one. A dream dreamt by an idiot.

That thought kept him silent as they drove through London.

Adam had never been to Edward Hackney's house and had not once considered that it might be only slightly smaller than Marsley House. The evidence of wealth was there not only in the Palladian architecture, but the sheer expanse of lawn that surrounded the home, protected by a tall brick wall.

The British Royal family had nothing on Hackney when it came to a palace. Adam was only surprised that Hackney hadn't purchased a grand estate away from London so the man could hold political country house weekends.

A line of carriages was parked on the far left side of the road some distance away from the house. It took them nearly a half hour to make the approach and pull into the circular drive. Once the door was opened by a liveried footman, Adam left the carriage and helped Suzanne navigate the steps.

He didn't know how women did it with all that material and flouncy skirt. He much preferred her naked, a comment that he might have made in another circumstance. He'd always been circumspect, but it seemed like his entire nature was changing.

"Your Grace," the footman said. "Would you like me to send word to your father that you've arrived?"

"That's not necessary," she said. "I'm certain he knew the moment we entered the gate." She glanced up at Adam. "My father knows everything that happens almost before it does."

That comment concerned him. It made him wonder if Hackney knew about Roger's actions in India. If Hackney was sponsoring Roger for Parliament, it seemed not only possible but probable that he'd been informed about everything in Roger's past. He'd want to know about any scandal or anything embarrassing that might hamper Roger's rise to power. Nor would Hackney want to be associated with anyone who could ultimately detrimentally affect his own reputation.

If Hackney had known about India, did that also make him a traitor?

Knowledge of a crime as well as the identity of the perpetrator should be shared with the proper authorities. The fact that Hackney hadn't done so made him guilty, but to a lesser degree. His actions hadn't caused the death of good soldiers and the massacre of women and children.

For that, Roger should be punished and Adam was going to make certain he was.

Chapter Forty-Nine

Suzanne was dressed in lavender, which her father had coaxed her to do. No doubt he'd think she had done so because of him. She was here, when she'd announced her intention not to attend. She was attired in a dress that was fashionable in its way and her hat, while not as large—or as outlandish as some, she noticed—had been designed by a famous London milliner. All in all, her father wouldn't be displeased by her appearance.

On the other hand, he was bound to become apoplectic when he saw Adam with her. When he realized why they were here he would be enraged.

How very odd that she was looking forward to angering her father.

Most of her life, she'd done everything in her power to be a peacemaker. She had acceded to his most unreasonable requests. She had been conciliatory and understanding. More than once, she'd sublimated her own wishes for his. She'd married a man she hadn't loved because he'd dictated it.

No more. Not again. Not one more time was she going to be the obedient, dutiful daughter. That behavior had garnered her nothing. Her father hadn't been more approving. He hadn't said anything kinder or nicer to her. Granted, her life had changed, but she couldn't say that it had improved.

Marsley House was a colossus. It didn't matter how many rooms it had. She could enter only one at a time. None of the objects, knickknacks, and belongings collected by the previous dukes added to her life in any way.

Nor did she care how many dresses she owned or how many hats, pairs of gloves, or shoes.

Money, possessions, and a title had never brought her joy. Only Georgie had.

If an angel appeared before her and said, "Suzanne Hackney Whitcomb, I give you a choice. All the money your father has given you, all the power and the prestige that your husband granted you, would you trade everything for the ability to see your son again? Choose."

She would have spoken before the angel finished. She'd have given anything—any amount of possessions or trinkets or even her life—for a moment with her son. To be able to tell him how much she loved him. To be able to hold him in her arms for just a few minutes.

She blinked rapidly. Now was neither the time nor the place to lose her composure. Adam reached out his hand and grabbed hers. He was watching her with a look of concern.

People did not hold hands at London luncheons. They did not gaze into each other's eyes the way the two of them were doing. She could tell that their behavior was eliciting curiosity and more than a few speculative glances.

What the rest of the world didn't understand was

that Adam was her lifeline right now. He added to her strength. He knew what she was feeling and realized how close she was to tears.

They entered her father's house, a place she'd never felt that she belonged. It hadn't been her home any more than Marsley House was hers. She held no affection for the stately architecture, the wide foyer with its stark white columns or the pink-and-gray-veined marble floor.

There were two dining rooms. One was small and accommodated a dozen diners. The other was much larger, given to occasions such as this, when thirty or more people would sit down to a meal lasting at least two hours. There, the grand mahogany table, a design her father had ordered and which had taken nearly a year to complete, would be arrayed with a king's ransom in silver, gold, and crystal. The three chandeliers above the table would be lit despite the brightness of the day, illuminating the emerald green of the wallpaper and the curtains that mimicked the lush growth of the gardens surrounding the house.

Everyone would come away from a Hackney luncheon with praise for the food, the company, the ambiance, and their surroundings.

For now, the guests milled about the public rooms, a drawing room decorated in white and gold, and the library now open to visitors as it was never normally.

Her father was evidently attempting to make an impression on the various dignitaries in attendance.

Adam suddenly stiffened. She followed his gaze to see a man surrounded by a group of other men, some accompanied by their wives. When the crowd parted slightly, she recognized him as Roger Mount. She recalled meeting him at the last dinner party. He'd been almost obsequious to her, an annoying man she dismissed almost as soon as they'd been introduced. His wife, she remembered, was the opposite. She'd insisted on telling Suzanne who her father was and then describing her garden in excruciating detail.

Roger was shorter than Adam, a stocky man equipped with a perpetual smile. He looked entirely normal if a little self-serving but, then, she had met a great many political men who were just the same. Had he been responsible for her son and George's death? He didn't look evil, but did evil have an appearance? Perhaps innocuous-seeming people were the most dangerous.

She would have approached him if Adam had relinquished her hand. She glanced at him again to see him studying her.

"That isn't wise," he said.

She didn't want to be particularly wise, but the chance to say that was gone when Adam squeezed her hand in warning.

"Daughter, you're looking lovely."

She glanced to her left to see her father standing there, flanked by his two secretaries, Jerome and Martin. She nodded to the men before greeting her father, turning her head slightly so that he could kiss her cheek, as was his habit.

This time he added a glare to the kiss. "Drummond."

Adam smiled. "Hackney."

"We need to talk. I believe you aren't who you're pretending to be."

"I know exactly who he is, Father," she said.

He stared at their joined hands. Any other time,

she would've released Adam's hand, but now she clung to it almost out of rebellion.

"Are you in the habit of demonstrating affection in public, Suzanne?"

"Are you in the habit of consorting with traitors, Father? Or even worse, being friends with the man who was responsible for your grandson's death?"

"What are you talking about?"

"Ask Roger Mount," she said. "Demand that he tell you the truth, unless you already know it."

Her father looked at Adam.

"He betrayed the East India Company, Hackney," Adam said. "And the regiment stationed there, not to mention hundreds of women and children. He sold information about the entrenchment to the rebel leader."

"That isn't possible," her father said.

"That's what I said when I discovered that my maid was poisoning me," Suzanne said. "On your orders."

"I don't understand." The look of confusion on her father's face was almost convincing.

"Do you deny that you gave Ella opium to give to me?"

"Of course I do. Why would I do that?" His brows drew together and his eyes narrowed. When her father was angry, the world knew it, and he was getting to that stage. Even his secretaries took a step back, ever so tactfully.

"You and I have had our differences, but you're my daughter. I'd never do anything to harm you."

She glanced at Adam.

"It's entirely possible that Ella was giving you the drug to control you on her own," he said. "The better to give her time to find the journal."

"You two aren't making any sense," her father said. "Opium? Journal? Explain yourselves. Especially the part about how Mount's a traitor. What's your proof?"

"One of the soldiers who served under the duke in India came to see him," Adam said. "I was attached to Manipora," he added. "We all suspected that someone betrayed us to the rebels. He identified Roger."

Roger was excusing himself from his coterie and beginning to walk toward them. He stopped some distance away, almost as if he sensed the tenor of the conversation about him.

"He's responsible for hundreds of deaths at Manipora," Adam said. "In addition, the duke confronted Mount with what he knew."

Her father stared at Adam for a long moment. "Was he responsible for the accident?" he finally asked.

"I don't know," Adam said. "One thing I do know is the extent of Mount's ambition. He didn't give a thought to the deaths of a few hundred people. A few more wouldn't concern him."

"I hope you're wrong," her father said. "But I'm damn well going to find out." Without another word, he started to walk toward Roger.

Chapter Fifty

❧

$\mathcal{H}$ackney approached Roger, stopping in front of the younger man. His expression must have warned Roger's admirers. One by one they began to move back, almost as if they were afraid the encounter was going to result in violence.

There was every possibility it would.

"Did you have the duke killed?" Hackney asked.

Adam had to hand it to Hackney. What he lacked in tact he made up for in fury. There was no doubt in anyone's mind that he was enraged.

Everyone in earshot—which was everyone he could see—was watching.

Roger said something in response, too low for Adam to hear. He released Suzanne's hand and made his way to the two men.

"I found the journal, Roger," Adam said in a low voice.

Up until then Roger had ignored his approach, but the moment Adam spoke, the other man turned to him.

He'd never seen a man's face change so quickly. It was like one side of Roger's nature flipped to reveal another, truer self. Something in the depths of his eyes flickered. His face stilled and became almost painted on.

"There never was an informant, was there?" Adam said. "The duke himself told you what he knew. He also told you he'd recorded the truth. No wonder you've been looking for the journal ever since he died." He asked another question, one that had occurred to him when he'd read the duke's words. "And me? I was dispensable, too. You probably had plans for me after I found the journal."

"I don't know what you're talking about."

There was no way this was going to end well. If nothing else, he needed to get Roger to another room, somewhere their conversation wouldn't be overheard. He'd spotted a former general and the Lord Mayor of London among the guests. The last thing the Silent Service needed was to have their mission or this assignment publicly known. He'd already said too much and Hackney didn't look like he was going to keep silent.

Suzanne approached, halting when she reached Roger. "You killed my son, didn't you? And my husband."

"Of course I didn't, Your Grace," Roger said. He didn't get a chance to explain—or prevaricate.

"You damn bastard!"

Edward Hackney pulled his fist back and struck Roger so hard that his nose became a geyser of blood. Roger stumbled, fell to his knees, and was hit again before he could right himself. Hackney looked as if he'd continue pummeling the younger man if Adam hadn't pulled him back.

"Let me go! That bastard killed my grandson. He deserves everything he gets."

"I agree, but now is not the time. Nor is it the place."

Hackney was wild-eyed, his face florid, his hands still balled into fists.

There wasn't a doubt in Adam's mind that Hackney wanted to hit him, too. If he did, he'd be hard-pressed not to return the blow despite the man's age. Maybe there was something in his face that indicated he wouldn't be as easy a target as Roger, because Hackney dropped his fists.

"Is it true?" Hackney asked. For the first time, he sounded his age. "Did he kill Georgie, Suzanne?"

She went to her father and grabbed his arm. Adam saw the minute her anger fled to be replaced by sadness.

Hackney looked tired and defeated. "I didn't know, Suzanne. I didn't know."

She nodded in response, patting his arm.

"You're one of his operatives, aren't you?" Hackney asked, glancing at Adam.

"No," Adam said, determined to clear up that point. "I was just attached to this operation."

He was acutely aware that he was broadcasting his role in the War Office to any interested party. He wasn't going to say anything else.

Bending down, Adam grabbed Roger under the arm, and hauled him upright. He gestured for one of the servants and sent him after their driver. He didn't trust Hackney's staff, but he knew Michael. He would help Adam get Roger to the authorities.

"What are you going to do with him?" Hackney asked. "He should be bloody well shot at dawn. Or blown from cannon."

Adam didn't say anything, but he wanted to ask if the former East India Company director had ever seen that particular death sentence carried out. It had been a favorite of the duke's. A man had to see it only once before deciding that he would do anything rather than view it again.

Suzanne still had his arm and was regarding her father with some concern. As well she should. Hackney's florid face had become nearly white.

Something caught his attention, movement on the edge of the crowd that had formed around them. He turned a dazed Roger over to Michael and stepped away, ignoring the questions that followed him.

It had been too easy.

Roger's capture, the knowledge that he was the spy, had all been too easy. Granted, searching for the journal had been a trial, but everything else? Something wasn't right and the feeling was only minutes old.

The man walking swiftly toward the door told Adam that his instincts were spot-on.

He began to push himself through the crowd. Just when he thought he'd lost him, Adam caught sight of Oliver sliding out the front door, heading for the iron gate.

He began to run.

Catching up to him just before he hit the street, Adam grabbed the other man's arm and whirled him around.

"You're the traitor. Not Roger. You."

Oliver didn't have Roger's ability to smooth his face of all expression. It wasn't difficult to see the sudden hatred in his eyes.

"But Roger knew, didn't he?"

"He didn't know," Oliver said. "He didn't know anything."

"But he figured it out soon enough, I'll wager. When? After the duke visited him? All his ambitions would go up in a puff of smoke if someone learned his secretary was guilty of treason. Nobody would believe that he hadn't known, too."

Oliver's only response was a smirk.

Roger had cautioned him about letting his personal opinion color his judgment on this assignment, yet that's exactly what he hoped Adam would do. He'd counted on Adam's dislike of the duke to blind him to the truth. He depended on Adam's thirst for some kind of justice to keep him focused.

It had almost succeeded. But for Suzanne, it might have.

Oliver didn't fight him as Adam dragged him back to Hackney's house. For good measure, he solicited the help of two of Hackney's burly footmen, but Oliver didn't struggle. He was one of those snakelike creatures who preferred operating in the shadows than being overt.

"Why did you do it?" Adam asked. "Was it the money?"

He half expected Oliver to remain silent, but the other man surprised him by answering.

"I wanted to go home."

He stared at Oliver in disbelief. "You wanted to go home?"

Oliver nodded.

"You were at Lucknow with Roger," Adam said. "You weren't even at Manipora."

"I wanted to come back to England. I didn't want to fight anymore. I wanted it to be all over."

Adam was left without a response. It was over, for all the men, women, and children who'd died that day.

Hackney broke through the crowd, Suzanne following.

"He's the real traitor," Adam said, glancing at Oliver. "He's the one who betrayed us at Manipora."

"And Roger?" Hackney asked.

"He's the murderer," Adam said. "I'm taking them both to Sir Richard. He'll know what to do with them."

Adam exchanged a look with Suzanne. He wanted to tell her goodbye and perhaps say something else. The moment wasn't one for intimacies. He had two traitors to bring to justice.

All he could do was smile at her, and say goodbye in Gaelic: *"Mar sin leat."*

Chapter Fifty-One

"Neither Mount nor Cater are saying that much," Sir Richard told Adam a week later.

They sat in Sir Richard's large paneled office in the War Office building. The windows were lightly etched to prevent anyone from seeing in, but done in such a manner that plenty of light entered the space.

The chair in which Adam sat was upholstered in material that felt like a tapestry. He guessed that the chair itself was an antique like Sir Richard's desk, the globe on a stand, and the replica of the ship that rested in the middle of the fireplace mantel.

The room was furnished more like a parlor than an office, with a comfortable-looking couch in the corner, a table with a lamp and chairs that were less old and softer than where he sat. The scent of leather and pipe tobacco seemed to cling to the walls, perfuming the air.

Sir Richard looked down at the stacks of papers on his desk before glancing at him.

"I think we can concur that they were both to blame. Cater for treason and Mount for trying to cover it up."

"And the accident, sir? Was it truly an accident?"

Sir Richard sighed. "We may never know." He met Adam's look. "I have my own ideas, of course, about that damnable business. I think it a bit too coincidental that the duke died when he did, after threatening to expose Mount. But I've no proof, Adam."

"Another instance of never knowing for sure, sir?"

"Exactly, Adam. It's the type of job we do. You've shown great discretion in this matter. Under difficult circumstances, I might add."

"Thank you, sir," he said.

His superior studied him for another few minutes. Adam knew better than to say anything until Sir Richard was ready for further conversation. The older man was not averse to silencing his subordinates with a hand gesture or a terse, "Be still."

Sir Richard Wells was a man of indeterminate years who never seemed to age, at least not since Adam had first met him seven years ago. His shock of thick white hair was always perfectly coiffed. His black suits never showed a speck of lint. He was the perfect representation of a senior government official with his craggy face and the lines that had been put there by concern and worry. A tall man, he had a habit of bending forward at the shoulders as if he'd been taught as a child that it was rude to tower over people. His dark blue eyes were shielded by bushy white brows that resembled two caterpillars crawling across his face.

They were currently meeting above his nose in a ferocious frown.

"I'd like you to consider taking a new position. One of a supervisory nature. It would mean that you weren't out in the field, of course, but we could use a man of your discretion and experience. Sometimes decisions are made without any input. Your presence would mean that we'd get the view from the other side, so to speak."

He had reported to Sir Richard for every one of his assignments except this last one. The man had always treated him well, respected his concerns, and communicated honestly and fairly with him. On this occasion, however, he thought that there might be something else Sir Richard wasn't saying.

His promotion might be masquerading as something else.

"In other words, Sir Richard, if I remain quiet about the massacre at Manipora, I'll get an office, title, and a promotion. Is that it?"

The other man leaned back in his chair, steepled his fingers, and regarded Adam with his usual somber look. Sir Richard didn't smile very often, and when he did it was mostly in recognition of some irony that amused him. He wasn't given to joviality or even a lightness of speech. Instead, he acted as if the weight of the world—or the Commonwealth's presence in it—was on his shoulders. It just might have been.

"Speaking out about Manipora now wouldn't be wise. Divulging Cater's or Mount's role in it wouldn't serve any purpose. Nor would the morale of the army be buoyed in learning that two of their own betrayed them. But to answer your question, no, this offer is not a bribe or an inducement to silence. Tell the story if you wish. I can't stop you, but I see no point in it. It will not resurrect the dead." Sir Richard looked away for a moment before redirecting his attention to Adam. "Although I can understand why you would wish it otherwise. Damned awful business."

Sir Richard had a capacity for understatement.

"I have no intention of saying anything, Sir Richard. I owe the army and you my life."

The older man shook his head. "A fortuitous arrangement in my case, Adam. You have shown yourself to be a great patriot all these years."

Adam bit back a smile. *Patriot* was another word like *hero* that was regularly bandied about. They both came down to doing what was right at any particular time. Choosing not the easiest course, but the correct one.

"I want you for this post, Adam. Not because of what happened in the past, but what is coming around the corner for us. I think you'd be the right man in the position."

"Then I accept, Sir Richard, and I thank you."

He wasn't a fool, however and Sir Richard knew it. They would butt heads in the future. If he took this position he wouldn't be an operative as much as a politician, and he was most definitely not a politician.

The older man stood, extended his hand. "It is we who should thank you, Adam. This promotion will make a change for you. Are you prepared for that?"

He nodded as he shook Sir Richard's hand. "I am, sir."

A few minutes later he took his leave, entering the hired cab for a ride back to his lodgings.

A week had passed since the scene at Edward Hackney's home. A week since he'd seen Suzanne. A miserable week in which he had been beset by insomnia, an inability to think straight, and a general dissatisfaction. He was in a deplorable mood according to Mrs. Ross, who'd labeled him dour. He couldn't argue with her.

He'd had various assignments in the course of the past seven years. None of them had been like the one at Marsley House, where he had been required to form friendships of a sort.

Surprisingly, he missed a great many of those people.

Mrs. Thigpen with her love of gossip and condemnation of the same. She'd never realized what a paradox she was. Thomas, earnest and brave, up for any adventure. He would have made an excellent soldier. He liked Daniel as well and would miss the young man.

He'd isolated himself over the years, and it was only after he'd left Marsley House that he realized how much.

He gave some thought to returning to Glasgow before his new position began, just to reacquaint himself with his roots. If nothing else, seeing Glasgow might center him, give him some appreciation for how far he'd come. His life hadn't been a straight trajectory. It had ebbed and flowed like a burn tumbling over rocks. At the moment it was ebbing and it irritated him.

Maybe the change of job was just what he needed. He'd be busy, his time and thoughts occupied so that he could forget a certain duchess. Or maybe he'd never be able to forget Suzanne.

The new position would mean that he would not have to go out into the field. He wouldn't have to pretend to be different people at different times with different goals and motivations. He would be a guide, possibly a mentor, certainly a boss over other men who would be doing the job that he'd been doing for seven years. In the army he'd been successful leading men and it had been almost natural for him. He didn't have a problem with the new position. It was the rest of his life that was up in the air.

SUZANNE ARRIVED AT Adam's lodgings, thanked Michael, and walked up the path to Mrs. Ross's front door with some trepidation. She'd never done what she was about to do.

She hadn't loved George; she hadn't even liked him very much. Loving her son, loving Georgie, had made her feel whole. When he'd died, she'd lost that feeling because he'd taken part of her heart with him. She would never get that part back and it was right and fitting that it was missing. Yet she could still love and still live.

That's what Adam had taught her.

She'd seen the worst of life. She'd been in the darkness too long and was grateful for any faint flicker of light. Adam was a candle, a bright flame that promised to keep burning.

Now all she had to do was take the greatest risk of her life.

Chapter Fifty-Two

$\mathcal{T}$he carriage Adam had hired slowed to a stop in front of Mrs. Ross's house. As he left the vehicle and paid the driver, he noticed another, much more expensive carriage parked across the street. Michael tipped his hat to him.

Adam stood there for a moment, frozen. Suzanne was here. Suzanne was here.

He almost got back into the carriage and commanded the man to drive around London for a few hours, anything but have to encounter the Duchess of Marsley.

They'd parted amicably enough, but she should have known it was final. The idyll had come to an end.

Now she was here.

He would have to say goodbye and leave no uncertainty in her mind.

He'd never before been a coward, but it was the hardest walk he ever made up to Mrs. Ross's front door. He didn't even get a chance to open the door before the woman herself opened it, frowning at him.

"It's an explanation I'm due, Mr. Drummond. You never said your cousin was the Duchess of Marsley. A duchess! I would have brought out my best china. And shortbread? I only served her short-bread!"

He didn't know what to say first, so he let his land-lady's words wash over him. Mrs. Ross scolded him for a good five minutes before he could make his way into the foyer.

"I put Her Grace in the visitors' parlor."

Not only did he have to encounter Suzanne, but he had to have a witness in doing so.

He was going to refuse his promotion. Instead, he was going to return to Scotland. He was going to wander among the sparsely populated Highlands. He was going to keep sheep as company. Not people. He might get a dog, but that was it.

He found himself guided into the parlor by Mrs. Ross's insistent hand on his elbow. He glanced at her, but she wasn't looking at him. Instead, she had a half smile on her face and an expression of determination in her eyes. He had the thought that he was being paid back for keeping Suzanne in his rooms over-night. He wouldn't put it past Mrs. Ross to dole out her own brand of societal chastisement.

"Thank you, Mrs. Ross," he said, pulling free. "You've been very kind."

There was enough firmness in his voice that she finally looked at him.

"Thank you," he said again. He entered the parlor, turned, and closed the door in her face. No doubt he would have to pay for that rudeness, too, but not right now. Instead, he had a greater problem: facing Suzanne.

She sat on the excruciatingly uncomfortable horsehair-stuffed sofa. Most of the furniture in this parlor—that none of the lodgers were allowed to use unless they had important guests—was in a particular shade of green. Unfortunately, not all the greens matched. He always thought of it as the bile parlor. Mrs. Ross, on the other hand, adored her furniture and considered the room to be the height of fashion.

The room smelled of Mrs. Ross's perfume, an odor of musk and woods that always made him want to sneeze. Today was no exception. He almost used that as an excuse for leaving.

Suzanne had already removed her hat and gloves, which were beside her on the sofa. There was no sign of her cloak, and the day was chilly enough to have called for one. No doubt it had been taken by Mrs. Ross and put in a safe place.

The kitten sat on her lap, eyes half-closed, his smile tinted with bliss. Adam didn't have any doubt that the cat was purring. Or that he resented the interruption. Adam was the recipient of a baleful feline stare before the cat jumped down from Suzanne's lap and disappeared behind the sofa.

Suzanne was as beautiful as she'd ever been, but there were signs of fatigue on her face. The shadows beneath her eyes were too dark and her face was too pale.

Had she been ill? He felt a spurt of fear that wouldn't dissipate no matter how much he told himself that her health was none of his concern.

"My father has agreed to fund Mrs. Armbruster's Institute and Foundling Hospital," she said, in lieu of a greeting. "Isn't that wonderful news?"

"Yes."

Success—he'd uttered one word. Surely other words were just as easy. Why, then, did it seem almost impossible to say anything?

He couldn't help but wonder how she'd managed the feat of getting Hackney to support two projects that could potentially be scandalous. Perhaps Suzanne had threatened to go public with the story of Roger Mount. Would she have done such a thing? Or was it the older man's way of reparation?

"Why?" There, one more word.

She smiled at him, one of those duchess smiles she'd given him at the beginning. An expression that really didn't mean anything since it was merely a momentary lifting of the lips.

"Does it matter? As long as good deeds are done?"

"Did you blackmail him?" He congratulated himself for speaking an entire sentence.

Both her eyebrows arched at him and her smile became genuine. "Do you really think I could do such a thing?"

"Why does the idea seem to please you?"

"Because it sounds utterly daring. Although, I must admit, I feel utterly daring right now. No, I didn't blackmail him. I did my best to convince him."

"Why?" Good lord, was he back to monosyllables?

"Because of a little baby by the name of Henry," she said. "I couldn't stop thinking about Henry. Any more than I could stop thinking about you."

He hadn't expected that.

"You didn't come to see me," she said, leveling a stern look at him. "I waited, but you didn't come. Neither that night nor the next day. Not for a week. Then, Adam, I realized you weren't going to come back to see me. I was part of your mission and your assignment was over."

Hardly that, but he didn't correct her.

"I don't think it's very fair that you've ignored me."

How the hell could anyone ignore her?

"I'm selling Marsley House," she added. "I'm taking your advice. I'm looking at property not far from here and I need your input, Drummond."

"Have you forgotten, Your Grace, that I'm no longer employed by you? I'm no longer your major-domo."

"Oh, do let's be serious, Drummond. You were never just my majordomo. You were my savior." Her voice changed, softened. "My rescuer. My lover."

What did she want from him?

"The sale of Marsley House will enable me to buy another house. I want a place of my own. Some place I've chosen that feels like home."

"Congratulations, Your Grace."

She startled him by looking up at the ceiling, then shaking her head.

"You're not going to make this easy on me, are you?"

"Make what easy?"

"I do not wish to live without you, Drummond."

He felt almost like he had when he'd been shot. He was in a state of shock, as if it was happening to someone else. Or like he was observing the emotions but not quite able to feel them.

"I don't wish to live without you," she repeated.

He stared at her. "You're a duchess."

"Do you hold that against me? I would gladly change my past if I could. But I can't."

"You're a duchess."

She rolled her eyes. She actually rolled her eyes at him.

"On this, Drummond, you must allow me some authority. I realize I'm a duchess." She spoke slowly as if he weren't capable of understanding her words. "There's nothing I can do about it. Nor do I seem to be able to alter my feelings about you."

He was incapable of speaking again. He'd never had this problem before, but she stripped every word from his brain.

She shook her head, stood, and circumvented the furniture to reach him still standing with his back to the door. Reaching up, she framed his face with her hands.

"I love you, Adam. I've been miserable away from you. I want to sleep next to you at night. I want to love you whenever I wish. I want to hold you when sorrow overtakes you. I want you to comfort me, too, but I also want to laugh with you and tell you silly things."

"Suzanne."

"I love you."

He had a feeling she was going to keep saying that until he responded in some way.

"Suzanne." He took a step to the right. She followed him.

"Do you not feel the same?"

"I was raised in a tenement in Glasgow," he said, letting his accent fall heavy on his words. "I made something of myself in the army, but I've not the fortune of your father. Or a title like George."

"So?"

She was the most stubborn woman.

"I can't give you anything, Suzanne. Not like you've lived. Not what you've known. I have a new position, but it still won't mean that I can give you what you're used to."

She smiled softly. "Are you married, Adam?"

"You know I'm not."

"Are you spoken for?" she asked.

"No."

"Then you can give me what I most value," she said. "You."

He closed his eyes and reached for her.

"This isn't wise," he said, just before kissing her.

Long moments later she said, "Oh, Adam, it's the wisest, most intelligent decision either of us has ever made."

He had to kiss her again after that.

He didn't know when he started saying the words, but they seemed to flow from him without conscious thought.

"I love you," he said as he kissed the tip of her nose. "I love you," he repeated when he trailed kisses from one cheek to the other with a stop at her lips. "I love you. I love you. I love you. *Tha gaol agam ort.*"

He enfolded her in his arms and rocked with her, the moment punctuated by silence and a sense of awe. This beautiful woman with her strong heart loved him. He must have done something right in his life to deserve her.

When he said as much to Suzanne, she only kissed him again.

He led her back to the sofa, moved her hat and gloves, and sat beside her. Only then did he notice she'd removed the ancestral ring that had been hers by right of marriage to the Duke of Marsley.

"I don't have any heirlooms," he said, picking up her hand.

The mourning ring was still in place, but he knew it represented Georgie, not her husband.

"I don't need any heirlooms."

"I haven't a title to offer you."

"There's only one I want, Adam."

He smiled, the first time since he'd entered this room. His life had not been what he'd expected. Circumstances and situations had challenged him and nearly destroyed him at times. Yet here watching him with a smile on her lips and joy in her beautiful eyes was the reward for every difficulty he'd ever faced and every dark night.

"Then be my wife, Suzanne. We'll be foolish together."

There was a slight noise at the door. He glanced at it, then back at Suzanne. No doubt Mrs. Ross was standing there with her ear to the door, ensuring herself of their propriety. Perhaps she had reason to be suspicious of the two of them alone.

If they were anywhere else more private, he might have given her grounds to be horrified.

"Come and see the house I've found," she said, standing. "It's just large enough, but not too large. Mrs. Thigpen says it's infinitely manageable and Grace is thrilled with the kitchen."

She held out her hand for him.

A new position. A new home. More importantly, a new life with a woman he loved and admired. Granted, that meant Hackney would be his father-in-law, but he could manage.

Standing, he pulled her to him. The house could wait for a few moments. Long enough for another dozen kisses at the very least.

Author's Note

$\mathcal{M}$rs. Armbruster's Institute and Foundling Hospital was located in Spitalfields, an area of London where many philanthropic ventures began. For example, the American philanthropist George Peabody began a foundation on Commercial Street in 1864 to improve the living conditions of the working poor.

St. Pancras Workhouse existed and is now St. Pancras Hospital. Unfortunately, the poor hygiene in the infant ward was so appalling that many babies died during their stay or after returning from foster care. Charles Dickens wrote about such parish treatment in *Oliver Twist*.

In the Victorian era it was possible to easily purchase cocaine, laudanum, opium, and arsenic. In the 1860s the publication of information about London's East End opium dens inspired various organizations to begin campaigns against the importation of opium. In 1868 the Pharmacy Act limited the sale of dangerous drugs to those registered to dispense them. However, few people ever spoke up about the addictive powers of those drugs during the nineteenth century.

Manipora was loosely based on the Massacre of Cawnpore (1857) now known as Kanpur.

Being a spy was not considered a gentlemanly occupation in the nineteenth century and was relegated to the middle classes, often former military men. Although the Secret Service Bureau wasn't formed until 1903, I imagined the frustration of military men, especially after the Crimean War and the Sepoy Rebellion.

In 1855 the Board of Ordnance had been dissolved and all duties transferred to the War Office. Both the Secretary of State for War and the Commander-in-Chief of the Army held equal responsibilities. Prince George, Second Duke of Cambridge, took on the job of Commander-in-Chief in 1856. Unfortunately, he was heavily resistant to any kinds of reform.

When you were stopped at the top, you developed other ways to get things done. In this case, I envisioned a loose grouping of men—the Silent Service—who worked for the empire with the tacit approval of men who would probably not support them if their actions ever became public.

The Schomberg House was divided into three sections in 1769. The three units were, at various times, homes for artists, a high-class bordello, a haberdashery, a fashionable textile store, a bookshop, and a gambling den. All three units were purchased by the British government in 1859 for use by the War Office, but were largely demolished in 1956. Only the facades remain.